'You dance with the grace of a water-sprite.'

Sir Rolf's ruggedly handsome features were set as unyielding as the stone battlements of a fortress, while his amber gaze travelled over her, insulting in its bold appraisal.

Meriel tensed, for no one had ever treated her with such disrespect, but she had never before been mistaken for a serving-maid.

'Would that I could tarry and take up the invitation of your dance, water-sprite, but duty calls me elsewhere this night. We shall meet again, sweet minstrel,' he vowed.

For as long as Pauline Bentley can remember, she has been captivated by history. She finds reliving the excitement of the battle of Crecy or a medieval tournament more exciting than the current news of the day. Born in Essex she was trained as a legal secretary, but always came away from visiting castles or manor houses with the desire to write about them. She now lives in Sussex and finds inspiration and relaxation during long walks over the South Downs with the family and dogs. She is married and has two children and a growing menagerie of pets.

Pauline Bentley has written three other Masquerade Historical Romances; *Cavalier's Masque*, *Lure of Trevowan* and *Shadow of Pengarron*.

SONG
OF WYCHAVEN

Pauline Bentley

MILLS & BOON LIMITED
ETON HOUSE   18-24 PARADISE ROAD
RICHMOND   SURREY   TW9 1SR

First published in Great Britain 1989 by Mills & Boon Limited

© Pauline Bentley 1989

Australian copyright 1989
Philippine copyright 1989
This edition 1989

ISBN 0 263 76356 0

Set in Times Roman 10 on 10¼ pt.
04-8903-86903 C

Made and printed in Great Britain

CHAPTER ONE

'WAIT, MISTRESS Meriel—not so fast!' a young woman's voice pleaded. 'The Earl of Sedbury will have my hide should he learn we have come so far from Eadstone Castle.'

Meriel broke off from her song and lifting her long gown above her ankles, danced round on her toes, her blue eyes bright with merriment as she regarded her breathless companion. Even on this hot summer's day the young Spanish woman was dressed in heavy velvet, and now her swarthy face was flushed from their hurried pace.

'But, Bella, we are still in sight of the castle.' Meriel pointed to the square keep standing watch over the desolate moor where the river curved in the shape of a horseshoe. 'My guardian is not expected until tomorrow. Having escaped the vigilance of the guards, let's stay awhile by the river. It's been weeks since I have been allowed to ride on the moor or leave the confines of the castle.'

'It is hard for you, I know,' Bella sympathised, but her accent became more pronounced, her tone warning as she went on. 'While Lord Sedbury serves King Henry in France, such measures must be taken for your safety. Now that his lordship has returned to England, things will change. You should not blame the earl for your misfortune, but rather Prince Richard, who is a bad son to raise an army against the king.'

Meriel glared mutinously back at the bleak battlements. Bella would always defend Sedbury, but her own resentment was too deep to be contained. 'Prince Richard's rebellion has nothing to do with my duress. I am treated like a prisoner because Lord Sedbury would have me wed the suitor he chooses, whether he be a pot-bellied despot or scrawny and hideously battle-scarred with the manners of a wild boar. I have told him I will not be a pawn whereby he can gain wealth and power!'

Tossing back a tress of midnight black hair which had fallen across her face, Meriel scowled, loathing both the sight of Eadstone's battlements and the life she was forced to live. Why had her mother, the Lady Maude, not stood out against her cousin and stayed at Wychaven? They had been the Earl of Sedbury's prisoners for seven years. Her heart lurched. Was it really so long since her father, Sir Arnulf, had died, and the earl had taken control of Meriel's and her mother's lives? A dull ache of longing plucked at her heart. Seven forlorn years! In all that time not once had they been allowed to return to their beloved Wychaven. Her eyes misted, the nearby woodland and flat moorland blurring as she conjured up an image of Wychaven Castle high on its cliff-top overlooking the sea. It called to her across the miles, its spell stronger than ever. It was a wild, un-tameable place—almost magical—for it was built close to the borders of King Arthur's legendary Camelot. She smothered a sigh. Unless she married, she would never see Wychaven again.

Refusing to be downcast on such a glorious day, Meriel stripped off her leather pattens and pale yellow hose. Continuing her song, she splashed her bare feet in the cool spring water which fed the river. Her voice rose sweet as a nightingale's in the last chorus and then, seeing Bella's anxious glances towards the castle, she frowned.

'You worry over-much, Bella. We are safe here—the moor is too isolated for more than the occasional traveller.'

Bella scanned the river bank and trees a short distance away, her voice heavy with unease. 'It was on such a quiet, carefree day as this that I was stolen from my home by the Infidels.' Her olive skin paled, and she shuddered. When she lifted her brown eyes to meet Meriel's gaze, they were clouded with remembered pain.

'I paid cruelly for my foolishness that day. Lord Sedbury is a good man. You anger him by your wilfulness.'

Guiltily, Meriel stood up. It would be Bella who bore the brunt of the earl's displeasure should they be discovered. Even though her companion was Sedbury's mistress, she was but a Moorish slave who had caught his fancy, and he treated her the same as all his servants. It was the gossip of the castle that Bella had become a dancing-girl and whore when she had been captured by the Moors.

'We shall return to the castle,' Meriel said, reaching for her hose and pattens. 'Sedbury has the devil's own temper, and I would not have it fall upon you.'

A guarded look shadowed the Spanish woman's eyes. She was only three years older than Meriel, and in recent months an unlikely friendship had become forged between them. Two years earlier, when Bella first arrived at Eadstone, she had looked very much the eastern harlot, with her gaudy clothes and her arms and throat festooned in garish jewels. The castle servants, although forced to wait upon her, deliberately shunned her, but Meriel, seeing the blankness of despair in her eyes, had been drawn to show her small kindnesses. She had been touched by the avid way Bella had responded, and it was not long before a change was apparent in the earl's mistress. Now, although her gown was of scarlet, Bella no longer wore her jewellery, and her hair was neatly braided and restrained beneath a veil and circlet. Out of the two of them, Meriel realised with a mischievous grin, on first impression a stranger would probably take them both to be strolling players—especially herself, with her black hair uncovered in the custom of unmarried maidens and her feet bare.

Meriel pushed her damp toes into her hose, but was stopped by Bella touching her arm. The shuttered look was gone from her dark eyes and she looked contrite. '*Madre Maria!* I am being overfanciful. England is not war-torn Spain. You have favoured me with your friendship, which I neither expected nor deserve, and I would not spoil your pleasure.' She forced a laugh. 'Let us enjoy ourselves while we may.'

Meriel looked at her anxiously; her friend's laughter was tinged with sadness. Did she miss her own people and family, or was it that she had come to love the stern man who had rescued her from the Moors but who could discard her just as easily once he tired of her? Even as the thoughts formed, they were cast aside as Bella began to clap her hands, her feet moving in time with the rhythm. She was like a brilliant butterfly seeking happiness where she might. Her fears of moments earlier had gone as quickly as they had appeared. Catching Bella's change of mood, Meriel, heedless of her bare feet, followed her intricate steps, their bodies pivoting and swaying in the exotic movements Bella had learned from the Moors.

Meriel shook back her hip-length hair feeling its weight swinging out behind her like a mantle as she gave herself up to the magic of the dance. The warm sunlight kissed her upturned face and, closing her eyes, her body dipped and twirled sensuously in the fluid movements. Her young body, too long cooped within the bounds of the castle, pulsated with the joy of the moment, the heady wine of freedom intoxicating her as she spun faster and faster. The magic took her, her mind soaring free of her body until it seemed that she was floating high above the tree-tops in a world where there was no darkness, only light. She pushed from her mind the dreary existence within the castle, the broken spirit of her proud but unhappy mother and the forbidding figure of the Earl of Sedbury who governed their lives. When she danced like this she found an inner tranquillity—the only true peace she had discovered since her father had died.

She crushed down the trend of her thoughts, and pictured herself a heroine in a troubadour's ballad, her blood throbbing through her veins as she dreamt of freedom, of adventure—of love... Lifting her arms, she slowed her movements, an ache of yearning clutching at her chest as she spread her arms to embrace an imaginary lover. She danced on, unconscious that the fine linen of her gown clung damply to her full breasts and hips while its hem swirled up to reveal tantalising glimpses of her slim ankles and calves. She forgot everything but the dream her dance evoked: the vision of a golden-haired knight riding out of the mist to rescue her from the clutches of the Earl of Sedbury. That in this year of 1187 she had reached the age of seventeen and was still unwed was because he had not received a rich enough offer for her hand. She shivered in the heat of the sun, rebelling against the thought of marrying a powerful but ageing nobleman. Yet how could she escape such a fate, if Sedbury willed it so?

Abruptly Bella's clapping stopped. Meriel spun to a halt, her arms still outstretched before her in silent entreaty to her dream-lover. Reluctantly, she dispelled the vision of her knight-errant and opened her eyes. Her heart skittered. She blinked once, twice, but still the image clung to her mind. Several feet away on the edge of the clearing, mounted on a white destrier, the sunlight shimmering over his uncovered fair head like a dazzling halo—was her knight! Foolishly, she blinked again. Neither man nor animal moved. It was a dream... It had to be!

The angular planes of the man's handsome face showed a cool self-possession not matched even by her esteemed kinsman. He was like Lancelot, Tristan, Charlemagne, merged into one. Her breath stilled, her body seemingly paralysed with a strange enthralment, making speech or movement impossible.

The man met the turquoise gaze, which seemed to hold all the mystery and allure of the Mediterranean Sea it resembled. The sound of her voice had drawn him to the river as surely as any siren's song from Greek legend. What manner of enchantress was this? Her black hair clung in damp tendrils about her wide intelligent brow and framed her delicate features, the sunlight giving its lustrous gloss the purply, blue-green tinge of a magpie's wing. With a brusque mental jolt he reminded himself of the falseness that could lie behind such beauty. He had been caught unawares—temporarily beguiled by the sensuality and enchantment of her dancing. He was immune to mere beauty, for it was a weapon used for self-gratification or, more often, for treachery and deceit. If her loveliness left him cold, he still found it impossible to drag his gaze away, for fleetingly, when she had first opened her eyes, he had glimpsed the sweetness of innocence and purity in the clearness of those crystal depths. He waited for the illusion to shatter, as he expected it must.

She remained poised, like a startled fawn about to flee to safety. But she did not move—except for the rise and fall of full uptilted breasts and the invitation in the breathless parting of her red lips. His senses stirred at the potency of her charms, which even his usual cynicism could not dispel, and his hands tightened over the reins. The unexpected encounter with this maid had diverted him. In the week since he had left Prince Richard's side he had ridden hard, sparing neither himself nor his men. He had been sent to warn Queen Eleanor of Prince John's suspected treachery, as her youngest son was again at the English Court. He stiffened. What would he not give to know the secrets now being plotted at King Henry's Court! Or was there a way? His glance swept over the slim, ethereal figure before him.

As he continued to regard her, Meriel felt her heart slow to a painful expectant thud. The breeze ruffled his shoulder-length hair as his horse impatiently pawed the earth. The sound of the shod hoof scraping on the hard ground broke the spell around her.

'Come away quickly, mistress,' Bella warned in a low voice.

With a start, Meriel dropped her arms to her sides. Her friend's warning unheeded, she lifted her chin, boldly meeting the man's forthright stare. She had poured her heart into her dance, which no man had been meant to see, but refused to show the embarrassment heating her skin. He was a trespasser upon Sedbury's land who had invaded her privacy. A scathing challenge sprang to her lips, only to wither unvoiced as the horse moved closer. Her flesh tingled with sudden apprehension. Apart from Bella, she was unprotected. Her throat dried. It had been madness to venture so far from the castle. Then her spine stiffened. All the laws of chivalry forbade any knight to force himself upon a lady. But something told her this was no ordinary knight—however chivalrous, there was a sardonic twist about his full lips which declared that he answered to no man.

Common sense told her to pick up her skirts and flee, but her limbs would not obey; she was held transfixed, captivated by the dream which had become reality. Her thoughts ran chaotically as he drew level. Despite his fairness, his straight brows and lashes were several shades darker and, beneath this startling contrast, eyes amber-bright studied hers as coldly calculating as a lion contemplating its prey.

'You dance with the grace of a water-sprite.'

His rich voice was like a caress, until with a jolt she realised he had spoken in English, the words slowly pronounced from lack of use, but without hesitation. That he had addressed her in such a manner, and not in the French favoured by the nobility, disconcerted her. Clearly he saw her as a servant-girl.

The grass was cold beneath her toes—a shaming reminder of her dishevelled appearance. To her annoyance, a blush stung her cheeks as her embarrassment grew. Of course he would think her such—her feet were bare, her hair unbound and . . . the blush deepened in intensity for, worse still, her gown was the plainest and oldest she possessed. To reveal her identity at this moment would be humiliating.

Biting back a retort, her glance flickered over his attire. His short nut-brown cloak was trimmed with gold thread, as was his fawn tunic. There was a leashed power in the easy way he sat his horse, as though man and beast were one, and his knightly bearing was unmistakable as he rested one gauntleted hand upon his slim hip. Her gaze dropped to the indigo silk caparison covering his charger's back, and her heart beat faster. It was emblazoned with a silver device: a rearing griffin, its wings outspread and front paws raised in attack. Recognising it, surprise sent a ripple of excitement through her, momentarily banishing her anger and discomfort.

Even in this remote part of Exmoor, word had travelled of Sir Rolf of Blackleigh, companion of Prince Richard. The third son of a northern border lord, he had scorned the ecclesiastical life which, as a landless younger son, was his destiny. He had risen from squire to knighthood and, now in his late twenties, was one of the most feted knights on the Continent, reputedly grown rich on the prizes won from knights captured in the tourney and in battle. If she recalled correctly, he had taken the cross two years before, and as a crusader served King Guy of Jerusalem, where his valour and largesse had won him acclaim. But what was he doing here?

From the corner of her eye, she saw Bella curtsy. When she did not likewise accord him the deference due to his rank, he lifted a finely-drawn brow. His ruggedly handsome features were set as unyielding as the stone battlements of a fortress, while his amber gaze travelled over her, insulting in its bold appraisal.

'The castle yonder—whom does it belong to?' he asked.

Meriel tensed at his arrogance, for no one had ever treated her with such disrespect, but she had never before been mistaken for a serving-maid. She conquered her ruffled pride—her bedraggled appearance placed her at a disadvantage and sealed her lips from revealing her own rank.

Spreading her skirt wide, she sank into a deep curtsy with all the reverence she would have accorded King Henry himself. Imperceptibly his eyes narrowed, suspecting her mockery, their topaz brightness silently questioning her challenge. Her heart tugged with a spasm of alarm. Behind that worldly promise glinted a chilling cynicism. Despite his outward calm, there was a steely

control that warned her he would be a dangerous man
to cross.

'If you have business with Lord Sedbury,' she
answered him in English as she straightened, 'I fear you
will not find him here, Sir Knight.' To her relief, her
voice showed none of the inner turmoil his presence
aroused. 'We do not expect his lordship until the morrow.
The Lady Maude will be pleased to receive you in his
absence.'

The wide mouth tightened grimly. 'I had not realised
this was Sedbury's land. I ride to Winchester and must
reach there before dark, and passed this way as the
shortest route. I heard your singing.'

'You go to visit Queen Eleanor?' Meriel interrupted,
her curiosity getting the better of her caution. 'Is she at
last to be released from her imprisonment?'

His eyes flashed at her impertinence. 'Her Majesty's
circumstances have not changed,' he replied curtly.

Bella moved forward to tug at Meriel's sleeve, her tone
urgent. 'I beg you, come away.'

Unflinching, Meriel continued to hold the knight's
stare and bit back a host of questions. It was not for
her to question a stranger on the king's motives for
keeping his queen a prisoner for over fourteen years.
Had the queen not incited the young princes to rebel
against King Henry on many occasions? 'Then I shall
pray for Her gracious Majesty. Her imprisonment must
weigh heavily upon her.'

There was a movement from the edge of the trees, and
Sir Rolf's squire rode forward, leading two packhorses.
Behind him a dozen men-at-arms were halted at the edge
of the clearing. Sir Rolf signalled for them to stay back,
an enigmatic smile tilting his lips as he regarded Meriel.

'For a minstrel-girl, you take an unhealthy interest in
matters of state,' he said in steely tones. 'Or perhaps you
see Queen Eleanor as deeply wronged and a romantic
figure for your ballads?'

A dart of fear lodged in her spine as her glance
flickered over the men at his command. They were all

above medium height and their bodies honed to muscular hardness from long hours of fighting or practising with their weapons. It would be an efficient military force, and she was at the mercy of their leader. Her hasty words had led her into a lethal trap and, worse, he believed her to be a minstrel, not of noble birth. Oh, why had she not curbed her curiosity as to what was happening in the outside world? What if Sir Rolf were not a follower of Prince Richard, and therefore of Queen Eleanor, as she had first suspected? These were dangerous times, and men were quick to change allegiance. Outwardly Sedbury sided with King Henry, but there had been more than one visit to this remote castle, when her guardian was in residence, by a messenger wearing Queen Eleanor's badge. Since the earl did not deign to confide in his ward, she could only guess at the depths of his intriguing. An indiscreet word could bring the king's wrath upon even the mightiest of his barons. She had only to scream, and the guards would ride out from the castle, but would they reach here in time?

Her chin came up in proud defiance. She had borne the brunt of Sedbury's rages too often to cower before any man, no matter how great the danger. But this was not her guardian! Her heart galloped as she forced herself to hold his stare. At her unspoken challenge, his mouth compressed so that it appeared like a bloodless line across his tanned features. The line of his jaw had set into a granite square, and his throat corded as a vein leapt into life, throbbing in the depths of a livid white scar that ran diagonally from his ear to disappear beneath his collar. This was a man who lived by the sword, a man who put honour before courtly finesse.

'You have not answered my question,' he drawled ominously.

Meriel's mind worked furiously to seek a safe and neutral answer. 'Queen Eleanor is much loved by our people, but no one can rebel against a king with impunity. I feel for her, as I would for any one with an agile mind and headstrong spirit, who has been a prisoner for so many years.'

'Spirit sympathises with like spirit.' Despite the lightness of his tone, there was nothing reassuring about his rock-hard features. A dark brow arched mockingly. 'Would that I could tarry and take up the invitation of your dance, sweet water-sprite, but duty calls me elsewhere this night.'

The great destrier side-stepped nearer and, as Sir Rolf brought it expertly under control, he smelt the heady tang of wild jasmine which perfumed her body. The urge to stay and take what she so blatantly offered was startlingly acute. He was a man of healthy pleasures and pursuits and, since his years as a squire, his choice of willing women had been there for the taking, though none had touched his heart—not even the fair Louise of Auvergne whom King Henry had tentatively offered as his bride several months earlier, though the discussions had abruptly halted when Rolf had returned to France. Louise was all he sought in a bride—she was virginal, beautiful and held vast lands—and yet ... A glimpse of innocence unsullied from this minstrel had sparked a craving deep within him, so that even now, with the illusion gone, he regretted the urgency of his duties which must take him away from so captivating a creature.

'We shall meet again, sweet minstrel,' he vowed, then, wheeling his horse, he touched his gilded spurs to its sides and cantered away without a backward glance. Strangely, though, the image of the raven-haired dancer stayed with him. There had been promise and beguilement in every fluid step of her dance that a man would have to be carved from stone to resist, but there had also been a mixture of innocence and naïvety—a clever ruse to enslave a man's senses.

Hot anger speared him that, tired and weary from his days of hard riding, he had almost fallen prey to her wiles. Had he not seen the destruction wrought by such false innocence and from one he had revered as an angel among women? The pain of disillusion gouged deeper.

Even after all these years, he could not forget or forgive.
It was the bitterest of all the lessons he had learned since
attaining his knighthood and began to make his own way
in the world.

Savagely he jerked his thoughts back to the present as
he urged his mount to a faster pace. There could be only
one reason why Sedbury kept such a prize hidden away—
so that he alone could enjoy her charms. Who is she?
he mused, curious despite his antipathy towards any
woman who feigned a virtue long since lost. Softly
spoken and with a natural grace that many a noblewoman would envy, there was also an untamed quality
about her. From her looks, she was most likely a minstrel. A plan began to form in his mind. Her talents were
wasted, shut away here. It was time Sedbury proved his
loyalty, and to that end, the minstrel-girl could be the
means they were seeking.

Meriel watched the riders turn away from the castle and
disappear through the trees in the direction of
Winchester. Within moments, the clearing was empty and
the sound of the horses faded into the distance. Still she
remained unmoving, her heart refusing to slow its frantic
beat. There was a hollowness within her. The knight of
her dreams had ridden into her life and then just as suddenly galloped away. Yet he had been no tender, solici-
tous lover, but a man hard-sinewed and battle-scarred,
handsome beyond her wildest hopes but with a tempera-
ment and heart forged from steel. He was like no man
she had ever known. Now he had ridden out of her life,
and he did not even know her name. And, worse, he
had thought her little better than a minstrel-girl! Her
cheeks flamed. He had seen her dancing when she had
believed herself unobserved and at a moment when her
soul had cried out to an imaginary lover. He must have
thought her wanton! Why had she not spoken out and
told him who she was? Now the opportunity was lost.
Her hands clenched with anger at the injustice that Sir
Rolf should think her so lowly.

'You are fortunate that the knight was true to his vows of chivalry,' Bella began excitedly. 'He made his interest in you plain—there was a moment I thought he would force his attentions upon you! Santa Maria! He was handsome enough to turn any maid's head, but why did you not tell him who you are?'

'And face his ridicule for being discovered thus?' Impotent rage shook Meriel's voice as she glared scornfully down at her bare feet. Snatching up her hose, she sat down on a boulder and hastily pulled them on.

Bella shook her head. 'Your life has been sheltered here. Men are not always so gallant. Clearly he thought you a servant—as such, he could have forced himself on you and you would now be dishonoured. If the Lady Maude or Lord Sedbury should hear of it . . .'

'Please, Bella, you will not mention it to my mother?' Meriel thrust her feet into her pattens and stood up, her blue eyes darkened with concern, but not for herself and what she had done. 'Lady Maude is not strong, and she worries unduly about my future as it is. Promise me you will say nothing? It would pain her greatly.'

'You have always shown me kindness,' Bella answered proudly. 'I shall not betray you.'

Moved by her friend's trust, Meriel looked wistfully along the path Sir Rolf had just ridden, her guard slipping as she confided, 'He thinks so ill of me, yet in other circumstances I would never have met him. Oh, Bella, is fate not cruel? Was he not the perfect knight?'

'Handsome, maybe, but perfect—I doubt it. There is something deeply hidden and controlled that eats at him.' Bella's brown eyes clouded with concern. 'I could feel it like a tangible presence. That one guards well his dark secret, but it reaches out from the past to give him no rest.'

'Enough, Bella!' Meriel did not want to hear the gloomy prophecy. 'You talk like a soothsayer. I shall not listen to such nonsense.'

'I cannot foretell what is to come, but I can sense danger when it shows itself to those I care for. Should you ever meet that knight again, you must be on your guard.'

'That is not likely,' she replied wistfully.

'He said you would meet again,' Bella pronounced. 'Such a one does not say such things unless he means them.'

CHAPTER TWO

EADSTONE, WHICH had never seemed like a home to Meriel, now appeared drearier and more isolated than ever. By good fortune, she and Bella had managed to return without their absence being noted and, in the days following her encounter with Sir Rolf, the castle routine dragged interminably. Even the Earl of Sedbury had postponed his return, having been delayed by deciding to visit Winchester, and word had reached them that he would now arrive within the hour. Meriel checked that all was in readiness, then joined her mother in the tower room. How drawn the Lady Maude looked, the whiteness of her wimple and veil adding to the pallor of her complexion! Each month away from her beloved Wychaven took its toll upon her mother's health. There were times when Meriel hated Sedbury for the ruthless way he had plucked them from their home and ordered them to live here among strangers. Wychaven was a rich prize, and since Sir Arnulf's death, its revenue had gone to swell the earl's coffers.

'Will you take up your lute and play for me, Meriel?' Lady Maude said with a smile, but her blue-veined hands fluttered nervously over her tapestry frame. 'Your voice is always such a delight, and you are a comfort in my loneliness, I shall miss you when you leave.'

A whisper of apprehension sped down Meriel's spine as her mother went on, 'When his lordship, my cousin, arrives, I must confront him over the question of your marriage. I cannot understand why he keeps you hidden away like this. You should be at Court.'

'I have no desire to go to Court. As to marriage...' Meriel hesitated, unwilling to distress her mother further. 'I know it is my duty to wed whom his lordship chooses—

but the thought of being bartered like a common serf for Sedbury's own advancement is degrading.'

'It is a woman's fate, my child. I, too, felt as you do, but although the first time I saw your father was when I stood by his side at the altar, I loved him from that moment.'

A transformation came over the Lady Maude as she spoke of her husband. The lines of worry eased from about her mouth and eyes, a soft glow spreading over the delicate lines of her oval face.

'But Sir Arnulf was young and handsome,' Meriel could not stop herself adding. 'He was chosen on account of his prowess in battle, and because his strength and valour would protect Wychaven from our enemies.' Her uncertainty of her own future broke through the years of hiding her dread. 'My father loved you, and took pains to ensure that you would be happy. Sir Arnulf had a kind and generous nature and was a true knight. Sedbury has no affection for me. What does he care for Wychaven, except its wealth?'

'At least at Court you will have some influence over your own destiny. You have wit, intelligence and beauty,' Lady Maude soothed her. 'It would not be the first time a clever woman has won the heart of the man of her choice.'

Meriel swallowed against the memory of a golden-haired knight on a white destrier that now mocked her. To cover her confusion she picked up her lute, unravelling the coloured ribbons decorating its neck which had become entangled, giving herself a moment to regain her composure. She no longer believed in dreams. She had been haunted by her encounter with Sir Rolf, and with each day her anger at her own stupidity had festered with the need to justify herself in his eyes. It made no sense. She had recovered from her shock of seeing her dream materialise, and certainly was not so foolish as to believe herself in love with Sir Rolf just because he resembled an image she carried in her mind. It was something about his manner that goaded her anger, and it had taken some days to fathom what it was. Beneath the taunting, she had been aware of his desire for her, but there had been something barely discernible in his attitude which had set her blood boiling. It came to her with a start: it was disgust. That silent condemnation ate into her, taking precedence over the image of her dream. If ever they met again, she vowed, he would swallow that insult!

'Unless I won the heart of a great nobleman, Sedbury would not agree to any marriage.' She clutched the lute tightly against her breast in mounting agitation. 'And, in such a union, Wychaven would become over-shadowed by other larger estates. Wychaven deserves better than that. Whomever I marry must love it as we do—as Sir Arnulf did. My husband must be worthy of Wychaven, not Wychaven of him.'

'Sir Arnulf would have been proud to hear you say those words,' Lady Maude said, a catch evident in her voice. 'At Court, you may find such a man!'

Meriel turned away, disturbed by the returning image of Sir Rolf, which she rejected impatiently. Never again would she indulge in foolish day-dreams. Sedbury would countenance no marriage of her own choosing, and life at Court held no attraction. It was rumoured that no woman, high born or low, was safe from King Henry's roving eye. If one were to believe everything one heard, even Prince Richard's affianced bride had not been spared. It was said that the reason Prince Richard and the French Princess Alice were still unwed, although the princess had been in England since childhood, was because the king had seduced Alice and she now lived openly as his mistress.

Knowing that once the Lady Maude set her mind upon a course, she would pursue it until she had won agreement from her daughter, Meriel plucked at the lute-strings, hoping to divert her mother's thoughts, but as she began to sing the opening line of a ballad, a fanfare blasted out from the gatehouse. The Earl of Sedbury had arrived. Replacing the lute on a stool, Meriel helped the Lady Maude, who rose stiffly from her seat by the fire, her step slow but dignified despite the rheumatism which had eaten into her legs from the years in the damp castle on the edge of the moor. Together they went outside to greet their kinsman as he rode into the inner bailey. The earl's snorting charger clattered to a halt, and at the abrupt way he swung down out of the saddle, Meriel felt a spasm of alarm. He was furious. Guilt speared her. He had come from Winchester. What if Sir Rolf were still there and had spoken of the incident by the river? Her palms broke out in a cold sweat. No, that could not be, she reasoned, trying to calm her unease. Just because she could not drive from her own mind the humiliation of that meeting, it would have no consequence to a wordly knight. Why, then, did that knowledge bring her no peace, only a greater sense of frustration at being unable to justify herself to Sir Rolf? She was being absurd.

As the earl approached, she bowed her head reverently and curtsied, as did her mother. Sedbury barely paused as he passed them by. 'I will see both of you in my chambers—at once!' he rapped out as he entered the keep.

Taking her mother's arm to help her to rise, Meriel felt a shudder pass through her frail figure.

'His mood does not augur well for us,' Lady Maude warned. 'Take care you do not anger him further.'

They reached the earl's chambers as he impatiently flung his cloak into the arms of a waiting servant and shouted for wine. He ignored their presence until a goblet was filled and he had drunk it down. Dressed in a long gown of emerald velvet lavishly trimmed with jewels and sable, Lord Sedbury, now in his middle forties, was a formidable sight. His dark hair, still thick despite his receding hairline, was swept back from his brow. At sight of the throbbing vein at his temple, the moisture dried from Meriel's mouth and her heart thudded with foreboding. He was not a patient or a tolerant man when his wishes were crossed. Although she was used to his irascible moods, she had never seen him like this, his whole body rigid with a white-lipped control that was frightening in its intensity.

'I like not what tales I heard in Winchester.' His bellow echoed up to the rafters as he turned his glittering black stare upon Meriel. 'It was you who was seen dancing by the river, was it not? The description of a black-haired, blue-eyed enchantress was very precise.'

Shame burned through Meriel as the memory of that day returned. 'Yes, but I truly thought we were alone.'

'A likely tale!' he snarled. 'I should have you thrashed for the disgrace you have brought upon our house. When I was summoned by Queen Eleanor, I could not believe my ears at the story I heard... You and Bella entertaining a knight outside the castle. What the devil were you up to?'

'Meriel!' Lady Maude gasped, so shocked by her daughter's behaviour that she dared to interrupt her cousin. 'Did I not forbid you to associate with that Spanish creature?'

Before Meriel could speak, Sedbury rounded on the Lady Maude, his cheeks suffusing with angry colour. 'She is your daughter—have you brought her up to run wild? Is this how you repay me for the years I have given you my protection?'

Lady Maude staggered away from her incensed kinsman, her hand covering her mouth in horror.

'My lady mother knew nothing of the incident!' Meriel burst out. 'And it was not as you say. Bella and I were by the river when...'

'So I understand from the tales carried to me.' Sedbury's mouth curled disparagingly. 'Has all sense of decency left you—surely you are aware that she is not a fitting companion?'

'Bella is my friend,' Meriel answered stubbornly. 'I own that it was wrong of us to venture outside without guards, but they were close by. We were not far from the castle.'

'You flagrantly disregarded my orders,' he thundered. 'The Lady Maude is too soft with you. I should never have given in to her pleas for you to stay with her, but sent you away to another household, as I did my own daughters, to learn the proper behaviour and obedience befitting your rank. As to Bella, she, too, must learn her place!'

'Bella has done nothing wrong!' Meriel cried, aghast, fearing her friend would be severely punished or even cast penniless from the earl's protection if he had tired of her.

'Has she not?' His scathing glare swept over her. 'What of this temptress's dance the queen spoke of? Did Bella dare to teach you her whoring tricks?'

'You misjudge Bella. She was never a whore by choice, but by fate!' Meriel indignantly defended her friend. 'Sometimes we dance together. I am not allowed to ride or fly my hawks unless you are present. I meant no harm or disrespect, but it is hard to spend so long confined within the castle.'

'Silence! You are not only disobedient but insolent, child,' Sedbury stormed. 'I will not have my orders questioned. You stay within the castle for your own protection. A sound whipping would beat this wildness out of you. However, for the moment, that cannot be. The damage is done. It is only by the greatest good fortune that Sir Rolf did not suspect your true identity.'

Sedbury paused, pacing the room for several moments in silence as he tugged angrily at his beard, before he shot Meriel a cold, calculating look and went on, 'The queen thinks you are a minstrel-girl and has summoned you to entertain her. I would have taken Bella in your place, but Sir Rolf missed nothing in his description of a black-haired siren. Bella is not nearly so dark, and it is likely that Sir Rolf will still be at Winchester when I return. I cannot risk antagonising the queen. King Henry's power is waning, and at this time it would be unwise to displease Queen Eleanor, who has great influence with Prince Richard, her favourite son.'

So that is why I am to be spared a beating, Meriel reflected grimly. My wily kinsman anticipates the wheel of fortune changing! While still paying lip-service to King Henry, he would not hesitate to win favour with the rebellious Prince Richard, who was heir to his father's throne.

Lady Maude wrung her hands distractedly. 'But Her Majesty is aware that Meriel is your ward. Surely she means her to be a waiting-woman?'

'I did not see fit to parade my ward's shame. Fortunately, it seems that Sir Rolf has been discreet and spoken of this to no one but the queen.' Sedbury's craggy brows drew down ominously. 'Her Majesty's needs are sparsely served at Winchester, and Meriel will attend her without delay. The child has a pleasant voice, and the queen is in need of diversion to pass away the lonely hours of her imprisonment. If Her Majesty is pleased, I shall of course explain the misunderstanding which has arisen. We may yet save the day—and your daughter's reputation.'

'This knight, Sir Rolf,' Lady Maude said shakily, 'can he be trusted to show discretion when he learns the truth?'

Narrowing his eyes, Sedbury ran his hand across his beard, his voice cutting like a dagger straight to Meriel's heart. 'I believe him to be a man of honour... If not, steps will be taken to ensure his silence.'

Meriel was stunned by the threat behind his words, and by her mother's calmness when she asked, 'When do you leave for Winchester?'

'Tomorrow. See that your daughter is prepared. Bella will accompany us. I should have taken her from here before this.'

'My lord, you cannot mean to cast her out!' Meriel cried aghast. 'She is not to blame.'

The earl fixed her with a freezing stare. 'Bella is not your concern, though it is to your credit that you defend her. I have no intention of depriving myself of Bella's companionship, so she will stay at my estate in Essex.

Some good may yet come of your disgraceful conduct.
You will serve Queen Eleanor in any way she commands. Now go and make ready, since we leave at first
light.'

Dismissed, Meriel did not risk antagonising Sedbury
further by questioning him upon what steps he meant
to use to silence Sir Rolf. She contented herself that Bella
would not be punished. But even that was little comfort,
as she realised that Sedbury would not hesitate to sacrifice her own reputation if he believed he would be dis-
credited, or her value to him was at an end. She was
useful to him only as a means to his own advancement.
It was a frightening thought.

And what of Sir Rolf? How could she face him if he
were still at Winchester? Her heart gave a traitorous tug.
If he had spoken to the queen of her dancing, how could
she be sure it was not common gossip? Would she arrive
at Winchester Palace to discover herself a laughing-stock
for Eleanor and her ladies? Unaccountably, she felt betrayed. When she turned to her mother to voice her
doubts, she was surprised by the brilliance sparkling in
the Lady Maude's eyes. It was years since she had looked
so animated.

'This is what I have prayed for,' her mother declared.
'You must serve the queen well and win her favour. It
is your chance to speak up to tell Eleanor about
Wychaven and that my cousin neglects his duty in finding
you a husband. Wychaven is your inheritance! Once you
are married, Sedbury will lose control of its wealth. I
fear his lordship aims too high for you. Sometimes I
think I shall never see my home again. More than once
Sedbury has suggested that my life would be better served
by entering a convent. He has already so banished his
ageing wife, and would not hesitate to do the same to
us. Only upon your marriage will Wychaven be returned
to us... and I can end my days there in peace.'

At such a poignant cry from the heart, how could she
dash her mother's hopes? She knew that Sedbury would
marry her off only when it served his purpose. Surely

her mother must realise that the queen held little power, shut away as she was. Yet the Lady Maude was relying on her. 'I shall do what I can,' promised Meriel.

The journey to Winchester passed in a haze as Meriel rode at Sedbury's side. She was parted from Bella, who had been ordered to keep to the back of the company. Throughout the long ride, he lectured her on how to behave in the queen's presence.

'You will appreciate the need for discretion,' he warned gruffly. 'On no account must you reveal who you are. Do I make myself clear?'

'I shall not shame you.' She bit back her resentment that he was treating her like a witless child. She was proud of her heritage and would do nothing to dishonour her father's name.

'See that you do not, or both you and the Lady Maude will find yourselves living out your lives in a convent. Until we leave Winchester, Bella will act as your maid. She has her orders and knows better than to disobey me. Let us trust we can leave here with your reputation untarnished. Then you will return to Eadstone, and Bella goes to Essex.'

The rebuke stung her, rekindling her anger towards Sir Rolf, who had been the cause of the ordeal she must now endure, and also the loss of her friend.

The earl fell silent as they entered the city by the West Gate and passed along the narrow streets towards the palace. It was market day, and the streets were crowded with cattle and poultry as well as pilgrims on their way to pray at the tomb of St Swithun in the cathedral. As they rode past the long, low, cathedral building with its squat tower, Meriel saw that part of its structure was swathed in scaffolding, where the masons were still at work. At any other time she would have delighted in what was happening around her, but she scarcely noticed the pushing crowds or the shrill cries of the vendors. The sunlight was momentarily blotted out as they passed

under an arch, and with a start, she realised they had
entered the palace courtyard.

When a page approached to help her to dismount, her
courage almost failed her, but she drew a deep breath
to still her tattered nerves. No one must guess the humiliation she was feeling. Graciously she accepted the
help of the page and, as she took her place at Sedbury's
side, her shoulders straightened as she defied anyone not
to acknowledge her true rank.

'You will not speak unless directly addressed by Her
Majesty,' he warned her sternly. 'And you will obey her
commands without question. Only when you have proved
your worth and ability to the queen will your true identity
be revealed.'

Meriel nodded, too ashamed to argue. Sedbury would
wash his hands of her if she failed to please the queen.
What did he have to lose? If she were disgraced, he would
banish her and her mother to a convent, and although
he would have to pay her dowry to the church, Wychaven
would be his to administer as he chose. Her head lifted
a fraction. She would not be cowed by his threats. When
she had presented herself to him that morning, he had
subjected her to a gruelling inspection. Although he had
permitted her to wear her sapphire silk gown, he had
commanded her to remove the girdle of gold and pearls
from her waist and also the ruby-studded circlet holding
her veil in place. His stripping her of the trappings of
her rank showed that he would disown her should she
prove incapable of furthering his ambition.

'You and Bella will remain here,' Sedbury explained.
'Before anyone is allowed to see the queen, they must
first present themselves to Sir Ranulph Glanville, her
gaoler. Until I return, you will speak to no one.'

When he disappeared into an inner room, Bella turned
large, anxious eyes upon Meriel. 'I fear I am to blame
that you find yourself so cruelly served. I should have
warned you of the dangers which lurk outside the life
of the castle.'

'You are not to blame, Bella. You tried to warn me, but I paid no heed. Whatever befalls, I brought it upon my own head.'

They fell silent as Sedbury returned, accompanied by the queen's stern-faced gaoler. Sir Ranulph eyed the two women dispassionately, then apparently satisfied that they presented no threat, he beckoned to a page before addressing the earl. 'He will take you to Her Majesty. I must ask you to report to me before you leave, my lord.'

Sedbury nodded stiffly, then followed the page to the queen's apartments. They were ushered into Her Majesty's presence, and Meriel caught her first sight of Eleanor. A wave of awe and reverence washed over her. The queen stood by a narrow window looking out towards the distant hills. Her face, framed by a white wimple and veil, still carried traces of her regal beauty despite her three-score years and the remarkable life she had led. This was the woman who, during her first marriage to King Louis VII of France, had travelled with him on the First Crusade to the Holy Land. When later she was set aside by her first husband because she had borne him only two daughters and no male heir, she was wooed and won by Henry, then Duke of Normandy and Count of Anjou, who was more than ten years younger than herself. Two years later, after King Stephen had died, Henry was proclaimed king of England. The Angevin empire ruled by Henry and Eleanor now ranged from the Scottish borders to the Pyrenees.

Meriel's legs trembled as she sank to the floor in a deep curtsy. It was to this woman that she must prove her worth. No one could doubt Queen Eleanor's courage, or her passionate nature. She had borne King Henry eight children: three daughters and five sons. If this regal and proud woman had ever loved Henry Plantagenet, Meriel suspected that she loved power more. After the birth of her last child, Eleanor had returned to Aquitaine for some years, and it was then that she had turned her sons against their father, causing him to imprison her as a punishment.

'Come forward, let me see you more clearly,' the queen commanded Meriel in French, emphasising the words slowly, as though to a child.

Her legs still shaky with the magnitude of the occasion, Meriel obeyed, her nervousness growing as Eleanor's sharp eyes studied her intently. 'Sir Rolf said you were beautiful. He was right. What is your name?'

'Meriel, Your Majesty.'

'You are well spoken, and understand French. Where did you learn such graces?' The words were rapped out quickly.

Meriel hesitated, wary at the line of questioning. Lord Sedbury had forbidden her to reveal her identity, and she felt as though on the edge of a precipice. The queen seemed to miss nothing, and she was forced to resort to half-truths. 'I—I have been in Lord Sedbury's household since I was a child. Father Bernard, his chaplain, was kind enough to tutor me when he saw I had an ear for languages.'

'You must have proved an apt student.' Eleanor sent Sedbury a thoughtful glance. 'You show a generosity towards your servants, Sedbury, that many of our subjects would do well to emulate. The child has grace as well as intelligence: potent weapons, if they are used in a noble cause.'

'What greater cause is there than in the service of Your Majesty?' The earl bowed gracefully. 'If the child pleases you, I am honoured to be the instrument of that pleasure.'

'In truth it is Sir Rolf who noticed her remarkable talent,' the queen rejoined, 'though I cannot blame you for keeping such a gem hidden away. Leave us now, Sedbury, I would speak with the child alone.'

The earl looked taken aback, but unable to disobey Eleanor's command, he cast a forbidding glare at Meriel, warning that it would bode ill should she in any way defy his wishes. And it was not just herself he was threatening. If she disobeyed, Lady Maude would also suffer. Signalling to Bella to follow him, Sedbury departed. Alone with the queen, Meriel's nervousness increased. What was expected of her?

Eleanor moved to a small inner window, which Meriel guessed overlooked a room or chapel below. For some moments the queen appeared lost in thought as she stared down. 'I was curious when Sir Rolf first mentioned you,' she said, turning back to study Meriel. 'Unlike so many of my knights, he spares little praise for us, the fairer sex. If your voice is as sweet, and your dancing as beguiling, as he says, you could serve me well. But first I would see how well you perform. Take up the lute from that coffer. You will entertain my guest.'

Obeying, Meriel followed her down a winding staircase to the hall below. 'If I should have to leave halfway through your performance, you must continue. It may be better if I judge your skills from the room above. You were described as a siren—even more than that: as a pagan priestess tempting the saints to perdition. If you fail to captivate the attention of my guest—and I truly mean captivate—your services will be of no use to me.'

Meriel was shocked at what Eleanor intimated. She was to play the seductress!

'You look surprised, but your innocence is part of your charm. I do have need of you, or someone like you. Would you fail your queen?'

'No, that would be unthinkable, Your Majesty!' Meriel declared passionately. It was not only the queen she would fail, but her own mother. She had no choice but to do as she was bidden. Eleanor had stated that she must captivate her guest—not seduce him. She clung to that thought.

It was too late to question further as they entered the hall. When Eleanor moved to a seat by the fire, Meriel caught sight of the man she must entertain, and her heart stopped. Merciful Holy Mother, let the floor open up and swallow me! She was expected to dance for Sir Rolf!

He straightened from his bow to Eleanor and his cool gaze turned to Meriel. His brow rose sardonically; he recognised her, and was obviously surprised at her rich attire, then he turned away as though her presence were unimportant. 'It is the wench,' he drawled. 'Will she serve your purpose, Your Majesty?'

An enigmatic smile touched the queen's lips. 'I have yet to judge her. A song first, minstrel, then it will please us if you dance.'

Meriel controlled the hot rush of rage that scoured her breast at the way Sir Rolf had turned so disdainfully away. How dared he ignore her! It was because of him that she must face this ordeal! Her fingers hovered over the lute-strings. He was not even looking at her, *but he would*! She would dance as she had never danced before, and make him incapable of taking his eyes away. Despite the aloofness he affected now, he was not indifferent to her—the meeting by the river had shown her that. It was time the proud knight was brought to account for the casual way he had meddled in her life!

CHAPTER THREE

As MERIEL strummed the opening chords upon the lute, the room seemed to expand in height and width and she grew small and insignificant. So much more depended on her performance than the personal score she would settle with Sir Rolf of Blackleigh. Not only her future, but the Lady Maude's was at stake. On countless occasions she had sung to entertain Lord Sedbury and her mother, but this was different...it was a judgement, not an entertainment.

Her stomach quaked in a sudden rush of nerves, and her throat locked in a tight spasm. To calm herself she continued to play for some moments, her eyes focusing upon a tall free-standing bronze candlestick several inches from Sir Rolf's figure. She willed herself to pretend that it was for the Lady Maude she must perform, and gradually the tightness in her throat eased. Her clear voice rang out sweetly as she began to sing of the love of Tristan and Iseult—the account of the knight's trials and sorrows to win his fair queen caught her imagination, giving her the confidence she needed.

Moving between Queen Eleanor and Sir Rolf, she was unconscious of the provocative sway of her hips as she sang of Tristan finally becoming the lover of his queen. Her voice throbbed with passion when the valiant Tristan was struck down in a jealous rage by the king, Iseult's husband, and her eyes misted as the song reached its final verse. She *was* Iseult—wretched and bereft, as she watched her brave lover die—her voice growing husky with heartache and longing. The last notes of the lute faded, and with a start Meriel found herself subjected to Sir Rolf's mocking gaze, the twist of his lips cynical as he looked askance at the queen, who was smiling.

'You have a delightful voice,' the queen remarked. 'Indeed you perform with such feeling that you put to shame many an accomplished troubadour. I have not heard that particular version of the story. Where did you learn it?'

'I composed it myself, Your Majesty.'

'You have many talents.' Queen Eleanor looked pleased. 'I believe you will serve me well. Now I would see you dance. Sir Rolf will play for you.'

Meriel glanced at the knight. Not by so much as a flicker of an eyelid did he betray his emotion at the request, but as he held out his hand to take the lute from Meriel, she sensed that he was far from pleased. When his long fingers brushed hers, the heat from his touch skimmed along her arm. Inadvertently she gasped at the sensation, and a light flared in his topaz eyes, faintly contemptuous, but also speculative, as he noted her reaction.

He strode to the window seat and, propping his foot on one of its scarlet cushions, struck a chord, his golden head bent forward as he adjusted the tension of the strings. Meriel gazed at him. He was more handsome than she had remembered. His short tunic was of green velvet, and black hose gartered with gold cross-bands encased his long muscular legs. His complexion was bronzed from the long months he had spent in the hot climate of the Holy Land. The same sun had whitened his hair to the paleness of ripened wheat. She waited, tensely, for him to begin to play. As he leant back against the window embrasure, a lion caged was the impression which struck her most forcibly.

Sir Rolf's tawny gaze settled upon her, the lean contours of his face unrelenting. Then, seeing the stiffness of her figure, the bleak line of his mouth relaxed into a challenging smile, his eyes sparkling with encouragement as he began. The change in his expression startled her heart to leap into a wild pounding. No longer condemning, his image was again that of the knight of her dreams. If she were to succeed in her task today, it

was to that image—and not that of a cold, sardonic
man—that she must dance.

Lifting the corner of her gown, she sketched a brief
curtsy to the queen, maintaining her position for some
moments to familiarise herself with the music. The
rhythm of the tune was strange, haunting and exotic—
possibly one he had heard in his years as a Crusader,
yet it echoed the tempo of the steps she had danced by
the river. Rising to her toes, she swayed in time with the
rhythm, her steps light and her movements sinuous as
she wove a graceful pattern backwards and forwards in
front of the knight. His expression remained closed, and
with a terrible sinking feeling she knew she was failing
to captivate him as the queen had instructed. The
coolness had returned to his eyes as her pace increased
and her gown swirled about her slender calves. She might
well have been a raw-boned washerwoman for all the
attention he paid her. A glance towards Eleanor confirmed her fears. Her Majesty was frowning. Desperation gripped Meriel. She must not fail! She increased
the pace of her spinning feet, the rhythm instantly taken
up by Sir Rolf. Her veil wafted across her face and she
snatched it from her head, holding it before her, at the
same time shaking her unbound hair so that it cascaded
in abandon over her shoulders to her hips. Through half-
closed eyes she looked sidelong at the knight. If anything, his expression was more stern than before.

Something snapped within her. How dared he ignore
her! It was his fault that she was in this absurd predica-
ment. What had he likened her to—an earth mother, a
pagan priestess, tempting saint and sinner? Did he then
set himself above the saints?

She conjured up images of Bella dancing when she
had first come to the castle. There had been wildness
and sensuality in every step and flick of her hips or
shoulders. The Lady Maude had voiced her horror at
the Spanish girl's depravity, but Lord Sedbury had
laughed in delight. Before the entire gathering, he leapt
across the dais table, his eyes ablaze with desire, and

swung Bella into his arms to carry her from the hall. That is how I must dance now, Meriel thought distractedly. There was no other way she would succeed. Her steps slowing provocatively, she held her arms wide, drawing the veil across her lower face, her body swaying like a reed in a gentle breeze, and her eyelids drooping in bold invitation as she slowly lowered the veil and willed herself to smile, offering him the sultry promise of a sensual pagan paradise. A muscle throbbed along the knight's bronzed cheek, and she knew she had caught his attention. Now she must keep it. She clasped the veil to her as though embracing a lover, then her hands moved provocatively over her hips and thighs. Keeping her gaze fastened upon his glittering eyes, she gave herself up to the magic of the world she had created. The music pulsated through her veins, its sweet notes trilling like birdsong through the sinews of her body until she became one with the sound, each note echoing the rhythm of her heartbeat and the sigh of her life's breath.

Sir Rolf watched the dancer, stirred, despite himself, at her grace and beauty. Where had she learned to dance with all the beguilement of the slave-girls of the east, yet retain an innocence that took away his breath and reason? Her body promised the joys of seduction while sustaining an air of mystery that set his blood racing. There was a subtle difference in her dancing now from that which he had witnessed by the river, and it intrigued him. Then she had been offering herself to a lover; now—although she was using all her skills to win his attention—there was a wildness, a desperation to her dance as she deliberately played the seductress. A hollow sensation rose from his stomach. Irrationally, he had wanted to believe in her innocence. But for all her falseness, the wench was undeniably captivating.

He moved away from the window, his expression carefully masked as he circled her, increasing the pace until her flushed face glowed from exertion and the dampness curled tiny ringlets of black hair upon her brow. They moved inexorably closer, circling, challenge meeting challenge, until their gazes fused in a conquest of primeval pleasure.

Meriel danced on, her lips parting as she drew deeper breaths, the presence of the queen forgotten. Every nerve fluttered with a tingling awareness that she had succeeded in captivating the knight. Her body floated on a wave of exultation as he caressed her with his eyes. She was aware of Eleanor leaving the room, but Sir Rolf continued to play, his eyes darkening as his fingers moved faster and faster. As she breathed in hot, heavy gasps, her feet kept pace with the wild rhythm he was creating for both her dance and her senses. Raising her arms above her head, she twirled round and round until the music reached its crescendo to end with an abruptness that left her senses reeling.

Still caught up in the ecstasy of her dance, Meriel watched Sir Rolf lay aside the lute as she sank gracefully to the floor in her final curtsy. Her breasts heaving, she fought to regain her tortured breath, unable to drag her gaze from his burning stare. There was suppressed energy and strength in the suppleness of his tall frame, but there was also a tangible force, totally masculine and sublimely dominant, that dried her throat with apprehension as he towered over her, his handsome features taut with desire.

All at once, panic engulfed her, and unsteadily she rose to her feet and took a step backwards. His hand shot out, snapping over her wrist. Wide-eyed she stared up at him, her heart hammering as he drew her closer.

'Do not think to play the innocent now, sweet sorceress,' he said huskily. 'I have no patience with false coyness. Your invitation was plain enough.'

'You mistake the matter, sir,' she breathed shakily, trying to pull free.

His hold tightened, jerking her up against his hard chest, so that she was forced to crane back her neck to look up at him, her shocked blue eyes dilated, meeting his mocking stare.

'Let me go!' she said, striking his shoulder with her free hand. He captured it effortlessly. His laughter cold as tempered steel, he forced it down to her side. Her gaze slid from his predatory lion's stare and she saw the long indented scar, the thickness of a finger, its whiteness stark against the bronzed column of his throat. He must have come close to losing his life from such a vicious wound, yet it looked several years old. He could not have been much more than a boy when it was inflicted. When, in spite of her struggles, she continued to stare at the scar, he tensed. Then, a crooked smile lifting the corners of his mouth, he centered his sardonic glance upon her parted, quivering lips.

'You have bewitched me—as you intended,' he murmured thickly. 'I take nothing that is not freely offered.'

'Please, you must listen! I...' Her protest was smothered as his mouth covered hers, ruthlessly silencing her explanation. His arms were like steel bars round her, trapping her arms at her sides and making further struggle impossible. Warm and insistent, his lips parted her mouth, his tongue finding hers, shocking her by the intimacy of its touch as he explored the sensitive silkiness within. Then his lips were moving down her throat, his fingers stroking the nape of her neck that was poignantly vulnerable to the expert caress which sent a tremulous heat spreading from her scalp to her toes.

Dear God, what was happening to her? His mouth was again ravaging hers. Frantically she twisted her body, trying to push free as his hands slid down the length of her spine, moving unhurriedly across her waist and ribs until his palm slowly stroked the aching fullness of her breast. An indignant gasp strangled in her throat, sounding dishearteningly like a tortured sigh. She had never experienced a man's kisses or a lover's embrace. The passion she had roused was frightening in its intensity, but her blood had turned to molten fire and a burning excitement flared deep inside, searing her more profoundly than her fear.

At his muffled oath, she found herself released. Turning his back on her, Sir Rolf bowed low as the queen approached. The havoc he had wrought upon Meriel's senses had made her deaf and blind, and she had not heard Eleanor return. She suspected, however, that she had been watching Sir Rolf's response to her dance from the window in her chambers. The amusement brightening Eleanor's eyes as she regarded them both confirmed her suspicions.

'I believe we have found what we were seeking, Sir Rolf,' the queen declared. 'You may leave us. Be so kind as to ask Lord Sedbury to attend me. I shall put my plan to him.'

He bowed. His fierce glance at Meriel warned her that she had roused a demon in him which boded ill should they ever meet again.

Once they were alone, Queen Eleanor's smile broadened, the calculating light in her eyes turning to merriment. 'You performed better than I dared to hope. Sir Rolf was quite won over, and he is not a man given to impulse. As a warrior, I believe only my son Richard is his equal; in affairs of the heart, no woman has yet captured his affections, unless...' her voice saddened, 'unless there is any truth that a woman inflicted that scar upon his neck. It would take an exceptionally brave or a very foolish person to risk questioning him upon the subject. He guards its secret more savagely than any insult to his honour.'

The sound of a heavy tread cut short the queen's speech, and the Earl of Sedbury swaggered into the room.

'Your minstrel pleases us well,' she said. 'So well that I would send her to my husband's Court as a token of my esteem for him, but in truth she will be my eyes and ears within that place.'

'I am overwhelmed, Your Majesty.' Sedbury beamed his pleasure. 'However, I must tell you that this woman is no mere minstrel but my kinswoman and ward.'

Anger flitted across the queen's pale face. 'She is a gentlewoman?'

'She is the daughter of my cousin, the Lady Maude of Wychaven, who is widow to Sir Arnulf.'

'Sir Rolf was convinced she was but a minstrel, and from the way she danced...' Eleanor shot Meriel a haughty glare. 'You have much to answer for, mistress—as have you, Sedbury.'

'I but obeyed Your Majesty's commands,' the earl protested. 'If it is a dancing-girl Your Majesty would send to Court, there is Bella who also accompanies me. She is of Spanish blood and was captured by the Moors. I bought her in a slave market, and she has been trained to...'

'Pray spare me the details,' Queen Eleanor cut in sharply. 'Your Spanish harlot will not do. It is this woman who suits my purposes. She will serve my cause at my husband's Court.'

'Our family are honoured to serve Your Majesty in any way we can. If Meriel is to go to King Henry's Court, I ask only that for the time being her true identity should be known only to yourself.'

Meriel almost choked on her efforts to stay silent. Clearly, after the way she had danced, the queen had a poor opinion of her ability to conduct herself as a gentlewoman, but she could not shame her mother by disregarding all she had been taught—she must not address the queen unless spoken to. Meriel chewed her lower lip, resentment flooding through her at the way she was being discussed as though she were not present. Obviously, her own feelings were unimportant. To dance for Queen Eleanor was one thing, but to be forced to act such a role at King Henry's Court filled her with horror. Sedbury had used her to win favour with the queen—and she would have little compunction in sacrificing her to King Henry's lust in order to have a spy at Court.

'Is it to protect your ward's reputation that you ask this, or your own, should King Henry suspect that you would betray him?' Queen Eleanor queried tartly. 'In deference to her birth, she must have some protection. Sir Rolf will escort her to Court, so would it not therefore be prudent if he knew her identity? With him as her champion, no one will dare to molest her.'

None save King Henry, Meriel fumed, unable to believe that her virtue meant nothing to them. Only her name must be safeguarded, for fear it would bring ridicule upon Sedbury. Of all the humiliations she had endured since that fateful day by the river, this was the worst!

'Surely it is I who should accompany Meriel to court?' Sedbury protested. 'It is not fitting for her to journey in the company of an unmarried knight, however chivalrous.'

'Sir Rolf has business at the Court on behalf of my son Richard. With respect, Sedbury, you have for many years been my husband's man, and have but recently shown your willingness to serve myself.' Her eyes hardened. 'There have been many betrayals, and I trust no one. Your kinswoman will also be a hostage, should you change your allegiance.'

The earl's face suffused with angry colour but his voice remained smooth and conciliatory as he knelt, placing his hands together and holding them towards the queen in a gesture of fealty. 'I pledge my life to serve you. I ask only that a female servant accompany Meriel to protect her good name.'

Apparently satisfied by his humility, Queen Eleanor placed her hands over his in acceptance of his homage before bidding him to rise. 'Your ward's role at Court will be that of a minstrel. It is not customary for such to travel with a lady's maid,' she contended. 'But is there not this Bella you spoke of? Could she not travel as Mistress Meriel's companion? And can she be trusted to be discreet?'

'I believe so.' The earl seized on this way to extricate himself from his obligations, but his eyes shimmered with a frosty light. 'My ward seems to have formed an at-

tachment to my—er—servant. It was because of that unlikely friendship that they were discovered by Sir Rolf
when he crossed my land.'

'Then so be it!' Eleanor nodded, dismissing Sedbury,
but put out a hand to Meriel when she made to follow
him from the hall. 'Stay, Mistress Meriel.'

The earl became as taut as a tightly strung bow, his
lips bloodless with fury that he had been dismissed like
a lackey. His thick brows drew together as he glowered
threateningly at Meriel.

When they were alone, Eleanor studied her shrewdly.
'You are hurt and angry that we seem to have discounted
your wishes upon this matter. But, in this, you must be
wholly for me—or against me.'

'I would give my life for you, Your Majesty, but . . .'

'But death is one thing and dishonour another, in your
young and inexperienced eyes,' the queen remarked. 'I
ask you to do nothing that other women have not done
before. Sir Rolf will protect you from the advances of
the courtiers.'

'And they will then think I am his whore!'

'I doubt any man would be foolish enough to voice
that opinion unless they wished to feel the judgement
of your champion's sword. Do you fear that your lost
reputation could cost you a husband?'

Meriel met her gaze squarely. Her churning anxiety
could no longer be contained. 'Not just a husband, but
my inheritance and my mother's happiness. Since the
death of my father, Lord Sedbury has not permitted us
to live at Wychaven. His steward exacts the revenues
from our estate to fill his master's coffers. To regain my
home, I must marry, and to a man capable of protecting
its vast wealth.'

'Wychaven is on the coast—south of Glastonbury, is
it not?' the queen probed. 'I remember Sir Arnulf—a
brave knight. Did he not drown?'

Meriel swallowed against a knot of grief lodging in
her throat. Even after all these years she missed the large
black-haired figure who had dominated her girlhood. Her

memories were full of the joyful hours when Sir Arnulf had taught her to ride and shoot a bow and arrow as keenly as any of the squires who served his household. One glorious hot summer, he earned himself the Lady Maude's censure by teaching Meriel to swim.

'Yes, Wychaven is by the sea.' Her voice was threaded with pain. 'There was a storm, and a ship was wrecked on the rocks. The men rode out from the castle to search for survivors, and discovered two children clinging to the outlying rocks. Sir Arnulf took a rope and climbed over the rocks to save them. He was tying the rope round the first child when a giant wave swept them all into the sea. Sir Arnulf was a strong swimmer, but the sea wanted her sacrifices that night. His body was washed ashore two days later.'

'He died a true knight.' A deeper warmth entered Eleanor's voice. 'Sir Arnulf's daughter deserves better than the fate Sedbury would condemn you to. Serve me well, and I will see that you are married to a man worthy to follow in Sir Arnulf's footsteps. Wychaven is a rich prize, and you are beautiful enough for any man to forgive a temporary indiscretion, especially when you have served a noble cause.'

Meriel bowed her head, battling to overcome her disgust at what she must do. How could she refuse to serve her queen? Perhaps, in Eleanor's eyes, what she asked was not so terrible. While married to the serious and monkish King Louis of France, Eleanor, high-spirited and exuberant, had led a frivolous life—fêted by the troubadours and enslaving the hearts of her knights. Although only the queen's enemies accused her of adultery, likening her to Messalina during those unhappy, unfulfilled years, her indiscretions had been part of the myth that surrounded this great lady whom Meriel felt privileged to serve. Even so, Eleanor had re-created the ancient Courts of Love that idealised perfect platonic love, yet by stirring the hearts of young unmarried knights to worship and venerate women of their choice, surely such ideals must have encouraged illicit relation-

ships outside the sanctity of marriage? Meriel was torn
by conflicting loyalties. Her mind and body rebelled at
playing the harlot, even for so noble a cause. It was impossible to banish from her mind the childhood image
of the perfect knight who would fall in love with her,
his strength and valour bringing Wychaven to greater
glory. Yet to fail her queen in her hour of need would
be a shame too heinous to be borne.

'What would you have me do?' she asked hollowly.

The queen's mouth drew down. She suddenly looked
every one of her sixty or more years as she paced the
hall, frustration at her enforced imprisonment evident
in the stiff lines of her regal figure. 'I must know what
is in the king's mind. There is speculation that he intends to divorce me. Do you know that we are even more
closely related than I was to King Louis? And that marriage was annulled on the grounds of consanguinity! For
years I endured the gossip of Henry's love for Rosamund.
The Clifford woman has been dead these ten years. I
will not stand by and be so humiliated again, this time
by my husband's infatuation for his own son's affianced
bride.' Eleanor paused, her eyes flint-hard as she went
on. 'If Henry intends to set me aside and marry the
Princess Alice, then I must be prepared. My son's birthright must be protected. Sir Rolf is here ostensibly with
an olive-branch being offered by Richard to end the conflict between him and his father. As Count of Aquitaine,
Richard is vassal to the king of France. It is the scandal
of Europe that Alice and Richard remain unwed, and it
suits our purposes that Richard is not seen to be ajudged
loath to accept his bride.' She struck a clenched fist into
her open palm. 'I will not be cast aside without a fight!
I have spent more years in England than Henry ever has.
It is I who governed in his absence—who toured the
countryside, winning the hearts of the people.'

'And you succeeded. The people would not tolerate
your being put aside,' Meriel declared.

'When did Henry ever think of anyone but himself?'
The queen's bitterness and frustration broke through her

reserve. 'I need someone at Court I can trust. You must know something of the rift that threatens to destroy my family.' She looked askance at Meriel.

The girl nodded, uncomfortably aware that the queen expected her to answer truthfully, and from the eagle brightness of Eleanor's eyes, she guessed this was to be a test of her honesty and integrity. 'I understand that, some years ago, King Henry divided his empire between your three eldest sons—but for Prince John, the youngest, there was nothing. As Prince Henry and Prince Geoffrey are now dead, there are only Richard and John left.'

She faltered as a spasm of grief contorted Eleanor's proud face. 'Ay, only Richard and John remain, and John is Henry's favourite, as ever Richard is mine. It bodes ill for the future, but I would hear it from your lips. Please go on.'

'On the death of Prince Henry, Richard became heir to England, Anjou as well as Aquitaine, which he governed in your name.'

'He loves it as I do,' Eleanor again interrupted, her voice edged with passion. 'The king knew Richard would never relinquish Aquitaine, but still he demanded that it be given over to John. Oh, I hated Henry for that! He knew it would hurt me for my lands to go to John. But Richard would never betray my trust. He held on to Aquitaine.' She paused, staring for some moments into the distance. 'I pray now that Sir Rolf can bring about a reconciliation,' she went on at last. 'Henry respects him, for Sir Rolf has never broken his vow of fealty to his king, despite his long years of friendship with Richard. Sir Rolf is a remarkable man. He has won the respect of both Henry and Richard by refusing to bear arms against one or the other. It could not have been easy to maintain such a stand, for both my son and husband have the devil's own temper. They have cursed and reviled him—and then in the end respected him for upholding his beliefs. Now Sir Rolf is the natural mediator between Henry and Richard, and I trust him, as I would no other, to heal the breach.'

The queen studied Meriel intently, her voice soft. 'I believe I can trust you, Mistress Meriel. Have you wit enough to fathom the king's devious mind? Could you lure Henry away from the charms of the Princess Alice?'

Meriel inwardly shuddered at her allotted role, her mind racing. 'You would have me become a rival to the Princess Alice?' she began hesitantly. 'Yet King Henry has many mistresses—taken and discarded at will. What chance has a minstrel to win his confidence, except...' she paused, warming to the idea, 'if I were to withhold myself from him? An easy conquest is too easily discarded.'

'You would dare to risk the king's wrath by rejecting his advances?' Queen Eleanor laughed. 'Oh, but it is a goodly notion, and one Henry is ill used to! This shows that I was not mistaken in you. You will need all your wits and resources, but Sir Rolf will be on hand giving you his protection, and this could indeed be the ideal ploy.'

'Why must it be Sir Rolf? Surely the Earl of Sedbury should be the...'

'I have explained all this to Sedbury!' Eleanor's eyes flashed at having her judgement questioned. Then, as though sensing Meriel's turmoil, her expression softened. 'I have to trust you. You have a look of honesty about you, and that is so rare. There is more than the king's infatuation with the Princess Alice which troubles me. Prince John—so aptly named Lackland—has returned to England. I must know if he seeks to steal Prince Richard's inheritance.'

As Eleanor returned to her caged pacing, the echo of the queen's words sent a shiver through Meriel. Eleanor's faith in Sir Rolf increased rather than lessened her unease. The knight had not hidden his interest in her. He had stood resolute against the Plantagenet temper and emerged the victor. She had roused a passion in him which would be all the more dangerous were it curbed

by his vows of chivalry to protect any maid in his custody.
She would be like a thorn eating into his flesh. And a
lion with a thorn in its paw was not humbled, or brought
low, but was twice as deadly an adversary.

CHAPTER FOUR

SIR ROLF stared at Queen Eleanor in astonishment, his teeth grinding together as he checked his rising anger.

'With respect, Your Majesty, I had intended to ride to Court with all speed. If I am to escort these two women, my pace must of necessity be slow.'

'But was it not yourself, Sir Rolf, who brought the minstrel-girl to my attention? She will be the perfect spy at my husband's Court, but she cannot work alone. She will report to you, and you will send your messengers to me.'

He conquered his growing anger. It had not dawned on him when he mentioned the minstrel-girl to Eleanor that his words would rebound upon himself. Aware of the queen's need to learn what was in the king's mind, he had spoken of the girl simply because a beautiful, seductive dancer had seemed the key. The subject had been brought up in passing while he was expecting to leave at once for Court. Instead, the queen had ordered him to remain at Winchester for a further three days. And now this! His pride smarted at the lowly duty he must perform. Yet as he saw in his mind the slim, provocative figure inviting him to make love to her with every step she took, his anger drained. His stay at Court could prove a pleasant interlude and not the drudgery he at first suspected!

'As always, Your Majesty, I am at your command!'

'And I know I can rely upon your discretion,' the queen added smoothly. 'The girl is not quite what she at first seemed. I need only say that I would have her honour protected. You will be her champion at court and guard her as steadfastly as you would guard the honour of your own sister.'

Sir Rolf stiffened like a pikestaff, his knuckles whitening as he closed his hands over his sword-belt. The pain as his buckle bit deeply into his palm went unheeded. Was Eleanor mocking him? His eyes narrowed as he braced himself against ridicule, but her expression did not change.

'How is the Lady Isolda?' Queen Eleanor asked.

'I have not seen her for four years. After the death of her husband, she became an anchoress. On the way to Court, we pass her reclusorium at the church in Cranhurst. I shall visit her then.'

'Your sister's piety is a credit to your family. She must have loved her husband dearly to shut herself away after his death on the tourney field. Did you not challenge Sir Harold's slayer?'

What rumours had reached these distant walls of Winchester of that fateful day in France? Rolf reflected grimly. Thierry d'Arbeux had struck Sir Harold from behind while he was unarmed after being unhorsed in a mêlée. After any such incident there would always be talk, but he had thought the gossip silenced for he had taken pains to challenge d'Arbeux in private, and apart from their squires and Isolda there had been no witnesses. That day something deep inside Rolf had been destroyed. From that moment the laws of chivalry and misconceived honour were but a sham to him. He had vowed to be true to no one but himself and his own conscience in the future.

'I could not let Sir Harold's death go unavenged,' he answered icily, trusting that his tone would silence the queen's further questions.

Apparently it did, but, as he was dismissed, his memories of the incident brought bitter bile to his mouth. His jaw set stonily. The past was over and done with, and the lessons learned had forewarned him of the fraility of trust. Overnight his naïvity had turned to cynicism, especially when a woman protested her innocence.

* * *

As the riders rode out of Winchester over the downs towards London, Meriel fought to overcome her misgivings at what lay ahead. Shivering in the early morning mist still lingering along the woodland path, she pulled her woollen cloak tighter about herself. To safeguard her anonymity she had left all the trappings of her rank behind at Winchester. Eleanor, having carefully scrutinised the few gowns Meriel had brought with her, had commanded that all the gold braid be removed and the jewelled girdles discarded in favour of brightly patterned woven bands, so that now Meriel felt strangely vulnerable in her new role. Used to unquestioning respect from Sedbury's men-at-arms, she was often subjected to sly glances and remarks from Sir Rolf's men, which made her uncomfortable. Normally, a chilling glare would be a warning to any man who overstepped the bounds of propriety, but, as a humble minstrel, misplaced hauteur would earn her their ridicule, not respect, so instead she retreated behind a barrier of assumed indifference.

She also missed her high-stepping palfrey, which would break into a smooth fast gallop at the lightest touch of her heels. The sluggish bay mare she rode was irritatingly placid. Pushing aside her dissatisfaction and frustration, she determined to accept her role with humility, for any show of untoward pride would bring failure to her quest.

Meriel stared ahead to where Sir Rolf led his score of men. Despite the chill air, he was bareheaded, and his flaxen hair drew her like a beacon. Unaccountably, her heart gave a curious twist. From the moment he had strode out into the palace courtyard that morning she had sensed his anger at having to escort her. Her shoulders had squared in silent defiance at his curt nod in her direction, and her resentment simmered when during the first few miles she had caught his critical gaze upon her, as though he expected her to fall from her mount at the first obstacle. He had ordered his sergeant-at-arms, Tom Kedge, to take Bella, who was an inex-

perienced horsewoman, on a leading-rein. She would give
him no cause to fault her own horsemanship. The man
had an insufferably low opinion of women, which grated
to the core of her being.

Their pace changed from a steady canter to a walk as
the track narrowed, leading down to the ford where the
river could be safely crossed. Ahead, Sir Rolf had turned
aside to wait as the first of his men entered the water.
To her surprise, she saw that the fast-flowing river came
up to the riders' girths.

'Give me your reins,' Sir Rolf commanded as she drew
level with him. 'I shall lead you across.'

'I can manage well enough.'

A light flared briefly in his tawny eyes as he met her
defiance with unconcealed amusement.

Some of Sir Rolf's antagonism towards the minstrel
mellowed as he stared down at her. The ride had brought
a rose-glow to her high cheekbones, and her kingfisher
blue eyes flashed with a proud fire. He had been surprised to discover that she rode as though she had been
born to the saddle, her hand light and expert upon the
reins. Even so, she was in his charge, and there was
something unsettling about the woodland on either side
of the river. It was quiet...too quiet! None of the usual
rustling noise of animals or chirping of birds accompanied the soft sigh of flowing water. The feeling
of unease that had been with him all day persisted, and
it was connected with the last heated exchange he had
had with Sedbury. The earl had been furious that he was
not to accompany them to Court, but it was more his
attitude towards the minstrel-girl that troubled Sir Rolf;
it was as though an unspoken threat hung in the air between them—one governed by malice. Clearly the in-
terview with Queen Eleanor had not gone as Sedbury
wished. He would make a vindictive enemy, and he had
for many years been close to King Henry. Could they
trust him? This place was ideal for an ambush, and
outlaws were known to be in the area.

'The current is swift.' He addressed Meriel, anxious to move on. 'I would be failing my queen if you chanced to drown only hours after leaving Winchester.'

'It takes more than a trifling stream to kill off a...' Meriel snapped her lips shut, appalled that she had almost revealed her identity, for the sudden memory of her father's being swept out to sea in a raging storm had caught her off guard. There was a shout ahead, and one of the soldiers fell sideways into the river. 'You had best look to your own men...' she began, but fell silent at seeing the arrow-shaft projecting from the man's back as he floated downstream. Then everything happened in a confused blur as men began swinging down out of the trees along the river.

'To arms!' Sir Rolf shouted, turning his mount back up the bank as his men began to wheel slowly about. 'You three get the women to safety.' Drawing his sword, he urged his horse past Meriel and Bella, his voice urgent. 'Rally, men! To me!'

Within moments, the peaceful ford had turned into a battleground, and Meriel's skin chilled at the cries from the wounded men. Sir Rolf was striking out at a red-haired ox of a man who, together with two of his companions, was attempting to drag him from his saddle. They might as well try to pluck prey from a lion's claws! The soft leather of Sir Rolf's tunic stretched tautly across the muscle-honed strength of his shoulders and arms as his sword flashed, lethal as lightning, down upon his attackers. The troubadours had not lied when they praised his skill at arms. Golden-haired and handsome as a demi-god, he fought with the unleashed fury of a demon. No blade seemed capable of coming close to him, and his opponents fell back, bloodied from his onslaught.

An arrow whined past Meriel's head, reminding her of her own danger, which had been forgotten in the enthralment of watching Sir Rolf fight. Urging her mare forward, she glimpsed Bella, white-lipped with terror, clinging to her mare's mane as Sergeant Kedge tried to

control the frightened animal. Then the mare reared up,
an arrow lodged in her flank. Bella screamed, and, her
arms snatching wildly at the air, she lost her hold and
slipped down into the water. Her head broke the surface,
but then, to Meriel's horror, she was again sucked under.

'Bella!' Meriel screamed, knowing her friend could
not swim.

The soldiers were all engaged in hand-to-hand fighting
with their attackers, and a hasty glance showed her that
Sir Rolf was still surrounded. Even Sergeant Kedge was
now being attacked and could do nothing to help.
Catching sight of Bella's pale face, her mouth wide as
she surfaced to gasp for breath before being dragged
under for the second time, Meriel threw off her own
heavy cloak. Mindless of the danger to herself, she leapt
from her mount in midstream. The water closed over
her in an icy flood. Her foot touched the rocky bottom
and she turned on her side, kicking out as she rose to
the surface in the shoulder-high water. She shook the
hair from her eyes, her vision blurred by droplets of water
clinging to her lashes. A few yards away, she could just
make out Bella's head as she struggled to keep it above
the water. Her own long skirts dragged against every
movement as she struck out towards her friend. Dimly
she heard the shouts and ringing of steel from the
fighting, but it now seemed in another world; all she
could think of was reaching Bella.

'Stay calm, Bella! Try to let your body float,' she
shouted desperately, praying her friend could hear and
take heed. Even as the words left her lips, she saw Bella's
head sink out of sight into the water. This time, to her
alarm, she did not surface again. Reaching the spot where
she had last seen her, Meriel gulped a long breath and
swam down into the gloomy depths. She could see little,
then her foot touched something soft. Her heart leapt
to her throat and even as her lungs began to burn from
lack of air, she swam deeper, grabbing at Bella's form
and dragging her to the surface. The pressure scalded
her lungs and her head seemed as though it was about

to burst as she kicked upwards. Her head broke free of the water. Gasping and spluttering, she gulped in as much water as air. The current was too strong for her to get her footing, and she heaved at Bella's inert form to bring her head above the water. They were being carried downstream away from the fighting, but she was too tired to swim against the current, weakening with every moment. Bella's weight was like a millstone. She had to get them on land quickly, or they would both drown.

Reeds grew along the far bank and there the water would be shallow, allowing them to hide from their attackers. Meriel concentrated all her energy upon reaching the bank, but, hampered by Bella's weight, she found the current prevented her from getting a foothold. She was a strong swimmer, however, and although they had now been swept round a curve in the stream from the fighting, she was making headway towards the bank. Dear God, let them soon reach the safety of the rushes! If she did not get Bella ashore quickly and revive her, it could be too late!

Then she grabbed at a thick branch growing low over the water, bracing herself against the current. Still clutching Bella, she managed to kneel on the river bed, although the water swirled about her waist, trying to drag her backwards. Her arms felt as though they were being wrenched from their sockets as she clamped them about Bella's waist and heaved her like a flour-sack into the reeds. Bella coughed, and, with a groan, vomited, clearing her lungs of the water she had swallowed. Meriel scanned the bank, assuring herself that they were safely hidden.

Bella pushed herself up on to her elbows, her breathing ragged. 'Heaven be praised!' Slowly her eyes lost their glazed expression as she stared at Meriel, who was watching her anxiously.

'Hush, Bella. Whoever attacked us could be close by.'

Bella nodded. Reaching out to grasp Meriel's hand, she raised it to her lips, her voice barely audible. 'I owe you my life. You risked your own to save me—a worthless harlot. I shall never forget this day, or the debt I owe you.'

Meriel shook her head. 'You are my friend. The men were all fighting. I did nothing special.' She gestured for silence, as the sound of approaching horses warned her of possible danger.

'Spread out and search the reeds. Their bodies must be found!' Sir Rolf's voice was unmistakable as he gruffly barked the order.

Shakily, Meriel stood up. 'We are both safe, Sir Rolf!'

He swung round in the saddle at the sound of her voice, his stern face relaxing with relief. As quickly, his lips thinned, his eyes glowing with a predatory light. A rush of heat rose from her neck to scald her cheeks. Her sodden gown would be clinging to every curve and hollow of her body as tightly as a second skin. Then his long dark lashes veiled his desire and, snatching off his cloak, he leaped from his horse and strode into the knee-deep water to drape it about her shivering figure.

A soldier came forward with a blanket for Bella to wrap round herself, and he helped her up the bank to the horses. Sir Rolf took Meriel's arm as she lifted her heavy skirts to wade through the water. Where his fingers circled her chilled flesh, they seemed to scorch every nerve-end.

'Both of you must change out of your wet clothes, and some of my men need attention to their wounds before we continue our journey.'

Meriel stiffened at the terseness of his tone. 'Obviously your men beat off our assailants. Were they outlaws, seeking to rob us?'

'They were not outlaws.' His tone hardened. 'Although we were meant to believe they were!'

'Then who were they?'

'You need not fear they will attack again.' He ignored the question, looking at her sharply, two grooves appearing at the side of his mouth to warn her she had forgotten her place. It was not for her, a minstrel, to question him. 'What madness possessed you to jump in the water after the Spanish woman?' he continued grittily. 'You could have been drowned. Have you forgotten how important your service is to Her Majesty?'

The rebuke stung. She *had* forgotten. But then her only concern had been for her friend. Shivering beneath the cloak, Meriel clambered up the bank.

'I could not let Bella drown,' she said, shrugging off the knight's hold, uncaring that her tone was as chilling and haughty as his.

'A brave deed,' he said with greater warmth. 'But dangerous.'

'We are both safe.' Her heart fluttered like a caged bird. He looked so stern and formidable. Surely the softening about his full lips could not be admiration? 'I must not delay your attending to your men. I can change later, once the more seriously wounded have been tended to. I have some skill in such matters.'

A groan drew her attention to the figure of a young squire propped up by a tree. His face was grey with pain, and her heart went out to him as she saw he must be two or three years younger than herself. An arrow had gone right through his upper arm, its wicked bloody point projecting some inches. Tom Kedge was bending over him, forcing a stick between his teeth for the lad to bite on. When the sergeant's hand closed over the feathered shaft, preparing to snap it off, then draw the arrow through the arm, the squire's eyes bulged with terror.

'A moment, Sergeant Kedge.' Meriel squatted at the squire's side and spoke very low, for his ears alone. 'You know that the shaft must be drawn, or your blood will become poisoned and you will die. Courage takes many forms. The pain will be intense, but it will be over quickly, I promise.'

She stood up and moved several paces away, the squire's calmer gaze on her. Tom Kedge moved quickly, snapping the shaft and drawing it through the arm in a single fluid movement. The squire went as white as a corpse, but no sound came from his lips and, as the sergeant tossed the broken arrow into his lap with an approving grunt, the squire's eyes glittered with pride.

'Whatever you said to him, I thank you,' Sir Rolf said from behind her. 'You gave him the courage to bear the pain in silence like a true knight.'

She turned to face him, her pulse quickening that there was no longer censure in his golden gaze. 'The lad merely needed a moment to prepare himself. The wound must be bandaged. I have a veil among my belongings that can be torn into bindings.'

'Then you must allow me to replace your veil when we are in London. A minstrel cannot afford to be so generous—but then I begin to suspect you are rather more used to luxury than to poverty. Sedbury must have been a generous master.'

The implication that he believed her to be the Earl of Sedbury's mistress stabbed like a knife at her pride. She fought to keep her temper, and lowered her lashes to conceal her fury from him. Remember that you are supposed to be a minstrel! she told herself firmly. No female servant could escape the attentions of her master; her duty was to serve and pleasure him in any way he chose.

His brows drew ominously together, his voice glacial. 'You have charms worthy of a king. That is why you have been chosen.'

Her head shot up, anger making her blood boil at this added insult, which could not go unanswered. She saw Bella shake her head, warning her to remain silent, but her temper would not be bridled, and there were many curious glances from the soldiers at her impassioned tone. 'We all serve as we are commanded. You condemn me, yet you know nothing about me. Nothing! I did not ask, or wish, to be sent to Court. If I have charms fit for a king, it is the role that you, not I, have chosen for myself.' Her voice took on a dangerous edge. 'I know my worth, Sir Rolf, and I am no one's mistress but my own.'

For a long moment Sir Rolf glowered sardonically at her. His amber eyes glowed with a fierce light—a light borne, she thought, of murderous rage and the burning hunger of desire. She should hate him for the contempt in which he held her, but deep inside a traitorous seed was sending down its roots, anchoring itself against all reason and impossible hope. Who in his past had tainted his regard for all women? How could she exorcise the dark demons which haunted him? Or why indeed should she want to? Yet she did! And with an intensity that left her shaken.

CHAPTER FIVE

'YOU MUST change out of your wet clothes, my lady,'
Bella urged as Meriel moved from one wounded man to
another. 'You will take a lung-fever and will be unable
to serve Her Majesty.'

Meriel saw that all the men had been tended to. Fortunately, only the first one had died from his wound
and, although three had injuries which would prevent
them fighting for some weeks, they would not prove
fatal. Satisfied that she could do no more to ease their
suffering, she clamped her teeth together to still her
shivering and followed Bella towards some dense haw-
thorn bushes behind which they could change.

She pulled Sir Rolf's cloak tighter about her chilled
figure and smelt the tangy muskiness of his body rising
from it. The masculine scent of his skin, mingling with
that of leather and horses, was disturbingly sensual, and
her fingers lingered upon the material until, with a start,
she realised that her thoughts were becoming dominated
by him. If she were to have any chance of succeeding at
Court with King Henry, she dared not let her emotions
become entangled with another man. It was time she put
her girlish fantasy of the dream-knight behind her. This
was the real world where only her wits could save her.

Bella, who was already in dry clothes, helped her off
with her gown and rubbed her body with a coarse cloth
to bring some warmth to her shivering limbs. As the
numbing effects of the cold dispersed, Meriel's thoughts
returned to the first moments of the attack. The images
were indistinct, since all her concentration had been on
Bella, but there was something indefinable which nagged
at her mind, and which continued to leave her uneasy
when they continued their journey. The feeling stayed

with her all day. The attack had delayed them for nearly two hours, and that night they camped in a clearing in the thickly wooded weald. The morning mist had dispersed to a hot summer's day, and the night was warm and bright with moonlight. After the evening meal, Meriel and Bella sat by the camp-fire a short distance away from the men.

'What troubles you, Bella?' her friend's unusual quietness prompted her to ask. 'It is more than your fright at nearly drowning, is it not?'

Bella hugged her knees to her chest, her voice low and taut. 'I have heard the men-at-arms talking. They say the attack was no ordinary one by outlaws to rob us.' She paused, clearly struggling to find the words to express her feelings. 'I think the solders are right in what they say. What if someone does not want you at Court?' She broke off, staring into the fire.

'But no one knows of the queen's plan other than those who are a party to it!' Meriel frowned at Bella's stricken look. 'Whom do you suspect, Bella?'

The Spanish woman looked down at her toes, her voice leaden. 'I am not sure... I do not understand this intrigue. I owe your family so much. Lord Sedbury took me from an evil life that I abhorred. I cannot change what I am, a ruined woman, but he has given me back my self-respect—I have great affection for him... To you, I owe my life. You have shown me friendship where others have scorned me. I fear for you... I am afraid of something I do not understand.'

Her eyes widened with fear and uncertainty and, as she held Meriel's puzzled gaze, her look was tormented. 'I pray you, be on your guard, mistress. It frightens me that your identity must be kept secret. It is as though those who should be protecting you have washed their hands of you.'

Meriel stared into the flames of the fire. She sensed that not only was Bella holding something back, but that she was torn by divided loyalties. In all the time she had known her, she had never spoken one word against

Sedbury. Did she suspect him? But that was ridiculous! Why, then, did the thought make her so uneasy?

Conquering her own disquiet, Meriel regarded Bella's anxious expression. 'Your fright in the water has made you fanciful, my friend. Sir Rolf and his men will protect me. They have proved their worth today.'

'These men live by the sword and are not easy to discipline.' Bella grimaced. 'There are many such in Spain. I have seen the way their eyes follow you. They respect Sir Rolf, and know he will carry out his threat to hang any man who tries to molest us. He is bound by his oath to the queen to protect your life. He, too, watches you. To safeguard your honour, you should tell him who you truly are.'

'That is not possible. I gave my word to both the queen and Lord Sedbury. And you must say nothing either— promise me?'

'If that is what you wish,' Bella answered, but her dark eyes slid away from Meriel's stare and, wrapping her cloak about her, she lay down, turning her face away, her voice strained. 'I wish you would reconsider, Mistress Meriel. Sir Rolf should know the truth.'

The events of the day swam round in Meriel's head, giving her tired mind no peace. The unease she had felt after the attack was still with her, yet its foundation continued to elude her. The men were beginning to settle down for the night, but her legs were stiffening after her hard swim and she was too restless to sleep. She stood up, needing to stretch her limbs, signalling to the two guards on duty that she intended to remain within the safety of the light from the fire. For some moments she paced the small space and then halted to stare up at the stars, and was suddenly overwhelmed with the need to see Wychaven again. Memories of her childhood crowded her mind, and she was again the fêted daughter of Sir Arnulf, cheered by the fisherfolk of the village whenever she accompanied her father on his rides. How had her people fared under Sedbury's yoke? The winters were hard for them. It was time she returned to Wychaven.

But to accomplish that she must first win herself a husband—and one who took pride in the land and her people. Perhaps, at Court, there might be a way, as her mother had suggested? Alas, she did not go to Court as Meriel, heir to Wychaven, but as a minstrel.

Her frustration grew. The years were slipping by—did her people feel themselves deserted? Her place was at Wychaven—not shut away in a remote castle at Sedbury's command, or even at Court. The muted sounds of the woodland hardly penetrated her consciousness. She yearned for the clash of the sea pounding on the rocks, and its sibilant whisper as the waves licked over the sandy cove. The harsh screech of the scavenging gulls and the rustle of the wind through the elm and alder grove— these sounds were the heartbeat of Wychaven, the song of Wychaven calling her to return.

She looked up at the stars, the same stars that would be shining over Wychaven, and all at once she sensed she was no longer alone. She tensed, her nose lifting like a deer scenting the air for danger. There was no sound to warn her that someone approached. It was in the intangible awareness which ran like a fiery finger down her back. There was no need to turn her head to know that Sir Rolf was standing behind her.

'It is not safe for you here.' His tone was impersonal, unlike the fire the moonlight revealed in his eyes when she faced him. 'You should stay closer to the guards.'

'I had no wish to disturb you. I shall return to my place.'

'I have not thanked you for tending my men's wounds.' Despite his words, his handsome face was set and suspicious. He looked at her steadily, blocking her path.

'I did little.' She shrugged his words aside. She could hardly tell him she had been brought up to tend the ills of her own people. 'Your men know well how to care for their injuries.'

The grimness of his expression sparked a chord in her memory of those first moments of fighting. She had glimpsed the face of only one of their attackers—now, as she again recalled it, she knew what had been troubling her all day. Surely she must be mistaken? But the man's lank red hair and battle-scarred face was very like one of Sedbury's captains! Had Bella seen him, too? Was that why she was so upset? But Sedbury had been eager to serve the queen...or was he? He had thought he would accompany her to Court. Did he now fear the situation would slip from his control, and that his hold over herself would weaken?

She dragged her mind back to the present, aware that Sir Rolf was studying her fixedly. 'You know many things one would not expect of a minstrel.'

'Part of our skill is to observe people and create songs about them,' she countered smoothly. 'The Earl of Sedbury's household is large.'

His straight brows drew down over his piercing eyes, and for a heart-tearing moment she thought he had seen through her disguise.

'Where did you learn to swim?' he surprised her by asking.

'In the sea at Wychaven when I was a child,' she answered too quickly, and, realising her error, resorted to half-truths. 'I was born on the Lady Maude's estate, which is by the sea. Her ladyship liked my singing and instructed her chaplain to tutor me. When Sir Arnulf died, the Lady Maude's kinsman, Lord Sedbury, became the guardian of her estates. Her ladyship took me with her when she was moved to Eadstone.'

'How long have you been at Eadstone?'

'Seven years.' A wistful note crept into her voice.

His frown deepened. 'Wychaven sounds special to you.'

She forced a shaky smile. 'Does not the place where we are born always seem unlike any other? Wychaven can be harsh and uncompromising, but its beauty is almost magical.'

'As is the water-sprite who longs to return there.' The taunting words were spiked with steel. 'You showed rare courage in saving Bella's life. You will need that courage in the days ahead at Court.'

His hand was warm as it brushed a stray tendril of her hair from her cheek, then it moved to her chin, trapping it between his forefinger and thumb as he tilted her face upwards. His full lips twisted with sensual promise, but it did not reach his eyes. 'The queen has placed you out of my reach—for the moment. It will not always be so. I have not forgotten the invitation offered in your dance, sweet minstrel. I intend to hold you to it.'

She stepped back, her eyes flashing with outrage. 'You presume too much, Sir Rolf!'

'Do I?' His eyes glowed with a cold infathomable light that chilled her to the bone. 'So now you think to set the knight aside in favour of the king! No woman uses me for her own ends, but I am patient. I can wait until your task is done at Court. Then I will hold you to that promise.'

'A lot can happen at Court,' she flared, refusing to give ground at his peremptory tone. She tossed back her hair and lifted her chin defiantly.

The hollows of his lean face tautened with barely restrained anger. 'Indeed it can! And you are there to serve the queen's needs, not your own ambition. Remember that, minstrel, or your false pride may be your downfall!'

Meriel's nails dug into her palms as she struggled to control her anger at his arrogance. She took a grip on her emotions, forcing herself to remember that she was supposed to be a servant. 'I have no false pride,' she muttered. 'Nor do I need lessons on how to conduct myself at Court.'

She held his glittering tawny gaze, her heart thudding wildly at having to curb her rage. Why did he always think the worst of her? And she sensed it was not just because she was a servant, but because she was a woman, that he treated her with such scorn.

'Life at Court is not the same as at Eadstone,' he responded curtly. 'Return to your place by the fire. We have many miles to travel tomorrow to make up for time lost today.'

He stood back for her to pass him, and they walked in silence to where Bella lay curled on the ground.

'Sleep well,' he said on leaving her. 'We rise at dawn.'

Her hands clenched as she watched him walk away, his tall figure lightfooted and graceful as he stepped over the bodies of his sleeping men. Her resentment flared at the assured way he made his claim upon her, yet strangely it was that very cool assurance in everything he did which set her pulses tumbling. A man of steel in body and soul, an unvanquished warlord of high ideals. Wychaven had need of such a master.

She stood rock-still. The thought had formed unbidden, startling and annoying her. Yet, was it so absurd? Her gaze remained upon him as he squatted by the fire. Then he looked across at her for a long moment, the firelight softening the rugged planes of his handsome face. Her heartbeat quickened. Why did he have to be the image of the knight she had carried so long in her heart? More maddening still was the knowledge that he was a warrior capable of wrenching Wychaven from Sedbury's clutches and holding it safely for her. To such a man it would be all too easy to lose her heart, but had he not made it perfectly clear that he despised her more than he desired her?

A secretive smile touched her lips as she lay down. Of course, since he believed her to be a minstrel, he would have a low opinion of her morals. But once he learned who she truly was, surely his opinion would change. The antagonism between them was through misunderstanding. To wrest Wychaven from Lord Sedbury, she must marry. And as she had no intention of wedding some ageing baron to satisfy the earl's thirst for power, why should she not marry Sir Rolf?

During the next two days Meriel began to wonder whether she had set herself an impossible task to secure Wychaven's future. Sir Rolf was cool but courteous, and never sought her company unless she was accompanied by Bella and they were in close proximity to his men. Although he had declared his intention of making her his mistress in the future, he would not break his oath to Queen Eleanor while she was under his protection. It was heartening to know he did not abuse the privileges of his rank. He lived by the same rules by which he governed his men, and would ask of them nothing that he himself was not prepared to do. That was the only leadership these hard men could respect, and they would give their lives for him.

They were also the qualities she needed in a husband, if Wychaven were to prosper. Only in dreams, or the songs of troubadours, did women of her rank marry for love. She must be practical—for although from their first meeting she had been physically attracted to Sir Rolf, she did not delude herself that she loved him. She respected him—surely that was more important? It was. At the turn of her thoughts, her heart gave a twist. She could tolerate a marriage without love, but could she bear it without mutual regard? The ache in her chest stabbed deeper. There lay the obstacle to her future. She gave herself a mental shake. To save Wychaven, she must first win Sir Rolf's admiration and esteem. Her blood raced faster at the challenge. Respect was something she suspected Sir Rolf accorded to few women, if any.

They were riding through a large village that was dominated by the tall buildings of a grey stone convent, and Meriel was surprised when the troop drew to a halt by the church outside its walls. Sir Rolf dismounted, and waited for Meriel to draw level with him.

'The good sisters here will provide us with a meal and lodgings for the night. We have ridden hard these last two days, and tomorrow we shall reach the Court.'

'I had not realised we would arrive so soon.' Meriel voiced her nervousness, stemming as much from his nearness as to what awaited her at Court.

'You need not fear you will fail Her Majesty. King Henry will be won over by your dancing, as the queen intended.' He smiled sardonically. 'As soon as we have the information Queen Eleanor needs, we shall leave.'

His brown cloak was thrown back over his shoulder and his leather jerkin was open at the neck, the whiteness of his shirt emphasising the healthy bronze colour of his skin. He stood, feet apart, his long muscular legs encased in tight-fitting hose and knee-boots, and hooked his thumbs over his sword-belt. The cool assurance of his manner irritated her, but under the impact of his handsome, commanding stare, it was impossible to be annoyed with him for long. There was something about his tone which made her ask, ingenuously, 'Does England hold so little charm for you that you are so eager to return to France?'

'Oh, England has its charms,' his topaz gaze slid appreciatively over her figure, 'but duty must come before pleasure. My duty is to Prince Richard, who has need of every man in crushing this new rebellion which has broken out in Aquitaine.'

'Instead, you are bound to play escort to a lowly minstrel,' she taunted softly.

Sir Rolf looked up at the minstrel's refined features, marvelling again at her beauty. She sat tall and proud in the saddle and was like no servant—or lady, he had ever met. His blood stirred. Oddly, he felt drawn to protect her. Why? Through duty? But no, it was something other than that. It was partly desire, partly the need to capture and hold on to an illusion. The absurdity of his thoughts mocked him. Here, of all places, he should know better!

'At the queen's command, I am your escort.' He stripped his voice of any emotion, but the blue-green eyes were as storm-tossed as a winter's sea as she held his incensed glare. 'Later, I anticipate the pleasure of my reward.'

'Your reward may be other than you think, Sir Rolf.' Instead of anger, her voice held the note of challenge. His eyes narrowed in warning, but her gaze continued to hold his, and there was nothing brazen about her cool stare, but a confidence that matched the courage she had shown by rescuing her companion.

Meriel looked past him to the low building attached to the north side of the church. 'Is that a reclusorium? Is there an anchoress within that church?' Her questions withered at his stony expression. Her pride smarted. She had asked nothing out of place. Refusing to back down, she continued in feigned innocence. 'I ask only because there is an anchoress living in a small cell in a churchyard near Wychaven who has been enclosed there for twenty years. Sir Arnulf gave yearly alms to her church for the poor, for the holy woman was given to visions, and had once sent word to him that she had seen the destruction of our fishing fleet should they set sail that day. They remained in port, and a freak storm blew up, sinking three vessels near Weymouth. I have often wondered what leads these men or women to shut themselves away from the world to live almost like hermits.'

'Many wish to atone for their sins,' he said brusquely. 'Others to find peace. The anchoress here is my widowed sister, the Lady Isolda.'

With a curt nod of dismissal, he turned towards the church, all thoughts of the minstrel dispersing as he entered the porch and stooped to pass through a low archway leading to the sparse chambers adjoining the church. He knocked on the shuttered window, and it was opened by a serving-maid.

'I am Sir Rolf of Blackleigh. I would speak with the Lady Isolda.'

The window was closed, and moments later a side door opened, and he was led into the chamber. A tall woman stood up from kneeling at a small window which overlooked the altar of the church. She was dressed in a simple gown of untreated wool, her proud pointed face sharpened by the close confines of a white wimple and veil which completely covered her fair hair. Her long elegant fingers tightly clutched the crucifix against her breast.

'Rolf! I had no idea you were in England.' Her voice echoed the coldness of their last meeting. In the four years since his sister had become an anchoress, she had become even more beautiful, and looked closer to his own age than to the ten years she gave him in seniority.

'How are you, Isolda?'

Her hazel eyes brightened with tears. 'You sound so hard and unforgiving—just like our father. Did you know that Lord Drogo came here before he began his pilgrimage to Jerusalem?'

'I saw Father in the Holy Land. He did not speak of you.'

'And you, Rolf, do you ever speak of me?'

She sounded defiant, but her lower lip quivered, her hazel eyes beseeching him to forgive her, and he almost faltered. He saw her again as the sister who had cared for him like a mother after their own had died when he was three years old. Then, she had been a generous creature who had given him his first pony when his father was away fighting some far-off war. Beautiful, witty, exuberant and always laughing, he had worshipped her as a saint among women—the perfect lady, she could do no wrong in his eyes, until... The memory was banished before it formed. The scar down his neck ached as he controlled his resurging anger as he remembered the way the laughing young woman had changed...

'Do you really care, Rolf?' she repeated as she moved slowly forward, her arms outstretched in supplication. She knelt at his feet. 'Can you forgive me?'

Meriel looked up at the sound of spurs ringing upon the stone flagstones. Sir Rolf stood in the doorway of the refectory used by the convent's guests, and beckoned to her. She stood up, but when Bella made to follow, he put up a hand to stay her. There was a setness about Sir Rolf's features that warned Meriel that his mood was unpredictable.

'Bella will remain here. The Lady Isolda wishes to speak with Mistress Meriel,' he said guardedly. 'She is granted special privileges, despite her seclusion, and wishes you to sing for her.'

From what little Meriel knew of female recluses, she realised that the Lady Isolda lived differently from most who deliberately cut themselves off from the world. But the Lady Isolda came from a great family. Meriel tried to remember all her mother had told her of this family, when it had been part of her education to know the names and relationships of all the noble houses. Although Sir Rolf, as a third son, possessed only the small manor of Blackleigh which he had purchased from the ransom moneys he had gained in France, his father held land in both Normandy and the eastern counties of England.

'The Lady Isolda is a widow, is she not? She was married to Sir Harold of...'

'You need not concern yourself with my sister's past life,' Sir Rolf interrupted her sharply, reminding her that she had spoken out of turn.

Blushing furiously, she followed him to the church, where a man-at-arms came and handed her the lute which had been tied to her bundle of belongings when they left Eadstone. She gripped it firmly, wondering how she was to win Sir Rolf's respect when even the simplest question uttered by her would be viewed as insolence, as she was forced to continue her role of servant.

The chamber she was led into was larger than she had expected, but only two small windows allowed the fading evening light into the room. When Sir Rolf stood aside, she saw a tall slim woman sitting in the shadows and curtsied.

'Come forward, girl!' The woman's tone was imperious and without warmth. 'Rolf, you did not tell me she was beautiful as well as talented.' She went on in French, clearly believing that Meriel would not understand her rapid flow of words. 'Is it Queen Eleanor's interest you serve by taking her to Court, or your own? I wondered at your unusual role in escorting a travelling minstrel. Even you, it seems, are not impervious to a pretty face.

And as to that, it is time you considered taking a wealthy wife. You are high in Prince Richard's favour, but what purpose does it serve you if you are given nothing in reward? Perhaps, at Court...'

'My sword is my fortune. There is no shame in that!' he declared with a heavy note of warning. 'I shall marry if, and when, it pleases me. It is not a subject I intend to discuss, especially in front of a servant who speaks our language.'

The Lady Isolda turned a sharper stare upon Meriel, who unconsciously held her head erect with the natural bearing of a noblewoman. Even though the Lady Isolda's face was partially hidden by the shadows, it seemed to Meriel that an amused smile touched her lips.

'A song, minstrel!' she commanded. 'Something of freedom, of an impassioned love, or the thrill of the hunt—all of which belong to a world lost to me.'

At his sister's words, Sir Rolf tensed, his handsome face shadowed with anger, and Meriel felt the tension crackling between brother and sister. Had they quarrelled before she arrived, or was it something deeper? The Lady Isolda spoke as though she were a prisoner, not an anchoress of her own free will.

Meriel glanced at Sir Rolf, now leaning with his arms folded against the wall, his expression rigid and uncompromising as he nodded for her to sing. Deciding upon an old Celtic legend, she struck up a lively tune and sang the song of King Herla who attended the wedding of the King of the Pygmies in an underground palace. As the story unfolded, she moved slowly between the two figures, stingingly aware of Sir Rolf watching her every move.

Unlike when she had danced for Queen Eleanor, she now completely ignored Sir Rolf's presence, her attention centred upon the Lady Isolda. Her voice sobered to a low throbbing tone as the song told that when King Herla and his courtiers were about to leave the feast, the king was presented with a small hound which he was commanded to hold in his arms, and not to dismount from his horse before the dog jumped to the ground. Back on the surface, the party róde long and hard, the land around them unfamiliar in the twilight. The king, seeing a shepherd, asked after his queen. The shepherd answered that there was no queen of that name, but that there had been, two centuries earlier. Meriel's voice rose as the rhythm quickened, as she sang of how several of the courtiers leapt from their horses and were immediately turned to dust. Isolda leaned forward, listening raptly as Meriel played on, her sweet voice trilling out King Herla's warning that none must dismount until the hound jumped to the ground. But the hound never did jump down, and Herla and his courtiers still roam the forests and hills. Meriel's fingers slowed upon the lute-strings, her head tilted sideways as she looked from Sir Rolf to his sister, and her tone dropped to a conspiratorial whisper. 'And there are some who do say that Herla still rides to this day, but they now call him Henry Plantagenet,' she finished, to the sound of the Lady Isolda's laughter.

Sir Rolf ran his hand across his mouth, hiding his own amusement at Meriel's allusion to King Henry's constant movements about England, which were the despair of his courtiers. The king rarely stayed in any place longer than a few days, and it was said his legs were constantly sore from the hours he spent in the saddle. The Lady Isolda clapped her hands, her laughter unrestrained.

'The girl has wit! King Henry is ever one to laugh at his own shortcomings. You have chosen well, brother. The king will be captivated.' The Lady Isolda stood up, her hazel eyes ringed by pale blonde lashes sweeping Meriel from head to foot as she walked towards her.

Belatedly, Meriel remembered to lower her gaze in a subservient manner. The Lady Isolda turned away, and when Meriel looked up, she was studying her brother in the same forthright manner, but her face revealed nothing of her thoughts. 'Your minstrel intrigues me, Rolf. I would speak with her until Vespers, but I am sure our women's foolish talk will bore you. You have no objection to my stealing her away from you for a time, I trust?'

'None at all.' He bowed, but despite his smooth tone, Meriel was startled at the hardness of his expression. He did not want her to stay with his sister. Did he think a common minstrel would taint this saintly woman?

Meriel's eyes burned with indignation, until, with a start, she saw the knight's brittle stare fastened upon his sister, not herself, and the hollow scar on his neck was starkly white against his darker skin, betraying the anger he was concealing, yet his departing bow was deferential. When he turned to nod briefly to Meriel, his eyes glowed like red-hot metal. It seemed for a moment that he would speak, then his dark lashes shielded his eyes and he left without a word.

Meriel watched him stride to the door, a slight frown forming on her brow. During the past days, she had studied him often. He had always been remote and self-assured, but now there was a stiffening in his usual supple movements, a barely discernible drooping of his proud shoulders which puzzled her. Surely he did not disapprove of the pious life the Lady Isolda now led? When the door closed behind him, she glanced at her and was disconcerted to find the older woman's assessing gaze upon her.

'I had not thought Rolf a knight-errant.' Lady Isolda seated herself on a stone bench by the window, and patted it for Meriel to join her. 'But you are no ordinary minstrel-girl, are you?'

Meriel sat down, feeling uncomfortable beneath the steady gaze of those hazel eyes that were bright with curiosity.

'No, I am not really a minstrel—but due to a misunderstanding, and the events which followed, I must for now become one.'

'And unless I miss my guess, this misunderstanding was brought about by Sir Rolf, was it not?'

'How could you know that?'

'I know my brother.' Lady Isolda smiled grimly. 'But there is much to your story which intrigues me. Will you tell me how this came about?'

Meriel briefly explained her first encounter with the knight by the river beyond Eadstone Castle.

'Who are you?' Lady Isolda persisted when Meriel hesitated to go on.

'Forgive me, my lady, but I cannot say.'

'But you are nobly born?'

'I am the daughter and heiress of a landed knight.' Meriel clasped her hands, feeling herself drawn into a trap.

'Does Sir Rolf know?'

Meriel shook her head. 'And he must not learn of it— not yet! Please, my lady, you will not tell him? My guardian was furious when the story came to light; he says I have disgraced his house. Only if I succeed in my allotted task am I to reveal my name. It is not just myself, but my dear mother who will suffer should I bring disgrace upon his name.'

'Men and their precious concept of honour!' the Lady Isolda said sharply. 'I doubt not this guardian of yours will bask in your success and use it to his own advantage. They care nothing for our feelings. We are not all meek chattels ready to do their bidding without question. But what a pretty pass your recklessness has brought you to!'

'I do not shock you, my lady?' Meriel voiced her surprise, for there was no condemnation in the Lady Isolda's tone.

'I have not forgotten what it is like to be young... To dream of a perfect knight.' She smiled warmly, inviting confidences. 'Would I be wrong to assume that you see my brother as the perfect knight?'

'He has many qualities,' Meriel began hesitantly. Despite the Lady Isolda's apparent friendliness, she was loath to speak of her private feelings.

'But, of course, he sees you only as a minstrel,' Lady Isolda remarked. 'Rolf insists on seeking a paragon among women, but all females are only human, with human frailities. For all that, he is not immune to your charms, or you would not be here now.' A speculative glow brightened her eyes, the fading light making her beauty more youthful—strangely worldly and sensual for these austere surroundings. 'I would help you if I can,' she said softly. 'No one knows my brother better than I. But I can do little if I do not know who you are. Your secret will be safe with me, I promise.'

Meriel wavered. How could she win Sir Rolf when she knew so little about him? But had not her father consulted the anchoress near Wychaven several times? The Lady Isolda would be bound by her holy vows not to break a confidence.

'I am Mistress Meriel of Wychaven, the ward of the Earl of Sedbury.'

'And Rolf truly believes you to be a humble minstrel?' Lady Isolda laughed softly. 'How blind can he be? Or does he simply wish not to see the obvious? He is proud and stubborn, once his mind has set upon a course.'

'The fault is mine, not his,' Meriel defended.

Lady Isolda leaned forward, her face like a beautiful but expressionless stone carving, as she prompted. 'The interests of my brother are close to my heart. Wychaven is a rich prize for any husband, but fortune alone will not win Rolf. He prizes virtue above all things, especially in any woman he would take to wife. Tell me— do you think you could win my brother?'

Startled by her bluntness, Meriel blushed. 'How could I? As a minstrel, in his eyes I am little more than a harlot. I have known no man, my lady, I swear.'

'Yet you find my brother arouses your interest? I think Rolf will have many surprises in store for him in the future.' The lengthening shadows hid the Lady Isolda's expression as she sat back, but her voice was impassioned. 'You would make Rolf the very wife he needs. Are you aware, though, that King Henry has intimated that he intends Louise of Auvergne to be Rolf's bride?

Her estates are on the borders of the Angevin empire. Of course, were Rolf to win her, he would rise high in the king's favour as justiciar and captain of a border army, but Louise is a pallid, convent-reared creature who would not suit Rolf at all.'

A spasm contracted Meriel's heart. The wealth of Wychaven was nothing compared to the greater glory Louise of Auvergne could bring to Sir Rolf. 'I knew nothing of this. Sir Rolf can hardly refuse such a generous offer.'

'Nonsense, my dear,' the Lady Isolda confided. 'Of course Rolf craves vast estates, but it is for you to make him want the woman who could bring them to him. In the next week or so you will be spending much time in my brother's company. I cannot say it will be easy to win him, for sometimes I think that his heart is encased in steel. It was not always so! Rolf is but a man—and therefore susceptible to a woman's charms. If ever you should have need of my help, Meriel of Wychaven, I will do what I can.'

Surprised by the Lady Isolda's championship, Meriel found she was trembling as excitement frayed her nerves. 'You are very kind, Lady Isolda.'

'I just wish my brother to have all he deserves in this life.'

On leaving the Lady Isolda's presence, Meriel felt light-headed. She would have expected condemnation from so holy a woman, but instead she had been welcomed and given unlooked-for support in winning Sir Rolf as her husband. She should be delighted, but somehow it left her with a rather unsettled feeling. Outside in the fresh air, other misgivings troubled her. The Lady Isolda had made it sound so easy. It would be far from that, especially if King Henry were intent on marrying Sir Rolf to the Lady Louise.

She frowned at seeing no sight of the two guards Sir Rolf had posted. It was almost dark, the yew and elm trees and high buildings of the convent changing to sinister shapes in the gloom. The Vesper bell began to toll as she picked her way across the churchyard, careful not to stumble over the exposed tree-roots. A twig snapped behind her. Startled, she turned, expecting to see one of Sir Rolf's guards. Her blood curdled when instead she recognised the red hair and bearded face of one of their attackers by the river. Backing away, she whirled, and lifting her cumbersome skirts high, ran towards the convent gate.

'Sir Rolf! Guards! Help...' Her scream was cut short as a rough cloak was thrown over her head and large hands grabbed her shoulder. Unable to see, she kicked out wildly. A meaty arm grasped her waist and she was lifted from the ground and flung over a man's shoulder.

'Let me go!' she gasped, her angry shout lost among the folds of the cloak. She struck out with her fists, making little impact against the stout leather of the man's tunic, her toes in her soft leather riding-boots bruising on her captor's thigh as her frantic struggles increased. The cloak stank of sweat and mildewed wool, and her lungs burned from the effort to breathe as the material pressed about her nose and mouth, stifling her.

Dimly she heard a gruff shout behind as her captor began to run back across the churchyard. Then other voices were all around her, angry and shouting, coupled with the ring of steel against steel. Her limbs were growing heavier as she fought for breath, but still she struck at him trying to impede his progress. Then her flailing hands brushed against a dagger-hilt hidden in the folds of his hood hanging down between his shoulders, which he probably used to launch a surprise attack upon an opponent. Desperate to escape, she tugged it free and, using all her strength, plunged it into his body below his ribs.

He stumbled, a foul oath rasping against her ears. At the same time, a vicious pain shot through her shoulder and side as her body collided with a tree-trunk. Red and orange stars flashed across her eyes, and she fought against the faintness that threatened to engulf her as her captor was abruptly jerked to a halt. There was a moment of weightlessness as she was tossed from his shoulder, then a sharp jolt when the last of the air was knocked from her lungs as her body crashed to the ground, and her senses deserted her.

'Meriel!' Sir Rolf's voice called from a great distance. Then, more loudly, 'Meriel!'

She opened her eyes. The suffocating folds of the rank cloak were gone, but she could just make out the pale outline of Sir Rolf's face and blond hair in the darkness. She tried to sit up, and winced at the sharp pain weaving through her skull.

'Keep still. You had a bad crack on the head,' he said, lifting her up and walking back to the convent.

Still dazed, she lay quietly in his arms, her head resting against his shoulder, but with each powerful stride he took she became more aware of the warmth and hardness of his body. The soft leather jerkin and linen shirt beneath were open to the waist, his skin still damp from the water he must have been washing in when he had rushed to her assistance.

'Did you recognise any of your attackers?' he asked, as they passed through the convent gate.

'Yes—one was among those who attacked us at the bridge.'

'I thought as much.' His voice hardened. 'That, too, was no ordinary attack.' He fell silent as they were surrounded by a group of anxious-looking nuns in the torchlit courtyard.

'The Holy Mother be praised that at least one of the poor lambs is saved,' the prioress cried.

Meriel started at the ominous words, suddenly fearful. 'Bella! Has something happened to Bella?'

'She's been taken,' Sir Rolf said gruffly. 'My guards were overpowered by several men who had scaled the convent wall. A nun discovered that Bella's cell was empty, and raised the alarm when she saw someone being carried through the gate. It was then we heard your screams. I fear these attacks are connected with our duties at Court.'

His eyes flashed, warning her to say nothing before the puzzled glances of the nuns. He strode past them towards the guest-house, and entered Meriel's chamber. Laying her gently down on the pallet bed, he sat on its edge, the single cresset oil-light throwing dark shadows across his lean features.

'Someone does not want you to appear before the king,' he declared gruffly. 'Were they Sedbury's men?'

Meriel swallowed against her rising dread. She had prayed she had been mistaken at the river, but who else would have had Bella and herself abducted? Although she had thought the earl eager to win Queen Eleanor's favour, there was more to this attack than that. Of course, Sedbury had wanted to travel to Court with her. If she won the king's favour, he would ruthlessly pursue the advantage, caring nothing for her lost reputation. By denying him, Queen Eleanor had robbed him of this chance. Sedbury would not openly strike against the queen, for of late the king's health was said to be ailing— and in such uncertain times, a man as greedy for power as her guardian would want to keep a foot in both camps. But was not her success at Court in Sedbury's best interest?

Her thoughts spun in chaotic confusion. 'What about Bella? Have you sent men after her?'

Sir Rolf leaned forward, gripping Meriel's shoulders. 'Some of my men have gone after them. Now, answer me! Was it Sedbury's men? Dear God, woman, do you not see the danger you are in?'

Frosty tentacles slithered down her spine. Was it only her reputation Sedbury was prepared to sacrifice for his own ends, or also her life?

'They *were* Lord Sedbury's men. The one who took me was from...' Her voice shook and her body began to tremble from the reaction of her ordeal.

Sir Rolf was watching her closely, his tawny-lion stare unnervingly close. Unable to hold his gaze, she looked down at her hands and was shocked to find them covered in blood. Wide-eyed with horror, she held them before her.

'I killed a man,' she groaned, her voice rising as she made to sit up, but was pushed firmly down on to the pillow. 'Dear God, I killed a man!'

'You did what had to be done,' Sir Rolf soothed. 'Had you not wounded him, he would have escaped with you before we could stop him. But it was not your hand that killed him. He was only wounded when we found you unconscious. Alas, he was struck down in the fighting before he could be questioned.'

Unaccountably, her eyes stung with hot tears at his comfort. A week ago she had been craving freedom from the mundane life at Eadstone; now she was thrust into a cruel, unforgiving world where only the strong or quick-witted could survive. Nothing in her sheltered life had prepared her for the intrigue and brutality which now surrounded her. She blinked away her threatening tears, angry at herself for allowing her weakness to show.

'That's better,' Sir Rolf said with an encouraging smile. He reached for the water-filled washing-bowl that had been placed in her cell by the nuns while she had been with the Lady Isolda. Dipping a linen cloth into the water, he gently wiped her hands. Even though they were clean, Sir Rolf continued to bathe them, his touch feathering across her skin, as he added in a low voice, 'Not many women would have had the courage to act as you did.'

The admiration in his tone, together with the sensual play of his fingers, gradually calmed her horror. Keeping her hand secure in his, he put the bowl on the floor, his expression enigmatic as he continued to stare down at her. The violent trembling which had gripped her body subsided to no more than the undulating ripples on a pond, brought on not by shock, but from the awareness of the man at her side.

He leaned closer, his face a handsbreadth from her own, filling her vision and her mind, as his eyes, heavy-lidded with desire, gazed upon her parted lips. Her breathing slowed with anticipation. Even in her innocence, she sensed the coiled passion controlled by his iron will. He lifted her hand, turning it palm upwards, his thumb languidly grazing the sensitive hollow. A gasp snatched in her throat at the tingling spiral of heat the light touch evoked.

'You are more tempting than an eastern *houri*—a nymph who leads a man to paradise,' he said hoarsely, swallowing hard as he kept a rein upon his emotions.

Her hand was released, but somehow it fell against his open tunic, the tips of her fingers touching the warmth and hair-roughened hardness of that broad chest. With a low groan, he gathered her into his arms, his lips descending, slowly caressing her mouth, savouring its sweetness with a mastery that roused a pagan wildness in her blood. The room blurred around her and the sounds of their surroundings receded into a muffled drone as she clung to him, unable to breathe, unable to think—there was only the thrill of her womanhood igniting, of a new world of sensations coursing through her veins which carried her spirits cloud-high. His kiss deepened, nectar-sweet, tongue teasing tongue, breaths mingling with the potency of a sorcerer's philtre turning her bones to liquid and her blood to a raging fire.

A shocked gasp from the doorway abruptly brought Sir Rolf to his feet, and Meriel sat up with a guilty start.

'Sir Rolf!' The prioress said sternly. 'I am shocked, deeply shocked. Do you forget where you are, and that this woman is under your protection?'

'Your pardon, reverend mother. Mistress Meriel was naturally upset after her ordeal. I had meant but to comfort her.' He smiled crookedly, its dazzling effect stopping Meriel's heart, and even the grim prioress appeared to be won over. 'I fear I was overcome by her beauty.'

'And she, no doubt, was moved by gratitude that you had saved her life. How fortunate that I arrived before you would both regret your actions.' She voiced her disapproval, before adding, 'Your men have returned, Sir Rolf—without the Spanish woman, I am afraid.'

'Then they must be sent out again at once.' Meriel stood up, her voice ringing with authority.

Sir Rolf swung round to face her, his eyes narrowing, all trace of the tender lover of moments earlier gone from their glittering depths. 'In your distress for your friend, you forget yourself, minstrel. I am not the besotted Earl of Sedbury to be twisted round your scheming finger.'

Meriel gasped, appalled that he seemed to think her the earl's mistress, yet her fears for Bella's safety overrode her shock. They could not abandon her friend to her fate. Before she could answer, the prioress stepped between them.

'Really, Sir Rolf, I must protest at your conduct. If it were not that your blessed sister were so dear to us, I would ask you and your men to leave. Have you no respect for this place or our vocation?'

'For you, reverend mother, I have every respect.' His words were clipped off short in an abrupt tone.

As Sir Rolf made to follow the prioress from the room, Meriel conquered her own anger at his change of manner, and put her concern for Bella before her hurt pride. 'Please, Sir Rolf, is there no chance of saving Bella? I meant no disrespect. Bella is my friend—my only friend.'

He halted, his knuckles whitening as they gripped the doorpost, and he threw her a scathing look over his shoulder. 'It is impossible to search in the dark. By morning, she could be miles from here. My return to France has already been delayed by my extended stay at Winchester. I cannot waste more time on a fruitless search for a serving-wench.'

At her stricken look, he pushed his hand through his hair, his voice terse with exasperation. 'If Sedbury's men have taken her, I very much doubt she will be harmed.'

'I pray that is so.'

'Then believe it.' His tone mellowed. 'Bella was not important to our plans. I think your master merely wanted to prevent you both from serving Queen Eleanor and to avoid being implicated himself. Your friend is safe. If they had meant to harm her, they would have killed her in the cell, not carried her off.'

Her gaze locked with his, knowing that he spoke the truth. In his own way Lord Sedbury cared for Bella, so he surely would not wish her harmed, and, by the same token, neither would he risk harming herself. He would lose his hold over Wychaven if she died, for it would then pass to the Lady Maude's eldest nephew. Obviously, for reasons of his own, Sedbury had wished only to prevent them from reaching Court.

The shadows about Sir Rolf's eyes deepened as he stared back at her. 'Her Majesty has great faith in you. Tonight you have once more shown exceptional courage. You deserve better than...' his voice was threaded with sudden fury, '...deserve a better master than that cur, Sedbury!' He gritted his teeth. The words had been dragged from him as though from a force outside himself. He knew her for what she was, and yet...

With a last glance, he swung on his heel and left. His anger at himself grew as he carried away with him the picture of her standing there—tall, proud and ethereal in the tiny cell, as though the danger from Sedbury's men had not threatened her. Her eyes were as brilliant as a warlock's fire, her cheeks still flushed from his impassioned kiss. During the attempted abduction, her veil had been lost and tendrils of hair escaped her thick braids to curl upon her brow and cheeks, its colour as rich and iridescent as a black pearl. She was beautiful—almost too beautiful to be human—resembling a creature of the old religions—a pagan priestess, an earth goddess, magical, mysterious, beguiling... treacherous.

Her beauty was a lure he could resist, but her courage had found a weak spot in his armour, which disturbed him more than he cared to admit. It was disquieting. Tomorrow they would be at Court. In a week or two he would be free of her for ever, and, long before then, with good fortune, he would have the consent of King Henry for his betrothal to Louise of Auvergne. His future and position would then be assured, for at last he would have a worthy estate to hold as his own. That was what he had fought his way towards for a dozen or more years. That was what mattered.

Or so he kept telling himself all through the long night as the memory of Meriel's lithe body clasped tight against him brought a fever to his blood. It is the land I shall have that is important, he swore through clenched teeth as he stared sleeplessly up at the ceiling, not the temptation offered by a black-haired siren. Especially when she is but a minstrel, and fair game for nobles and servants alike in any household. But, tarnished or not, he did want Meriel, and with an intensity which made sleep impossible. His desire was heightened by the abstinence forced upon him by Queen Eleanor when he had vowed to protect the minstrel.

He frowned. Why should the queen take such pains to protect the virtue of a minstrel-girl? There was much about Meriel that was swathed in secrecy. There was fierce pride and a mysterious aloofness about her which intrigued him. Since he had seen her dancing by the river, he had been haunted by the vision of her loveliness and the promise her body offered. Then she had been like a living flame, beckoning all to enjoy the pleasure of her sultry heat, but there was also ice within her complex nature. Always courteous, she had with a freezing glance silenced the ribald comments of all but the most battle-hardened of his men, and even they had shown her a grudging respect when she refused to respond to their baiting. Before I return to France, he vowed, she shall honour the invitation of that dance and my desire will be slaked, thereby freeing me from the dark magic she has cast over me!

Whatever illusions of splendour Meriel might have had about the elegance of Henry II's Court dissipated within moments of her arrival. They had followed the king's party, who had been out hunting all day, into the palace courtyard. The lead figure, a stocky, untidily dressed man, had leapt from his horse and strode unceremoniously over to Sir Rolf. To Meriel's astonishment, Sir Rolf slid from his horse and knelt in the muddy courtyard as the man approached. Surely this unkempt rangy-figured man with a thickening waist could not be King Henry? But as he pushed back the hood of his cloak, despite the grey streaks, the fiery Plantagenet hair was unmistakable.

'Sir Rolf!' the king boomed, clasping the shoulders of the knight and heaving him to his feet, his face turning ruddy as his voice rose menacingly. 'I suppose you come from that devil-spawned son of mine who continues to defy me? And you stopped to visit Eleanor at Winchester without my permission.'

Sir Rolf stiffened at the rebuke, and for a horror-filled moment Meriel held her breath, fully expecting him to be arrested and thrown into prison. Some inches taller than the king, he looked straight down into King Henry's eyes, his golden gaze shimmering with answering fury. 'My messenger was sent ahead to inform you of my intention to visit Queen Eleanor. I received no word that my visit would be viewed with disfavour.'

'You tread a dangerous path, Sir Rolf. Richard is again waging war against me in France.'

'I have never drawn my sword against your men,' Sir Rolf answered stiffly.

'Yet you still side with Richard?' King Henry thundered, harsh lines carving into his brow and about his mouth.

Sir Rolf's stare did not waver. 'I have been favoured by your son's friendship for many years and have risen high in his service. He is the greatest warrior of our age. I am privileged to serve the Lionheart, but he knows that my first allegiance is to you, Sire.'

'God's bones, Sir Rolf, in any man but yourself I would have his skin flayed for a traitor!'

A deathly silence fell upon the courtyard as the king's words resounded about them and sovereign and vassal outfaced each other. Meriel trembled, her body chilling as though coated by a thick layer of frost. Sir Rolf stood tall and proud, his gaze fearless as a lion's, silently challenging the king. Fearfully, she glanced from one to the other. Both men looked carved from granite. Sir Rolf would not protest his innocence. It was as though he were daring King Henry to do his worst, and be damned! And all present knew what a disastrous path that could lead to. Had not Thomas Becket so defied King Henry? He had met a martyr's death in his own cathedral, because four knights had obeyed the king's wish, spoken in the heat of anger, to be rid of his archbishop.

The tension in the courtyard could be sliced with a dagger, then Henry slapped Sir Rolf heartily upon the back, a blow which would have brought a less stalwart man to his knees. 'Would that all my subjects were as loyal as you! It is time I rewarded such fidelity. And what way is more fitting than a wealthy bride?'

'Your Majesty honours me!'

Sir Rolf's deep and easy laughter stung Meriel. Moments earlier she had thought his death was near at hand, and now that he was reprieved, she felt a constriction about her chest. Why should the news of an impending marriage strike her so hard? There would be knights aplenty, other than Sir Rolf, for her to choose a husband from at Court. As she watched Sir Rolf being led into the palace, the king's arm still about his broad shoulders, an irrational anger scoured her. The future of Wychaven hung in the balance because Sir Rolf had meddled in her life. How easily he had forgotten her presence, her status as minstrel rendering her too lowly and unimportant to mention!

Without waiting for assistance, she jumped to the ground, her anger rising as pain shot through her jarred ankle. Throwing her reins to a waiting page, her simmering glare met Sir Rolf's gaze. He and the king had paused by the doorway, and both men were looking back at her. A rebellious spark of pride flared within her. Sedbury, Queen Eleanor and Sir Rolf might have reduced her to the role of minstrel, but she was still a

noblewoman for all that. She was too angry to pay heed
to the eyebrows Sir Rolf had raised in her direction, and,
summoning her brightest smile for King Henry, she sank
into a graceful and reverent curtsy. He inclined his head
in acknowledgment, his cool assessing gaze flickering
appreciatively over her just long enough to assure her
that his interest had been pricked.

Why, then, did the knowledge fill her with dread? That
was why she had been brought here: to help Queen
Eleanor, and her own secret scheme to try to save
Wychaven. But at what cost? The awesome reality of
becoming the object of King Henry's lust set her body
trembling with abhorrence until it felt as if the earth
itself quaked beneath her feet.

'Mistress Meriel, are you all right?' Sergeant Kedge
asked.

She took a grip upon herself and drew a long steadying
breath, forcing a smile to her quivering lips. 'I have never
seen His Majesty before, or been to Court. I fear it has
overwhelmed me.'

'Sir Rolf will not thank me if you are taken ill.' He
looked at her sternly, but his tone was not unkind. A
battle-hardened man of some forty years, he was
awkward in the company of women, but increasingly
over the last days he had spoken and treated her with
deference. 'The man whom Sir Rolf sent ahead is waiting
to take us to the lodgings he has found in the town. You
will feel better once you have rested.'

Meriel remounted, and following Tom Kedge, was relieved not to have to share the overcrowded accommodation in the palace. As they rode into the street, she
heard her name called. Puzzled, she looked over the
heads of the townspeople towards the city gate, where
dozens of carts were entering, filled with provisions for
the palace. She froze in astonishment as a dark-cloaked
figure waved frantically at her. Then her puzzlement gave
way to a cry of relief and joy as the woman stood up
and climbed down from the cart.

'Bella!' Meriel shouted against the noise of the busy street, and urged her mare forward. 'Thank God you are safe!' Leaping from her horse, she hugged her friend close. Bella stood tense and ill at ease in her embrace, and with a frown, Meriel stepped back. 'Are you hurt?' Bella shook her head, refusing to meet Meriel's gaze. 'What is it? We thought you had been taken by Lord Sedbury's men. How did you get here?'

The woman raised her head, her dark eyes stricken with anguish. Meriel gasped. One of her eyes was partially closed from a vicious-looking bruise, and her cheek was cut.

'It was you those men were supposed to abduct, not I,' Bella said. 'Lord Sedbury is furious that the queen did not trust him. The attack by the river was also by his men. He sees you as an enemy, not an accomplice, and has returned to Court to try to regain King Henry's favour.' She glanced furtively over her shoulder as though fearing they would be overheard, and lowered her voice. 'Because I owe you my life, I had to warn you. You must do nothing against his lordship's interests.'

Meriel studied Bella, her stomach lurching. 'I cannot betray the queen's trust, or the future of Wychaven.'

'Mistress, you must be careful!' Bella's swarthy complexion drained of colour.

'Do not worry, my friend. I know my kinsman!' Meriel answered. 'I am safe enough if he thinks he can still use me. Always he is the same—he must have a foot in every camp. Henry's health is supposedly failing, and who will succeed him—Richard or John? Sedbury would not wish to be seen to have too openly supported the loser.'

'*Dios!* It is not as simple as that.' Bella's voice choked with fear. 'If Lord Sedbury believes you will do anything against his interest, he will stop you in any way he can. You are in grave danger!'

CHAPTER SIX

ROLF CAME out of the king's chamber, his ears still ringing with the force of Henry's rage. It was the worst storm he had ever weathered, and he was not even certain whether he had emerged unscathed. Henry had completely disregarded Prince Richard's terms of reconciliation that he had brought to England, whipping himself into such a black temper that he had thrown himself down on the rush-covered floor, his face puce and his eyes bulging, as he kicked and screamed with demonic fury.

More shaken by the episode than he would admit to any man, Rolf had kept his voice calm and somehow ridden out the tempest. What had shocked him most was the weakness of the king once his rage had blown itself out. Henry had sunk on to a chair, hollow-cheeked and deathly pale, the vitality drained from his usually bright intelligent eyes. Rumours of his ill health had not been exaggerated: Henry could not continue to give way to such rages, and survive. Rolf had looked past Henry's slumped figure to a sinister wall-painting of an eagle and four birds, which was similar to one he had seen at Winchester. The old eagle's body was being attacked by three of the birds, while the fourth scratched at its eyes.

'Ay, you may well look upon that painting,' Henry had announced darkly. 'The old eagle is myself, and the eaglets represent my sons, who have not ceased to pursue my death—not the least of them John, whom I love most of all. Look well, Sir Rolf, for my sons will be the death of me.'

There had been no warmth in Henry's voice when Rolf was dismissed, and with gut-grinding frustration he could feel his reward of Louise of Auvergne slipping from his grasp. It was a grave setback, for not only would Louise have brought him vast lands, but she was a quiet, convent-bred girl, pious and comely enough to content any man. And, more important, at fifteen, she was too young to have been tainted by the world.

'Sir Rolf!' The voice of Sir William Marshal, the king's most trusted familiar, cut across his thoughts. 'It would appear that the breach between our sovereign and Prince Richard remains.'

Rolf turned with a sorrowing smile to greet the knight, who was aged about forty. This man, like himself, had risen from being a younger son and near obscurity to become, through his prowess at the tourney, the king's faithful friend. It was William Marshal who had inspired Rolf's own efforts to win greatness for himself: what another could do, so could he. 'I fear it is so, Sir William. The rift is too deep, and little love is lost between them. I prayed it would be otherwise.'

'As have I, Sir Rolf,' Sir William answered heavily. 'One day Prince Richard will be a worthy king of England, but not before his time, I hope.'

'Perhaps, between us, we can find a way to restrain our fiery masters from pitting themselves against each other—unless, that is, Henry were to name Prince John his successor.'

'That would be a disaster for us all,' Sir William retorted swiftly. 'Richard is the rightful heir.'

'I shall inform him that you mean to stand by him.' Rolf eyed the knight warmly, for in recent years the mutual respect between them had turned to friendship. 'When the time comes, Richard will need advisers such as you.'

Since other courtiers were hovering within earshot, he turned the conversation. Despite his own disappointment, he was nevertheless delighted at the continued advancement of Sir William. But as he strode out of the palace and mounted his destrier to ride to his lodgings at the inn, his thoughts remained bleak. God willing, the minstrel-girl could sweeten King Henry's mood!

Two days later Meriel stood in an alcove of a bustling corridor of the palace awaiting a summons to attend the king. She had been waiting for three hours, and her nerves were frayed almost to breaking-point. She was surrounded by people, yet so alone. Just what had she walked into?

This was nothing like what she had expected—if only Bella were here to reassure her! But her friend had been so distressed at any mention of her coming into the palace that Meriel had been loath to force her. Since her abduction, it was as though a vital light had gone out of Bella. She was withdrawn, acting willingly as lady's maid to Meriel, but she was so quiet and uncommunicative that she was obviously deeply troubled. Any gentle probing as to the cause threw her into an even deeper state of anguish. Guessing that Sedbury had very likely ordered Bella to keep him informed of her own and Sir Rolf's activities, Meriel did not pursue the matter. Her heart went out to Bella, who was in an unenviable position that was tearing her feelings of friendship and loyalty apart, and sadly it had destroyed the intimacy of their relationship. Now, more than ever, Meriel longed for a confidante, someone she could trust, and with Bella so withdrawn to the point of discouraging confidences, her own position at Court was harder to bear. Instead, she had to keep her thoughts and emotions even more rigidly concealed.

So far, Meriel had not seen the Earl of Sedbury, but this was her first visit inside the palace. She had no wish for a confrontation with him, but she had given her word to Queen Eleanor, and she would not break it. Neither would she allow her kinsman to browbeat or frighten her into giving up her fight to reclaim Wychaven.

The waiting seemed endless, and, embarrassed by the curious glances in her direction, mostly from the male courtiers and members of the household, she moved further back into the shadows of the gloomy corridor. On several occasions some man went beyond curiosity and ventured near. Fortunately, a movement from one of Sir Rolf's men who were always near was enough to send them away. The servants, at least, were now too busy preparing for the evening banquet to pay her much heed. The longer she was forced to wait, the more the noise, bustle and the stamping tread of soldiers throughout the rambling palace strained her nerves. Why had she been kept waiting so long? She schooled herself to remain calm, but without the protection of her rank, the palace was a frightening and hostile place.

The guard at her side jerked smartly upright from lounging against the wall, alerting her to Sir Rolf's approach. She had not seen him since they arrived at the palace two days earlier, for he returned to the inn late, after she had retired for the night, and was gone before she rose each morning. In the dimness of the torch-lit corridor his pale blond hair shone like the midday sun, and her heart gave a curious tug of confused emotion. He was dressed formally, in an indigo short tunic bordered with gold thread, and black hose. The leashed power in his every movement was both reassuring in that he had been chosen as her protector, and nerve-tinglingly threatening to her senses. As she stepped forward into the light, an unguarded spark of pleasure lit his eyes, then his lashes hid their expression and his voice was brusque.

'You made quite an impression on His Majesty in the courtyard the other day. It will please him if you dance at the banquet tonight.'

A chill bit into Meriel's flesh at the horror of so public an ordeal. 'At the banquet?' she cried, aghast. 'I could not!'

'What treachery is this?' he demanded sharply. 'It was for this reason that you have been brought here.'

'To dance before the king, yes ... but not to parade myself like a common whore before the entire Court!'

He stared at her for a long moment, his eyes blazing. 'Is Sedbury behind your change of heart?'

'No! I have not seen my...Lord Sedbury,' she corrected quickly, in her anguish almost betraying her kinship.

'Then why would you betray the queen's trust?' He gripped her elbow and pulled her towards him.

'I would never betray Her Majesty! It is simply...' Her voice broke beneath his furious glare. 'Oh, what's the use of trying to explain—you would never understand!'

'Try me!' he growled.

His face was rigid, and she could feel the tension in his body as he leaned closer. Her throat ached with the need to tell him the truth, but she could not. She had given her word to Sedbury. Whatever his schemes for her, she must take care not to endanger her mother. It was too soon to place all her trust in Sir Rolf, who served Queen Eleanor, and she, knowing her identity, had ordered her to continue this role of deception.

'I have never performed before so many.' No longer able to hold the fierceness of his tawny gaze, she lowered her eyes.

'Your nervousness will disappear once you begin,' he said less harshly. 'The others are unimportant; it is Henry you must impress.'

'But the others' stares will be upon me.' She shuddered in disgust. 'It is degrading.'

'It is your trade,' he glowered suspiciously. 'You are a minstrel. A dancer!'

'I have often sung to entertain the Lady Maude, and occasionally Lord Sedbury and his guests,' she countered, matching his enraged glare. 'But when I dance, it is for myself, to find peace and a release from the restrictions placed upon me.'

He closed his eyes briefly, then said, 'I find that hard to believe! Your dance was exceptional. An invitation to paradise for any lover.'

'I thought I was alone on that occasion, except for Bella.' Her face flamed with embarrassment. 'That was your interpretation of my dance, not mine.'

'Then explain your performance at Winchester!' His gaze travelled mockingly over her tense figure.

It took all her will-power to hold his stare. How could she find the words to describe the madness that had possessed her that day? She tipped her chin higher in defiance. 'I danced at the queen's command. Lord Sedbury had told me I must please her in all things. *She* said that I must capture your interest. If I failed, I would be of no use to her.'

'And you were angry,' he persisted, loosening his grip upon her arm, but not releasing her. 'I remember that. Why?'

'I did not ask you to meddle in my life, Sir Rolf!' She stood perfectly still, unflinching, as he towered over her. His mood had subtly changed in a way she could not fathom. He was still suspicious, but the anger had gone from his eyes and he was looking at her... Sweet heaven! He was looking at her with a mixture of curiosity, and something else—a longing which pierced her senses. Her mouth was dry, and she gulped, but somehow she found the strength to go on. 'Yes, I was angry. The peace and security of my life were threatened by your interference, and when I arrived at Winchester you looked through me as though I did not exist.'

'Ah! That pricked your vanity!' His lips hardened into a grim smile, the dangerous glitter back in his eyes. 'And you thought to bring me to heel?'

'I had to prove myself to Queen Eleanor—nothing more.'

'Nothing more!' The violence beneath his words grated across her overstrung nerves. 'You underestimate your skill, or your ambition. Dance like that at the banquet, and dukes and earls will be vying with the king for your favours!'

She struck out at him with her fist, hurt and furious at his callous words. Her knuckles cracked as they

thudded against his chest. Capturing them with infuri-
ating ease, he held them in an iron grip. 'Curse your
arrogant hide!' she wrenched out through a jaw locked
tight with fury, her body rearing back from him. 'I have
done nothing that you should hold me in such contempt! I have sworn to do my duty by Queen Eleanor,
but I will not dance at any banquet. And nothing you
say, or do, can make me.'

She fell silent at the rigid set to the lines of his face.
His voice was low, crackling with a huskiness that carried
a threat more blood-freezing than a shout. 'But you *will*
dance. For your sake, seeing that it worries you to
perform so publicly, I shall arrange a private audience
after the banquet. You will dance for the king then!'

She relaxed slightly; she had won a small victory, but
was still a long way from winning his trust. 'Thank you,'
she said unsteadily, conscious that his hands were still
clamped about her wrists. His straight brows drew frac-
tionally together as he stared down at her, arrestingly
handsome as his expression softened.

'What a surprisingly complicated creature you are!'
He released one hand to stroke a long black curl of her
unbound hair.

'That is because you do not know me.' Her voice was
oddly breathless.

His lips twisted in a taunting smile. 'Is that another
invitation, sweet siren?'

Somehow, without either of them apparently moving,
she found their bodies touching at thigh and hip; their
arms imprisoned against their chests the only barrier between them. The intrinsically masculine scent of him
filled her senses. His moods were more variable than the
winds, and his emotions infuriatingly guarded. Famed
warlord that he was, he showed little of his true self to
the outside world, but, despite that steely exterior, she
had glimpsed brief moments of tenderness such as this.
Her heart capered wildly. Was it possible to turn his
desire for her into a deeper need, and thereby win for

Wychaven the master it needed? The challenge was irresistible!

With Bella acting so strangely, and Sedbury a real and dangerous force to be reckoned with, she needed someone in whom she could put her faith, yet Sir Rolf in many ways was a threat more lethal than Sedbury could ever be. She swallowed to keep her voice even. 'You have a habit of twisting my words and actions to suit yourself, Sir Rolf. As you reminded me a few days ago, I am at Court to serve Queen Eleanor. I have to succeed. But . . .'

She stopped. How could she speak of her dread, say that she found it humiliating to play the role allotted to her? Or that she knew that, although he desired her, he believed she was little more than a strolling player, used to selling her favours, and he despised her for it? To save Wychaven, she had to succeed, and he was part of that plan. But, by winning King Henry's attentions, she had a despairing feeling that this proud knight would hold her in contempt all his life. What did that matter if she still had Wychaven? Yet, senselessly, it did.

Rolf watched her, his gaze speculative as he waited for her to continue. Foolishly, her eyes pricked with frustrated tears. Having given her word to the queen, she must not fail her. Her face set into a mask as she managed a tremulous smile. 'There is too much at stake for me to fail. Sir Rolf,' she lifted her gaze beseechingly, 'will you play for me when I dance for the king?'

He did not reply immediately, his golden gaze scanning her features. Tipping her chin up with his forefinger, he turned her face towards the light of a burning flambeau. 'There is more that troubles you than dancing for the king. If it is Sedbury, I shall not let him harm you. I shall play for you, if it is what you wish.' His tone was overlaid with an unfamiliar note almost touching upon protectiveness. As quickly as she had detected it, it was gone, and the cynical twist again thinned his lips. He was looking over her shoulder towards the sound of footsteps. Meriel turned to follow his gaze, and her heart shuddered. Lord Sedbury was approaching.

She curtsied, and from the corner of her eyes saw Sir Rolf give the briefest of bows in acknowledgment of the earl's rank. As she straightened, she met her kinsman's glare without flinching. A raised vein pulsated upon the broad expanse of his balding crown, and his chill gaze swept over her. With Sir Rolf at her side and the corridor filling with courtiers making their way to the Great Hall for the banquet, Sedbury did not pause in his swaggering stride, but in the few moments that his eyes held hers, there was no mistaking the warning, or menace, in their depths. He had not acknowledged her as his ward, and it would be inconceivable for the great and noble Earl of Sedbury to talk with one of his servants in so public a place. That threatening gaze, more telling than words, had reminded her that there were not only her safety and future at stake, but also her mother's. Meriel dug her nails into her palms to control her rage and frustration. She would not be frightened by Sedbury into jeopardising Wychaven! If she succeeded in charming the king, the earl would soon be heralding her as his kinswoman, but in the meantime, as far as he was concerned, she was on her own.

Sir Rolf laid his hand upon her shoulder and gently eased her round to face him, his handsome countenance serious. 'I do not trust Sedbury. Take care, Meriel. Go nowhere without one of my men in attendance.'

'Since I am now at Court, his lordship will not openly act against Queen Eleanor's wishes. Providing I do nothing contrary to his wishes, I am safe. But you forget, Sir Rolf, that I am bound to Lord Sedbury's household. It is there I must return when my duty to the queen is done.'

His gaze scorched her with its intensity. 'There are other alternatives—you need not return to Sedbury's household. I would give you my protection,' he said softly.

'Sir Rolf, are you suggesting that I should become your mistress?' she answered with bitter irony. She had begun to see him as her husband and the master of Wychaven, and he was merely hinting that he would set her up as his paramour! Still, it proved he was not immune to her. If only she could keep her wits about her and learn the information Eleanor needed, while keeping Henry at bay...there might be a chance of achieving her goal. A provocative smile tilted her lips. 'Surely I am mistaken at your intention? Did I not hear His Majesty promise you the reward of a rich bride?'

'That will not be for some time. Besides, marriage is a contract. My family is an old and powerful one. I will protect my bride's land; she, in turn, will provide children to inherit that same land. It has nothing to do with us, which will be another kind of arrangement altogether.'

The simple honesty of his words should have heartened her. Clearly, he had no romantic attachment to Louise of Auvergne—one wealthy bride would be as acceptable as another to him, or so it would seem. But her heart twisted with pain. Why should she feel that ache? His view was that of most members of their rank.

The warmth of his hand spread a languorous heat through her entire body. How could she collect her thoughts when she was aware only of the broad breadth of his shoulders, of the magical power of that compelling golden gaze? Mentally, she shook herself. One did not marry for love, but for position! Suddenly the cold-heartedness of it all left her empty and dissatisfied.

'Sir Rolf!' Sergeant Kedge interrupted the intimacy of the moment as he hurried to join them. 'His Majesty is asking why you are not at the banquet.'

Sir Rolf nodded, dismissing the soldier. His thumb stroked Meriel's jaw and halted at the corner of her mouth, his eyes darkening to the colour of fresh honey as he gazed down at her. Her heartbeat slowed with the expectancy of his kiss, and unconsciously the tip of her tongue moistened her lips. A flicker crossed his lean features before he drew away his hand and stepped back, clearing his throat before he spoke.

'The king will not remain at the banquet for long. I shall send one of my men with something for you to eat, and shall return as soon as His Majesty commands your presence.'

Meriel watched him walk away, anticipation cascading through her. Sir Rolf might control his desire for her beneath a will of iron, but he did desire her! She ran her forefinger over her chin, which still tingled from his touch. Was it possible that her plan for marriage between them could become more than a legal contract? She stilled the erratic pounding of her heart the thought provoked. She was allowing her plans to turn to hope—and that was wrong. It was very unlikely that the king would agree to such a match.

Less than an hour later, Meriel stepped into the royal apartments, her legs trembling as she beheld Henry's stocky figure. He did not stop pacing the length of the chamber, or look up from the papers he was studying, as she sank into a low curtsy. With an abstracted wave of his hand, he gestured for her to rise. Straightening, she was surprised that she was much of a height with him. Her nervousness increased. He was not how she had imagined him from the stories she had heard. His attire, although of the finest quality, was carelessly worn, and his hands looked as rough and coarse as those of a servant. But, within moments, her first impression began to change. Even with his reddish hair beginning to grey, and his freckled face lined with ill health and disillusion, there was a magnetism about his restless figure. She started at the violence with which he flung the parchment aside, his prominent grey eyes bloodshot and flashing like flaming arrows as he rounded on herself and Sir Rolf.

'God's bones, when will my sons give me rest!' His gravelly voice lashed over them. 'Richard is again plotting with King Philip of France, my most virulent enemy. They eat at the same table, sharing the same dishes, and at night they sleep in the same room. What say you to that, Sir Rolf?'

Meriel felt her flesh cringing and her knees knocking together in the crossfire of that blistering tempest. Somehow, by gripping her hands together, she stood tall, her nerves almost snapping, only glad that the king's rage was not directed at herself. Sir Rolf, however, stood his ground, unyielding as a siege-engine, calmly holding his sovereign's furious glare.

'The news grieves me, Sire, that Prince Richard takes up arms against yourself. The Lionheart will never relinquish the lands he believes to be his birthright, but it is not too late to come to terms with him. Does not his determination to defend his rights not make him the very warrior your empire needs to hold it together?'

'Even now you defend him!' Henry roared, bluish spots appearing on his darkening cheeks as his temper rose.

'No, Sire, I understand what drives him,' Sir Rolf declared evenly, the rigid set of his square jaw betraying the effort it was costing him to control his own temper. 'The Lionheart has qualities most men only dream of possessing. If his strengths far outweigh those of lesser men, then his weaknesses...' He allowed the sentence to hang as his tawny eyes continued his challenge. 'He is a Plantagenet. He will never act like an ordinary man.'

Meriel gulped spasmodically. This time, surely, Sir Rolf had gone too far! She bit back a gasp as Henry slammed a clenched fist down on a table, oversetting a wine flagon.

'Ay, Richard is from the devil's brood,' he grated out, his eyes glazing as he watched the spilled red wine drip on to the rushes, his expression concealing his bleak thoughts.

With a shiver, she recalled the Angevin legend of King Henry's ancestry—that he was descended from Melusine, a lady of unearthly beauty who married a count of Anjou and bore him four children. The count adored his beautiful wife, and the marriage was a happy one, seemingly perfect, except that Melusine never stayed within a church for the consecration of the Host. This puzzled the count and, determined to silence the jealous voices within his Court, he decided to put his countess to the test. He summoned her to attend the church, and when she prepared to leave at the moment of the consecration, four armed men laid hold of her. Even as they seized her mantle, she shrugged it from her shoulders and, gathering two of her children in her arms, rose and flew through a window, never to be seen again. A strange story, and one that Meriel would have thought King Henry would dispute, instead of allude to. But then Henry himself was a paradox, unpredictible, quick to anger and equally quick to reward. Her stomach knotted with foreboding. She had to pit her wits against such a man!

Then, as suddenly, his mood changed. He set the flagon upright with a thud, the vitality sapping from him. 'Philip of France feeds the feud between my sons and myself. It is to his advantage, for divided we are weakened. It is time I returned to Anjou and made Richard see reason.'

Henry turned to Meriel, abruptly changing the subject. 'Sir Rolf highly praises your dancing. Does your talent, I wonder, match your beauty?' his hoarse voice growled as his gaze travelled appreciatively over her figure. 'The burdens of state weigh heavily upon us. Dance! Make me forget my troubles, if only for a few moments.'

He moved to the table, his hands idly picking over the papers spread upon it, and Meriel fought against a sickly rush of panic. She inhaled deeply, seeking an inner calmness which eluded her. The enormity of what Eleanor expected of her was daunting. This was the king—a man who had forged a vast empire with his cunning and administrative genius. Standing frozen to the spot, she cast an imploring look at Sir Rolf.

He put the strap of the lute over his shoulders, propped one long, shapely, muscular leg on a stool, and positioned his fingers over the strings, an encouraging smile tilting the stern line of his mouth.

She drew strength from the compelling force of his stare, that willed her to dance as she had never danced before. She dared not look in the king's direction. A faint rustling of paper told her that his mind was still upon the documents on the table. Her arms felt weighted as she lifted her skirt, not high enough to reveal her ankles, but enough to prevent their heavy folds from hampering her movements. Drawing a steadying breath, she nodded for the music to begin.

Softly, like water lapping against a lake's edge, the notes drifted over her, and to her surprise, Sir Rolf's velvety baritone voice began the opening verse of a short love-song. He had sensed that her nerves had betrayed her and was seeking to put her at ease before her dance began. The tension eased from her stiff muscles, his consideration bringing her the calmness she so desperately needed. Gratefully she regarded his tall, powerful figure, but his head was bent, his hair falling forward over his brow in a silver-gold fringe, shadowing his eyes. Her heart quavered, the smooth richness of his voice setting her blood pulsating, then her spirits revived at its haunting, seductive tone. When her own voice joined his, blending in perfect harmony, their gazes linked, and she found herself caught in the web of those seductive tawny depths. Drawn by a longing so intense that her body seemed to float, she moved towards him. But a slight raising of one dark straight brow rebuked her and, with a start, she recalled that it was the king she must captivate.

With a graceful dip and sway of her hips, she turned to face Henry, who had stopped studying the documents. His restless fingers still fidgeted with a large seal, but his grey eyes sparkled with interest. Sir Rolf stopped singing, and when he increased the tempo of the music, her dance began. Through provocatively lowered lashes she kept her gaze upon Henry, her smile brightening as the music seeped into her bones and she relaxed beneath its magic. The king's figure was partly hidden in the shadows, and in the flattering light Meriel glimpsed the rugged manliness that had been his in youth. Shadows softened the squarish bearded face, slimming the deep barrel chest and the stocky bandy legs of a man who spent hours upon horseback. Strength and vitality emanated from him, despite his recent illness. The fury had gone from his eyes. By the deepening gentleness now filling them, it was easy to understand why his mistresses were as numerous as ever. Few women could fail to be moved by his sheer physical presence.

If this new image the king presented made it easier for her to dance, it did not ease the growing ache in her heart each time her steps took her close to Sir Rolf. She dared not risk looking at him, but was perplexingly aware that, as the king's interest sharpened, the knight was becoming withdrawn, the lute strumming out the wild rhythm with a violence that puzzled her. From time to time she saw Henry glance behind her to him, his eyes at times speculative, at others faintly amused. As she arched back her body and stretched her arms over her head, she risked a sidelong glance at Sir Rolf. The fine layer of hot moisture coating her body from her exertions chilled instantly to ice. His handsome face was set in a rigid mask, but the scar upon his neck was stretched tight. What had she done now to enrage him? Had she not captured the king's interest? Was that not what she was supposed to do? What everything since leaving Winchester had led towards?

When she sank into her final curtsy, her breathing coming in ragged gasps, she knew from Henry's broad smile that she had succeeded in the first part of her task. Yet the knowledge brought her no joy, for when he gestured for Sir Rolf to leave them, the lute-strings twanged in a harsh discordant note as he lifted it over his head. She had done as the queen desired, but at the same time she felt she had lost something more precious...the hard-won respect she had so fleetingly earned from Sir Rolf.

At the sound of the door thudding shut, an arrow seemed to embed itself in her heart, and her eyes fluttered shut with the pain. When she opened them, she inwardly flinched. Henry had silently moved closer, and his prominent grey eyes were studying her narrowly.

'You have pleased me well, my dear,' he declared, and, nodding towards an inner door, continued, 'The bedchamber is beyond. Go and prepare yourself.'

Meriel blenched, gagging upon a rise of nausea in her throat. She swallowed, and somehow found the strength to stand up.

Henry folded his arms across his chest. 'Does your king not find favour in your eyes?'

His harsh voice grated in her ears. Having witnessed the violence of his rages, she had no wish to unleash his demonic fury upon herself, and yet how could she go through with what was expected of her? Her legs seemed to have lost all power. 'Sire, you honour me,' she wrenched out with an effort. 'I am overwhelmed.'

'Is this not what you expected?' His prominent grey eyes narrowed alarmingly.

Meriel swallowed painfully as the king moved closer, his hand reaching out to smooth a tress of her hair. It took all her will-power not to flinch, and she kept her eyes averted. The tress was dropped at once.

'You are appalled at the idea of my bedding you!' He rasped. Startled, she looked up. His eyes were flashing dangerously. 'Do you think I do not know an unwilling woman when I see one?' he demanded. 'Or a virgin? You were not dancing for me tonight, but for Rolf of Blackleigh. Eleanor sent you, did she not?'

Meriel took an involuntary step back as the king's words lashed over her. She had been a fool to believe she could dupe him. She had failed miserably, and the consequences of that were harrowing. Not only her life was in jeopardy, but Sir Rolf's also as an accomplice to the plot—perhaps even the queen's. Her mind reeled as she desperately sought the words to placate him.

'Answer me!' Henry thundered, angry colour flooding his face. 'Tell me why Eleanor sent you. And who you are. Sir Rolf may have convinced himself that you are a dancing-girl, but you are not. This night smacks of treachery, and I would know the truth!'

CHAPTER SEVEN

'No, your Majesty, there was no treachery, I swear it!' Meriel protested, indignation smarting her eyes at the very thought. The fear of rousing the king's temper was forgotten in righteous defence of her innocence.

'I am pleased to hear it.' King Henry's high colour faded, but his eyes were overbright, warning her she was treading a perilous path. 'But Eleanor does nothing without reason. Were you sent to spy for her? To learn of my plans for dealing with that treacherous son of mine, Prince Richard, so that he could be warned and escape my wrath?'

'No, Sire,' Meriel protested vehemently. 'Why, that would be tantamount to *treason*!'

'Precisely!' Those steel-grey eyes assessed her every movement. 'I think you had better explain yourself.'

Somehow Meriel found the courage to hold the king's incensed gaze. She had failed the queen miserably, and now Henry believed them all to be traitors. It was disloyal to betray Eleanor's fears to the king, but if she remained silent, they would all be judged guilty of a more serious crime. Henry was too shrewd to accept half-truths. Besides—her conscience mocked her—it was unthinkable to lie to His Majesty. She drew a deep breath, praying that the queen would understand that she had to speak out.

'Queen Eleanor is distressed by rumours concerning another matter, one which touches her future more directly.'

Henry moved towards a falcon tethered to a stand in a corner and began to talk softly to the hooded bird as he stroked its feathers. 'Go on,' he ordered, without looking back at her.

Without the king's assessing gaze upon her, Meriel found it easier to speak out, but how much could she say without being disloyal to Eleanor? 'This rumour concerns the Princess Alice, Sire,' she began hesitantly, carefully choosing her words. 'Since the French princess and Prince Richard seem no nearer to taking their marriage vows, and in view of the number of years Princess Alice has been in England, the queen fears that in the interests of diplomacy... you might feel it necessary to annul your marriage and appease King Philip by marrying the Princess Alice yourself,' she finished in a rush, bracing herself for Henry's rage to descend.

Instead, a boom of laughter filled the room, startling the falcon, who flapped its wings in alarm. Henry took a moment to calm the frightened bird before crossing the room to stand in front of Meriel. 'So that wily old eagle has sent a dove to do her bidding!' He tugged thoughtfully at his beard as he restlessly paced the room. 'Even in prison, Eleanor continues to intrigue and to give me no peace. She eats into me like poison, yet once...' His gruff voice set Meriel's taut nerves on edge. 'By the eyes of God! Once she was my helpmeet, a woman beyond comparison, until those clever wits of hers dabbled in that which was not her concern.'

He swung about, his mood changing as abruptly as his constant motion. Meriel held her tongue, sensing that she would learn more by remaining silent and listening sympathetically. 'For what it is worth, you may tell Eleanor that the marriage stands. I've reared one devil's brood who are continually at my throat. Two warring sons are enough; what need have I to breed more? It would serve only to destroy all that I have worked for.' His stare darted over her proud form. 'Now I would know your name and why you came to Court as a minstrel!'

At first Meriel skimmed over her story, but, to her discomfort, the king probed deeper, questioning her on everything, until the candles burned low and he knew the whole story.

'So, Meriel of Wychaven, you find yourself discovered. You are the Earl of Sedbury's ward. What did he seek to gain by taking you to Winchester?'

Meriel suppressed a sigh. Would the king give her no peace until every last detail had been dragged from her? 'I know not my kinsman's mind, Sire,' she hedged, 'but surely only a foolish man would ignore a command from Her Majesty.'

'You say Sedbury keeps your mother a virtual prisoner at Eadstone, refusing her request to live out her days at Wychaven? Yet you are loyal to Sedbury when I give you a chance to denounce him. And you, yourself, are long past marriageable age. You speak with passion of your home. Do you resent not being mistress there?'

'Naturally I miss Wychaven and worry about my people, whom I have not seen for so long. But I do not believe Sedbury plots against you. Indeed, once I left Winchester, he was determined that I should not reach Court. Twice he sent men to abduct me, and failed.'

Henry nodded, apparently satisfied, and Meriel began to breathe more easily.

'Why did you agree to serve Eleanor?' He changed back to attack with a swiftness that disconcerted her.

'It is my duty to serve Her Majesty. I could not see that by so doing I was in any way doing you a disservice, Sire. From what I know of Sir Rolf, he would never agree to be party to anything which would touch upon disloyalty to yourself.'

'How ably you defend your champion,' Henry persisted ruthlessly. 'Do you bear Sir Rolf no ill will that it is because of him you were caught in this web?'

Meriel's eyes slid from the king's shrewd gaze. 'No, Sire.'

'But you have been ill used.' His voice gentled, and she again met his stare. 'You deserve better than to bear the brunt of Sedbury's anger once he learns that your identity is known to me. Marriage would free you from him, would it not? Your father was one of my most loyal and brave knights, and you have much of his courage.

Few men have stood their ground before me, and even fewer women.' He lifted a hand to touch a lock of black hair tumbling over her shoulder, and regret showed in his eyes. 'You are very beautiful and very desirable. It is easy to see why Eleanor chose you. I'll not be the one to abuse you further, unless...' His eyes bored into hers, judging her reaction to his unvoiced invitation.

'Sire, my wilful escape from the guards at Eadstone was the cause of all that has happened to me since. I am honoured by your attention, but if I am sometimes wilful and reckless, I trust I never forget the reverence due to my father's memory. When I marry, I would go to my husband still a maid.'

Henry lifted a speculative brow. 'For a woman as beautiful as you, who also brings with her vast lands and wealth, few men would complain. There are even some who would willingly see their wife installed as my mistress, for the influence and position at Court it would give them.'

The muscles of her face stiffened and her stomach lurched. Did he intend to wed her to such a man, and so still seek to win her to his bed?

He turned from her, his voice dismissive. 'You have been honest with me, Mistress Meriel. Would that all my subjects were so truthful. Tomorrow I shall speak to Sedbury. You will stay at Court until I leave for France at the end of the week—I would have you dance and sing for me again.'

Meriel curtsied and backed from the room. Once past the two men-at-arms guarding the outer door to the king's apartments, she let out a long breath of relief. Unconsciously, her head lifted more proudly. She had hated the deception, and now the king had released her from it. But until he spoke to Sedbury, it would be wise to tread carefully. If, as was likely, Henry set sail for France before her mother was freed from Eadstone to return to Wychaven, she dared not risk rousing her kinsman's wrath.

The corridor leading to the king's apartments was unusually deserted, for there were always several courtiers
waiting with petitions. A stifled yawn from one of the
guards, and a page curled up on a coffer fast asleep,
warned her of the lateness of the hour. Catching sight
of Sir Rolf leaning against the wall, she was surprised
to find that he was waiting to escort her personally back
to the inn. Her step lightened with pleasure at the thought
of his company. Had she not learnt the very news Queen
Eleanor had sent her here to discover? That meant that
Her Majesty's fears would not be realised. Despite the
stoniness of Sir Rolf's expression as he watched her approach, she smiled broadly.

'You look pleased with yourself, Meriel!' His voice
sounded like cracking ice. 'But then the length of time
you have been closeted alone with Henry proves how
successfully you must have captivated him.'

Meriel bristled at his tone. 'I do not like what you are
implying, Sir Rolf.' She was too excited by the triumph
of learning that Eleanor was not to be put aside to pay
much heed to his ill humour. Glancing over her shoulder
to ensure they could not be overheard, she dropped her
voice to a whisper. 'I have learned that Henry has no
intention of parting from Eleanor. Was that not the
reason why I was brought to Court?'

His eyes darkened, and a muscle pulsated along the
rugged jaw. 'You have learnt much from a single
meeting. Henry is devious, and usually reticent as to what
lies in his mind. Your charms must indeed have proved
exceptional.'

Meriel stared at him in astonishment. The chiselled
hardness of his face was plain enough to read. He
thought she was the king's whore! Indignantly she burst
out, 'I trust you did not think I...'

'I know our king!' he growled. 'And the invitation
offered in your dance!'

She opened her mouth to continue, but seeing his
amber eyes flash fire, she kept silent. Nothing she said
would convince him otherwise. He believed all women

could be bought at a price. Her chest felt as though it were being crushed beneath a heavy boulder, and in defiance she retorted cuttingly, 'How observent of you, Sir Rolf. But then you were the first to pay heed to my dancing.'

He stared down into her oval uptilted face, knowing that his anger was unreasonable, but unable to conquer it. Her eyes, blue and clear as the Mediterranean, were raw with pain—pleading, as only a woman could, for him to believe her innocent when she was as guilty as hell! Irrationally, he wanted to believe her. But had he not been similarly deceived—not just by one woman he had cared for, but by two?

The first was still a raw wound deep within him. But the second betrayal, by the widowed Lady Sibyl, had merely hardened his distrust of the female sex. In the three years of his relationship with her in Aquitaine, he had occasionally suspected her of infidelity, but whenever he challenged her, she wept and pleaded innocence, declaring passionately that she loved him and only him. She had the face of an angel and the body of Venus, and it was all too easy to believe her.

Rolf steeled himself against the beguiling beauty of the minstrel-girl, his thoughts sardonic as he reflected again on the falseness of the Lady Sibyl. On his last visit to Richard's Court, although her pleas of love had been more impassioned than ever, he had been challenged by three knights, each claiming to be her current lover. Bloodshed was avoided by arranging to meet all of them in a tavern in the town. When the other three also realised that so many now shared the Lady Sibyl's favours, they had been quick to see the absurdity of fighting over her and had spent the night drinking together. The incident nevertheless destroyed what was left of his faith in a woman's word.

That Meriel did not answer his challenge, her eyes brimming with a censure which matched his own, unsettled him. She did not plead, but, knowing Henry as he did, and that his carnal appetites were voracious, it

was unlikely that any woman could spend so long alone
with him and emerge untouched. And Meriel—curse the
wench for her insolence in reminding him!—had he not
chosen her because of her seductive charm? Why, then,
did he feel such unreasonable disappointment? Or an
anger at her more acute than that aroused by Sibyl's
betrayal. He, who had never envied any man either his
lands, title or position, envied Henry this night for possessing a minstrel-girl.

'You have served Queen Eleanor well.' He kept his
voice even, but the strain of maintaining an outward calm
taxed him hard. 'I have not fared so well on Prince
Richard's behalf. I must seek another audience with
Henry before we leave.'

'The king intends to leave for France before the week
is out, but he has asked that I stay at Court and dance
for him again.'

Sir Rolf locked his jaw against his churning anger, a
tense silence falling between them as they returned to
the inn.

The next afternoon Meriel was again summoned to the
king's presence, and was disconcerted to discover both
Sedbury and Sir Rolf with him. From the atmosphere
in the room, the meeting had so far been stormy. Meriel
was raised from her curtsy by the king, the expression
in his grey eyes surprisingly mellow, alerting her that the
dissension stemmed from either the earl or Sir Rolf.

Her glance darted to the knight. His form and
expression could have been carved from stone—except
for his eyes, which swept over her with a scathing, blistering heat filled with derisive anger. Startled, she looked
across at Sedbury. His face was flushed, his lips bloodless
with anger above his dark beard. Meriel shivered. The
glare he turned upon her was murderous.

The king with his usual restlessness paced the room.
'Mistress Meriel, the matter of your identity has been
resolved, and to allay any further confusion, you will
be formally presented to me at the banquet tonight by

the Earl of Sedbury.' His hoarse voice was tinged with amusement. 'At the same time, I shall have the pleasure of announcing your betrothal to the Earl of Loxstead.'

Shock made Meriel's head jerk up, her stomach grinding as her plans crumbled to dust. She had never heard of the Earl of Loxstead, and from Sedbury's expression it was definitely not a match he would have chosen. A dull ache enclosed her heart. She did not want the Earl of Loxstead; she wanted... Her glance returned to Sir Rolf, the pain in her breast deepening. She wanted him, and until this moment she had not realised just how fervently she had set her heart upon such a match. He stood with his thumbs thrust into the ornate silver and gilt sword-belt, his expression shuttered. No doubt he was enraged that he had been made to look foolish by not knowing her true identity. As she gazed into his lean, handsome face, her heart was wrenched in misery, knowing that this was the only man she wanted for her husband... that this was the man she loved!

'Mistress Meriel,' the king said more sharply, 'does this marriage not please you? Is it because you do not know the Earl of Loxstead? It is a recently created earldom.'

Again she heard unaccountable amusement in his tone, and through a haze of wretchedness she struggled to speak. 'Your Majesty honours our family by so exalted a match.'

'No, I but right a wrong done to you! I value loyalty above all things—especially so since my own sons have turned against me.' Henry picked up a land deed from the table and studied it. 'You show little curiosity about the man you are to marry,' he fired at her suddenly.

'I am rather overcome, Sire, by the unexpectedness of it,' she managed to force out.

'The lands given to Loxstead in reward for his years of self-sacrificing service border the estate of Wychaven to the west and north. Your marriage is an ideal alliance, since his estate matches Wychaven's acreage. As you are probably aware, these lands fell to the Crown in the days of King Stephen. The castle upon them is wooden and in poor repair, and the land has been sadly neglected. There are also manors in Kent and along the lower reaches of the River Thames.'

At least Wychaven would still be a valuable and strategic fortress and would lose none of its importance, which she had feared would happen. She knew the land King Henry spoke of, which the Earl of Loxstead now possessed. It was rich and fertile pasture, but sparsely populated. Wychaven would prosper from this match, but the thought gave her no pleasure.

All three men's eyes rested upon her, waiting for her response. The king speculative, Sedbury glowering and Sir Rolf... There was no saying what was going on behind that frozen expression.

'You must hold the Earl of Loxstead in high regard, Sire, to have raised him so high, and you have conferred a singular honour upon a humble knight's daughter.' She was surprised that her voice could sound so unruffled when her heart seemed about to break. 'May I ask when the marriage is to take place?'

'I have a mind to attend your wedding. The contracts were drawn up and the settlements agreed this morning. Since I could be some months in France, I suggest the marriage takes place three days hence, but, of course, it is a matter for you and your betrothed to decide. What does Lord Loxstead say?'

Meriel swung round, expecting a stranger to emerge from the inner room. The doorway remained empty and her heart somersaulted as she heard Rolf's deep voice cut across the silence, the words seemingly dragged reluctantly from him. 'It will be in three days, if you wish it so, Sire.'

Meriel could not believe her ears. The room whirled dizzily for some moments. Rolf was now the Earl of Loxstead, and in three days they would be wed! Her throat worked to dispel a tight knot of emotion as she faced him. What she saw in his face turned the tightness

to leaden clamps. It was obvious that he did not desire
this match and was being forced into it by the king.

'Then in three days it shall be,' Henry declared with
a boom of delighted laughter, apparently unaware of the
tension in the room.

The king watched the three of them file from the room,
his lips twitching with amusement. So Sedbury thought
he could intrigue with Eleanor and not earn his censure!
Well, he had lost his hold upon Wychaven and its vast
revenues this day, neither had he gained an alliance to
further his quest for power. There was little love lost
between Loxstead and Sedbury. Henry's eyes narrowed,
recalling the fury of the knight when he had learned
Meriel's identity and that Sedbury had been content to
barter her future. Yet what had made that fury then turn
against the woman herself, when Rolf had learned she
was to be his bride? More than that, he had glimpsed
an inner torment, which that proud face had quickly
shielded behind a rigid mask.

Henry frowned. Having witnessed the attraction between the two, he had thought to honour Sir Rolf and
also punish him just a little for his devotion to Richard,
by forcing him to accept a wife whose lands were in
England, away from the influence of the prince. It had
pleased him to give Rolf a wife who was not only wealthy
but young and attractive, and a woman he obviously
desired. He had certainly not expected him to react with
scarcely bridled fury. Henry shrugged his puzzled
thoughts aside, his mind filling with the preparations to
be made for his journey to France and the course he
must take to bring his eldest son to heel. The Earl of
Loxstead now had the lands and title his loyalty had long
deserved, even if he did not want the woman who
brought half of them to him. It was for him now to make
what he would of them.

Once outside the king's chambers, Meriel intended to
speak with Rolf. The knowledge that he was so opposed
to their marriage tortured her. In three days they would

be man and wife, and it was not her nature to sit by and let events take their course. She had to know why he did not want her as his bride, for only then could she begin to win him entirely as her own.

Rolf strode through the ante-chamber without a pause, but before Meriel could catch up with him in the corridor, William Marshal called to him and he joined the company of four other knights. From the way Sir William clapped him heartily upon the back, it was obvious that, in the curious manner of these things, news of Rolf's elevation to an earl was already known.

Meriel drew to one side, unwilling to bring attention upon herself until she had spoken with Rolf. A low snarling voice close to her ear set the hairs on her neck pricking with a different kind of fear.

'So you think to outwit me!' Lord Sedbury pronounced darkly, his hand bruising her shoulder as he spun her round to face him. 'You disobeyed my orders. This is not the marriage I had planned for you.'

'Perhaps not,' Meriel countered, her eyes burning with indignation as she glared at him. 'Lord Loxstead will never be your minion, but you must agree that the marriage has far-reaching possibilities. Loxstead is favoured not only by King Henry, but also by Prince Richard. One day Richard will be king of England—he may not look kindly upon those who have pandered to his father and discounted the wishes of Queen Eleanor. I would have thought you would desire to have stronger links with Prince Richard's court.'

Sedbury scowled. 'Richard could lose England by rebelling against Henry. There are many who see John as our future king, and Loxstead is no favourite of his. I do not give this marriage my blessing. You cannot flout my wishes and escape the consequences. You always were too wilful for your own good, and the Lady Maude too lenient with you. It is time, I think, that your mother began her life of seclusion.'

'No!' Meriel burst out, the colour draining from her face. 'She has done you no harm. You cannot banish her to a convent. She will live at Wychaven.'

'You sacrificed your mother's freedom by disobeying my wishes,' Sedbury jeered. 'The Lady Maude will do as I decree. She is my kinswoman. It is to me that she has sworn fealty.'

'I shall go to the king and demand...' She bit back a gasp of pain as his hand dug into her forearm.

'You will do nothing. Or I shall take steps so that you never see your mother again.'

'Sedbury!' Lord Loxstead's voice rang with challenge. 'You appear to be causing my betrothed no little discomfort. Release her, if you please.'

Meriel felt her torment ease as Rolf sauntered over to them. However much he resented their marriage, he had seen her distress and come to rescue her. Was that not a good sign for the future—that with time he might accept her? Sedbury appeared to ignore him. His grip tightened cruelly upon her arm, and she gritted her teeth to stop crying out from the pain. Then brusquely he released her, his long face, sallow against Rolf's healthy sun-weathered countenance, set in derisive lines.

'How quickly you champion Meriel!' he scoffed. 'But then you have much to thank her for. Am I truly to believe you did not know her identity? It was a masterly stroke to get her to charm Henry. Of course, once she was compromised, the reputation of a lady of gentle birth must be safeguarded. How better could a grateful sovereign reward a loyal and understanding subject than by giving him an earldom and a wealthy, if tarnished, bride!'

'My lord, that is all lies, and you know it!' Meriel began, but her words were lost as Rolf moved forward, grabbed a fistful of Sedbury's long velvet gown and pushed him hard against the wall. The bravado died in Sedbury's eyes as he met the fury of Rolf's incensed glare.

'Take back those words, or you will answer for them with your life, Sedbury!'

'Perhaps I was over hasty,' Sedbury mumbled, but the malice remained bright in his eyes, 'and you were an innocent party to this chit's scheming. She would stop at nothing to enrich that precious Wychaven of hers. And, no doubt, during that intimate hour she spent with Henry last night, she suggested the very lands he deeded to you with your title. You are wily enough to keep both Henry's and Richard's favour. The fox and his vixen. You are well suited.'

Meriel watched Rolf's face harden, and her heart spiked with agony. Sedbury's spite had hit upon the truth. That was indeed what Rolf believed of her, or a greater part of it.

'My Lord Loxstead, I pray you, do not listen to his lies! Lord Sedbury does not want this match any more than you do. He seeks to provoke a fight, so that your actions will displease His Majesty.'

Furrowed lines of temper were carved on each side of Rolf's mouth as he glanced at her. Imperceptibly his eyes softened, as though he were ashamed that she had guessed the truth of his reluctance. She quickly looked away so that he could not see how much the knowledge hurt her. Rolf released Sedbury, who disdainfully smoothed the crumpled velvet of his gown, and when she risked looking in her betrothed's direction again, there was no mercy in his tawny gaze, as he ground out, 'If the king wills this match, so shall it be. But I warn you, Sedbury, none but ourselves and His Majesty knows of Mistress Meriel's visit to Henry last night. The guards were both men I have ridden with in the past, and I can count upon them to remain silent. I will tolerate no hint of scandal to be attached to my wife's name. And should any be spread abroad, I shall hold you accountable for it.' He bowed stiffly to Meriel. 'My guards will continue to watch over you at the inn, Mistress Meriel. For the sake of propriety, I shall find rooms elsewhere.' Signalling for two of his men to escort Meriel back into the town, he marched from their presence.

Unable to bear the sight of him walking away, and aware that several curious glances had been following the angry scene, Meriel looked down at her ringless hands.

Sedbury laughed cruelly. 'I wish you well of him, Meriel. He will stand none of your wilful ways, nor your wanton conduct. From what I hear of our new Earl of Loxstead, he prizes virtue in a woman above all things. You may yet find yourself shut away—like his sister!'

What did he mean? The Lady Isolda was an anchorite—a holy woman! She watched Sedbury, still laughing, move away, and then her mind was distracted as the two guards fell into step behind her. Her head tilted proudly, and her mind raced to overcome the problems the day had brought as she, too, walked from the palace. She had won for Wychaven the master she had sought, but it had happened too quickly, with too many misunderstandings unresolved between Rolf and herself. She had earned the enmity of the Earl of Sedbury, and, by so doing, her mother's future looked bleak indeed.

Inhaling deeply, she strove to calm her growing panic. Each problem must be met and dealt with on its own grounds—one step at a time. Perhaps she might yet placate Sedbury, and Rolf... A ragged sigh escaped her. Rolf might take a little longer to win round. She chewed her lip in grim determination, her blood quickening at the challenge. She would start at the banquet tonight.

CHAPTER EIGHT

MERIEL FROWNED at hearing the voices of the guards waiting in the inn courtyard to escort her to the palace. She looked down at her gown and sighed at the plainness of it. Although unadorned, the material was of the finest linen, and she knew its kingfisher-blue colour exactly matched her eyes and enriched the blue-blackness of her braided hair.

'Oh, Bella, just when I needed to impress Lord Loxstead, I shame him instead! It is humiliating that I appear as his betrothed for the first time in public, dressed as simply as a tiring-maid and without a jewel to my name. When I think of the jewels Sedbury made me leave behind at Eadstone, I could scream with vexation.'

'There's no need to scream, mistress,' Bella laughed, as she straightened from rummaging through one of the three bundles of clothes they had been allowed to bring with them. Triumphantly, she held out a sapphire- and diamond-studded girdle and a thick gold circlet. 'The Lady Maude asked me to smuggle these into my belongings. She hoped you might have use for them at Court. There are also two rings—a sapphire and a large ruby.'

'What would I do without you?' Meriel squeezed her tightly. 'That is just like my mother to have me prepared for every eventuality.' Her frown returned. 'Yet things have not gone as she would have planned. Wychaven will be free of Lord Sedbury's tyranny upon my marriage, but not so herself.'

'Lord Loxstead is a good man,' Bella said, fastening the jewelled girdle about Meriel's waist. 'He does not fear my Lord Sedbury. You worry over much. Loxstead desires you. It is natural for such a man, at first, to resent being forced into marriage. But how can you fail to charm him? You will be the most beautiful woman at Court; every man will envy Lord Loxstead his good fortune.'

With the gold circlet in place over a gossamer-fine wimple and floor-length veil, and the two rings on her fingers, Meriel felt more confident. For the first time since she had met Rolf she was dressed as befitted her rank, and she defied him to find fault with her appearance, but, even so, her smile was wistful as she walked to the door. 'With all my heart I pray you are right. But it will take more than beauty to win the admiration of Lord Loxstead. He is so cynical, and distrustful of women.'

'And does that not make him all the more fascinating? Mystery is the most seductive charm of all.' Bella spoke from a wealth of experience, her dark eyes tinged with sadness. 'It is what we were taught when we had to sell ourselves in the bazaar.' She shrugged, putting the painful memories of the past behind her, and her smile was mischievous. 'Do not give all of yourself at once—always keep something back. Satisfy, but continue to tantalise, and his fascination for you will be heightened, his need become the greater.'

During the short ride to the palace, Bella's words resounded through Meriel's mind. It was sound advice, but when she entered the Great Hall she doubted whether it held the secret to break down the barriers of Rolf's distrust and prejudice. Through the haze of smoke from the central fire and dozens of burning flambeaux, she saw Rolf standing a half-head taller than Sir William Marshal or any other of the knights gathered round him, and her heart quivered. He was contained, self-possessed in a way that set him apart from the other courtiers. A lion leashed through loyalty, but untamed.

With the queen a prisoner and no sign of the Princess Alice in attendance, there were few women at Court. Meriel's arrival caused a stir among the men nearest the door and spread like a ripple. She held her head high, standing cool and reserved, waiting for Rolf to recognise her. When he followed the glances of his companions towards her, his eyes widened in surprise and fleeting pleasure. Excusing himself, he walked with long cat-like strides to her side. As he lifted her hand to his lips in greeting, she met the full force of his sardonic gaze sweeping over her. Their tawny depths sparked with self-mockery.

'Had I seen you thus that day by the river, there would have been no disputing that you were of gentle birth.' His low voice was laced with warning. 'Yet that day I glimpsed the real you—an enchantress weaving a spell to entice a knight to save her precious Wychaven. At least the pretence was stripped from you that day and you danced with honesty.'

She bristled, that he touched so close to the truth. 'I was still a wilful girl, dancing to find peace in an impossible dream. The world has taught me much since then.' Her gaze locked with his. 'Not the least of which, that, as a woman, I can be bartered and manipulated to suit the ends of powerful men. You seem to have conveniently forgotten that I could have had no knowledge of your presence on Lord Sedbury's land. You put that particular interpretation upon my dance, not I, but I will not deny that Wychaven and the welfare of my people are important to me. If you took the trouble to know me better, Lord Loxstead, you might learn that honesty is also something I hold most dear.'

A fanfare of trumpets announcing the arrival of the king prevented him from answering. After Henry had taken his place at the centre of the dais table, Rolf offered Meriel his arm, the coldness in his eyes melting a few degrees. 'Come, His Majesty awaits your official presentation and the announcement of our betrothal. The eyes of the curious are already upon us,' he warned. Beneath the light touch of her hand, the muscles on his forearm were steel-hard with tension. 'They will take great pleasure in noting that Sedbury is not present for the announcement.'

A quick glance about the hall showed her that he spoke the truth. 'My kinsman seeks to shame me by his action. I defied him. He had other plans for Wychaven.' Bitterness crept into her voice even as she fought to hide her alarm that Sedbury was angry enough to risk the king's displeasure by refusing to acknowledge her. What else was he planning? 'It grieves me that his lordship should also snub you in so public a manner,' she went on. 'Despite the misunderstanding from our first meeting, you have always treated me with honour. I fear this will not be the last trouble Lord Sedbury may cause.'

A muscle leapt beneath her fingers and then relaxed. They were almost at the step of the dais, and anything they said would be overheard by King Henry, who had stepped forward at their approach.

Rolf presented Meriel to him, feeling her hand flutter with nervousness as his deep voice announced their betrothal. The Hall seemed to recede about him as he stood with Meriel at his side, while several of the courtiers came forward to congratulate him. The anger with which he had first greeted the king's proposal—that Meriel and not Louise would be his bride—was still simmering below the surface. But he had been startled at the serene beauty of his betrothed when she entered the hall. Her poise and elegant grace alone should have shown him she was a noblewoman. How could he have thought her a strolling player? The lemon-scented fragrance of her body wafted over him, and he saw envy and the disturbing darkening of desire in the eyes of every man who paid his good wishes to him.

He watched Meriel parry their flattery with a blend of demure innocence and sharpness of wit, which was devoid of flirtation. When a knight, bolder than the rest, was more coarse in his compliments, her magnificent eyes flashed with a cold blue flame, so that he stammered and fell back disconcerted. Her smile charmed everyone, but he was delighted to discover that it was at its brightest when it settled upon him and, with it, the promise of paradise. However, he knew the falseness of that seemingly innocent smile! The scar on his neck throbbed as disillusion returned. The thought of possessing Meriel as a mistress had been exhilarating, but the qualities he enjoyed in a mistress were different from those he sought in a wife. Yet he could not afford to anger King Henry by refusing to marry the wench.

It was already dark outside when Meriel arrived at the royal chapel for the quiet private service Lord Loxstead had insisted upon. She did not mind not having a grand wedding, but this seemed almost furtive. A prickle of foreboding chilled her spine. It was a further sign of Rolf's reluctance to marry her. She glanced back at Bella, standing directly behind her, her swarthy face still puffy from the hours of weeping throughout the night. It was another disquieting reminder of the change in her life. When Meriel had returned to the inn after the banquet, she had found Bella huddled in a corner, sobbing, her gown in tatters across her back. Sedbury had come there during her absence and beaten her for not informing him of his kinswoman's plans, as he had ordered. He had then consigned her to the devil and withdrawn his protection. Appalled by his treatment, Meriel had sat up all night tending to Bella's wounds and seeking to reassure her. She had not hesitated to offer her friend a home and a place at her side as maid and companion. But it was more than Sedbury's callous treatment of his former mistress that upset Meriel; she could not shake from her mind that he was unlikely to surrender Wychaven without exacting a bitter price.

Her misgivings grew as she looked to the side of the altar rail where the Earl of Loxstead stood with Sir William Marshal and the king. Rolf, immaculate in a leaf-green short tunic and cloak, both bordered in heavy gold thread, and matching green hose, kept his back to her. His thick, neatly trimmed mane of hair was freshly washed, shining like newly minted gold over his broad shoulders. A tide of love flowed over her as she walked slowly to take her place at Rolf's side. This was the knight of her dreams, and in a few moments she would be his wife. But those dreams were a distant memory, and reality was more sobering. Loyalty to the king had forced this marriage upon him. Given time, she knew she could break down the barriers of distrust. Most disturbing was the legacy of Sedbury's hatred, which her dowry brought. The road ahead was a rocky one. Undaunted, she squared her shoulders. She was prepared to use her skills and charm to exploit her attraction for Rolf. She would do battle with every means at her disposal to ensure that he never regretted their marriage.

The royal chaplain, round of face and even rounder of body in his long grey robe, beamed at her as she took her place at Lord Loxstead's side. As he began to recite the marriage service, she looked up at Rolf, wondering what thoughts were going through his mind. The sculptured perfection of his lean face was relaxed, his lips parting to reveal white even teeth as he smiled reassuringly at her. But the smile did not reach his eyes, and although he spoke his responses unhesitatingly, her heart clenched at the trace of resignation in his deep voice. Having spoken her own vows proudly, almost defiantly, she suddenly found herself embraced by the king.

'A goodly match between two loyal families!' He grinned over her head at Rolf. 'Now I claim a kiss from the bride.'

The king's beard grazed her cheek and chin as his moist mouth pressed down upon hers, his lips lingering longer than custom demanded. Meriel stiffened, and as Henry released her, she met the icy fury of her husband's glare. His eyes still glacial, Rolf faced the king, his legs braced slightly apart and his body taut in silent warning that he would tolerate no man, not even a king, taking liberties with his wife. The king's brows drew together ominously, his cheeks flushing with ruddy colour, and the air in the incense-laden chapel was suddenly overlaid with tension.

Sir William Marshal stepped forward, clearing his throat. Ignoring Rolf's glower, he planted a brief kiss upon Meriel's cheek, saying heartily, 'Fortune smiles on you, Lord Loxstead.' He clasped his friend warmly about the shoulders, and Rolf dropped his gaze from the king's.

Meriel smiled gratefully at the older knight, who had tactfully intervened to break the building antagonism between Rolf and the king. The atmosphere in the chapel lightened, and when Henry turned to leave, Sir William went on as though the dangerous moment had never been.

'You have a beautiful wife, the envy of every man at Court, and lands which are a tribute to your loyalty to His Majesty. None deserves more than you the bright future this day offers.' He looked to where Henry had paused in the doorway of the chapel. When the king continued on his way, they all followed, Sir William adding, 'His Majesty grows impatient to attend a meeting of his counsellors, and I must join him. And you, my friend, have yet to kiss your enchanting bride.'

The breath caught in Meriel's throat as Rolf stepped in front of her, the gathered knights blocked from her vision by his towering form. His bronzed complexion was unusually pale as the bawdy jests from the others demanded the kiss. One hand circled her waist, the other lay against the slim column of her neck as her head eased back, her lips parting in unconscious surrender. A muscle throbbed alongside the scar in his neck, warning her of his controlled anger beneath the outward calm.

He did not kiss her at once. His eyes, carefully shielded by long dark lashes, studied her intently. When his mouth fastened upon hers, cool and firm, lightly sampling the suppleness of her lips, her heart lurched. It was a cold passionless gesture, almost brutal, because custom demanded it. His lack of emotion was an insult!

Rebellion sparked deep within her. Although aware of the watching knights, she knew she had to prove to Rolf that his kiss was more important to her than the king's. Sensing that he was about to pull back, she slid

her arms round his neck, her fingers pressing down as
she rose on tiptoe, moulding their bodies closer. The heat
and hardness of his body pressed against her thigh and
hip, her every nerve-end enflamed by the potency of his
touch and the heady masculine scent of his skin. The tip
of her tongue tasted the sweetness of his lips, then, more
daringly, probed deeper, recalling how he had kissed her
at the convent. She explored the hot inner softness,
briefly teasing and caressing, until she felt the answering
quiver of passion ripple through his powerful frame, and
his arms tightened about her. In that single moment of
his response, her blood raced like liquid fire, and
somehow she found the strength to pull away.

A ribald jest and laughter from the king resounded
over their heads as they drew apart. Her cheeks flamed
with high colour because she had found the courage to
play the temptress before them all. Rolf's hand briefly
lingered upon the crook of her neck. His golden eyes
flecked with topaz were harrowed. Whether from regret
or some deep inner torment she could not tell, for the
next instant their expression was once more unfath-
omable and bleak.

King Henry summoned a page to bring forward the
goblets of wine he was holding. 'A toast to your union,
Loxstead.' He used Rolf's title with pleasure. 'I shall be
some months in France. When I return, I look forward
to visiting your lands. By then the new castle we spoke
of, to be built some miles inland on the river north of
Wychaven, should be well under construction.'

'The work will be put in hand at once,' Rolf declared
smoothly. 'Unfortunately, I am not at liberty to put my
own interests first. Your Majesty cannot have forgotten
the duty I bear to Prince Richard. I must return to France
without delay. The building plans will be sent to me there
for approval.'

His voice was resolute, and when he turned to Meriel
with every apparent sign of regret, she knew he was
acting a role for the benefit of the king. She felt a sudden

panic as she anticipated his next words, knowing he did not intend her to accompany him.

'My wife has long been absent from Wychaven and is naturally concerned for the welfare of our people. She will remain in England. I have every faith that the work at the new castle will progress well under her guidance.'

The king's colour heightened. 'We do not expect such self-sacrifice from our subjects,' he said harshly. 'Richard will understand your desire to remain in England. You have a new wife, and need time to put your affairs in order.'

'With respect, Sire,' Rolf returned coolly, 'Prince Richard expects my return within the week. There are some who would see the honours you have bestowed upon me as a sign that I have forsworn my allegiance to the Lionheart. I would assure him that my devotion remains as strong as ever.'

So she was to be abandoned! Meriel's flesh pricked with a rush of humiliation. It was true that Wychaven needed her, but it needed its new lord more. Her pride reared up hot and defiant. She glanced, as though for reassurance, towards Bella, but she had already left the gathering to go ahead and check that all was in readiness at the inn. Meriel crushed down her hurt. Rolf did not want this marriage. Was this his way of putting her aside? She could understand his resentment, for he was stubborn and proud...and, worse, for the moment, highly prejudiced against her—believing her to have been the king's mistress. Well, their first night would prove she was a virgin! And, given time and patience, she was confident that she could overcome his distrust. Sadly, time was what she was being denied.

'By the eyes of God, Loxstead!' Henry grated out his favourite oath. 'One day you will push my forbearance too far. You insult your bride.'

'Sire!' Meriel stepped forward to soothe the mounting tension. 'With respect, I cannot be insulted when Lord Loxstead's duties take him from my side to serve yourself or Prince Richard. Indeed, I am honoured to govern our vast lands in his absence. A new wife likes to prove her capabilities to her husband.'

The king eyed her sternly, his gaze darting over both Rolf and herself for a long anxious moment. He nodded in acceptance, his voice sardonic. 'Do you hear that, Loxstead? Your countess is eager to take up the reins of rulership of your domains. She has much about her which reminds me of Eleanor's thirst for life when I first met her. *There* was a woman capable of leadership! And look where her love of power took her. The only time she was not causing me trouble was during the years she was producing children. Let that be a lesson to you.'

'I shall bear it in mind,' Rolf answered with equal cynicism. 'The countess will leave for Wychaven in the morning.'

'So soon?' Henry queried. 'A pity—I had hoped she would dance for me again before I left for France. No matter; I shall look forward to that pleasure when I visit Wychaven.'

Meriel sensed, rather than saw, Rolf stiffen at the king's words. Surely he should be delighted that he intended to visit them. Or had he taken Henry's wry humour amiss, suspecting that His Majesty hinted at a future liaison between himself and her?

'We shall keep you no longer from your bride, Loxstead,' the king went on, his tone impatient. 'Come, Sir William, the last of those documents must be dealt with before the day's end. What would you advise upon the . . .'

The king's voice faded as he and Sir William disappeared around the corner of the corridor. Rolf took her arm, his long stride adjusting to hers as he skilfully led her through the inquisitive groups of courtiers offering their good wishes.

'Forgive us, good sirs, if we are impatient to leave the palace,' he joked lightly, his arm sliding about Meriel's waist, as several knights, their faces flushed with wine, barred their progress, 'But the hour grows late, and the countess and I leave Court early tomorrow.'

A chorus of bawdy jests followed them as they proceeded to the bright moonlit courtyard, where the horses were waiting to take them to the privacy of the inn. When several of the knights followed, expecting to accompany them to enjoy the ribald sport which usually accompanied a couple's bedding, Rolf swung round, his voice edged with steel. 'A vat of the finest burgundy wine awaits you in the Great Hall to drink to my marriage. Take your fill, good knights, but my wife and I would be left in peace this night.'

A slightly-built figure in gold velvet richly encrusted with jewels came forward into the courtyard, his dark-bearded face thin and set with malice. Meriel instinctively moved closer to Rolf as she curtsied, her heart lurching as Prince John's pale, lecherous glance roved over her figure.

'Have you risen so high, Loxstead, that you would deny us our harmless sport?'

Rolf inclined his head in the briefest of bows. 'Your Highness, I had not realised that you had returned to Court.'

'An overnight visit, to assure my father of my good wishes. My brother is gathering his army, and His Majesty leaves for France in two days to confront him, so I hear.' He looked pointedly at Meriel, and smiled slyly. 'I have not met your delightful bride. It would pleasure me to attend the nuptial rituals at the inn.'

'We are honoured by your interest, Your Highness, but the king himself has decreed that we shall have our night of privacy. I leave at first light on His Majesty's business.' His voice had just enough deference to soften the insolence of his words. As he spoke, Sergeant Kedge and several other of Rolf's men stepped forward from the horses, their hands resting on their sword-hilts.

Prince John's eyes flashed like white lightning in the moonlight, and although Meriel was glad she would not be forced to endure the embarrassing ritual of a group of drunken knights escorting Rolf to her bed, she could not help but reflect that Prince John was a dangerous man to thwart. For some moments Rolf and the prince took each other's measure, and Meriel's skin prickled with awareness of danger. Prince John was known to have a vindictive streak when his temper was roused. Rolf showed no sign of backing down, and although she admired his courage in refusing to pander to the whims of a royal prince, she dreaded what might be the outcome. To Meriel's surprise, Prince John smiled wryly.

'You stick by your principles, Loxstead. A rare quality in these turbulent times. Until now, I thought William Marshal its only possessor. It is always heartening to know that there are men who can be trusted to remain loyal to those they serve. Go to enjoy your wedding night in peace, if that is what you wish.'

Rolf waved aside a groom, and placing his hands about Meriel's waist, lifted her up to her saddle. Although the gesture to those watching would appear a tender one, his gaze did not hold hers, and when he swung astride his own destrier, the suppressed violence of his action caused the horse to prance. Expertly it was brought under control, and they trotted from the courtyard. Once they had passed under the portcullis of the palace gatehouse, he looked across at her, his dark brows frowning.

'I had thought to tell you of my plans at the inn.' His tone, if not apologetic, was conciliatory, giving her hope that she had misinterpreted his anger, and that it was towards Prince John, not herself. Prince Richard was spending all his time in Aquitaine and defying his father—it had long been rumoured that Henry was considering leaving his realm to his younger son, and Prince John made no secret of wanting England for himself. Rolf cut across her thoughts. 'The marriage was arranged with such haste that you must realise I have matters to resolve in France before I can join you at Wychaven.'

'I, too, have found it unsettling to discover myself wedded so soon,' she answered sweetly. 'Of course you must return to Prince Richard, but will you not even visit Wychaven? And I must also reassure Queen Eleanor that Henry does not intend to put her aside in favour of the Princess Alice.'

The tendons of his neck corded. 'I shall spend two days in visiting my estate to give instructions to the steward. To do so, I must leave early tomorrow and cover the distance in three days. After my inspection, I immediately take ship to France. Naturally I would not expect you to undergo such a rigorous and punishing pace. A dozen of my men will escort you and your maid at a more leisurely progress, first to Winchester. All will be in readiness for you at Wychaven when you arrive.'

The finality of his statement brooked no argument. Meriel bit her lower lip to stop her heated reply. If she forced Rolf's hand now, he would be entrenched in his decision. Better to wait. Tonight was her wedding night. In the few short hours given to her, she would not only become his wife in deed as well as name, but must captivate him so entirely that he could not bear to have her from his side. The incisive set of his square jaw warned her that it would take more than charm and wiles to conquer this lord's heart.

Upon arrival at the inn, the men-at-arms were dismissed, and the landlord and his wife bustled forward to add their good wishes. Rolf curtly thanked them, and taking Meriel's arm, led her to their chambers. As they entered the ante-room, Bella straightened from putting the final touches to a table laden with cold meats and fruit.

'Leave us, Bella,' Rolf commanded. 'Your mistress will ring when she has need of you.'

Bella curtsied, her swarthy face beaming with joy. As she rose and hurried quickly past them, Meriel reached out to stay her. The air was heavy with the scent of freshly picked roses and wild flowers which were strewn about the chamber. 'The room looks beautiful. Thank you, Bella.'

The door clicked shut behind her maid, and Meriel was at last alone with her husband. Rolf selected an apple from the table and bit into it, his expression serious as he studied her in silence. Meriel swallowed against a knot of nervousness lodging in her throat, her own appetite deserting her at her husband's inscrutable features.

'There is much we have to discuss before I leave for France,' he said curtly, as though addressing his men.

Meriel forced a bright smile as Rolf poured two goblets of wine, extending one to her, but he was careful that their hands did not touch. For the first time since they had met, he appeared ill at ease in her company, but this marriage had been thrust upon them with such suddenness that her own head fairly reeled with the shock. She drank deeply from the goblet, the smooth liquid calming her jagged nerves.

'The whole night is ahead of us, my lord,' she said huskily, reaching across him to pluck a grape from the fruit dish, aware that the lemon-scented freshness of her hair would waft provocatively over him. 'I am eager to learn of your plans for Wychaven and the new castle to be built to the north.'

He was frowning when she turned back to face him. Tossing the apple-core into the brazier burning in the centre of the room, he locked his hands over his sword-belt. It was as though he were exercising control over every movement. She knew he was capable of almost inhuman restraint, but she had the impression now that he was deliberately setting up barriers between them. Somehow she had to break them down, for beneath that guard, he had shown her a man who was tender, sensual and passionate. She knew that he desired her, so why was he now so cold and remote?

The heavy gold circlet pressed tightly against her brow, and she removed it, laying it together with her veil and wimple on a nearby coffer, while she summoned to mind all Bella's advice on arousing and keeping a man's attention.

'My instructions will be awaiting you at Wychaven when you arrive,' Rolf explained, seizing upon the practical as he sought to blot the tempting loveliness of Meriel from his mind. Yet, even as he spoke of his plans, he

was acutely aware of her every movement. Of the fullness
of her breasts outlined against her silk gown as she lifted
her arms to pull the pins from the midnight-black braids
looped over her ears. Thick as a woman's arm, the plaits
fell to her hips as she pulled them over her shoulders,
her agile fingers unravelling them, until, with an al-
luring shake of her head, her tresses tumbled free to reach
to her knees like a shimmering silk mantle. He concentrated hard on what she was saying, but his gaze was
drawn to the provocative sway of her hips as she moved
about the room.

'The land around Wychaven is good pasture,' she informed him, 'which, if stocked with cattle, would swell
the estate coffers.' She paused, her pearly teeth tantalisingly nibbling the end of her forefinger in a way that set
his pulse racing. He drew long shallow breaths to still
the desire flaring deep within him as her throaty voice
continued to speak of her home. 'The fishing fleet could
also be extended along the coast and the catch sold in
the nearby towns.'

Her sound reasoning of what was best to improve the
estate income surprised him, as did so many things about
her, yet it changed nothing. She had brought him the
lands and wealth he had striven so long to achieve, but
she was also tainted with the one flaw he found unac-
ceptable in a wife. He had seen how her quick mind
outwitted the unwary, how her obvious charms captivated and beguiled. Therein lay the poison. He desired
her as he had desired no other woman. How easy it would
be to fall beneath the spell of those magnificent sea-blue
eyes which could shimmer with pretended innocence.
Other eyes from his past mocked him, and the familiar
pain of that long-ago betrayal channelled through him,
hardening his heart and resolve.

'It is not just of the estate I would speak,' he began,
his temper flaring at the sudden deafening noise from
the street below their window. Shields were being battered with sword-hilts and the shrill notes from hunting-
horns blasted the serenity of the night. Some of the

knights and courtiers denied the bedding ritual were taking their revenge by disturbing the peace of the bride and groom.

'How long will that noise continue?' Meriel asked, clapping her hands over her ears in mock horror, but her eyes were merry with laughter.

'As long as it suits them,' Rolf ground out savagely, his own humour at the situation swept aside as his plans were frustrated. He had intended to leave at once for his estates. The king had forced him to marry Meriel, but that did not mean he must bed her. If the marriage remained unconsummated, it could be annulled. But he could not leave the inn while the revellers remained outside. He would not shame Meriel so openly; he could at least spare her that.

He looked around the room, startled to discover that she was no longer there. The sound of her soft footfall came from within the bedchamber. The promise of the delights that awaited him, should he step through that door, rekindled the fire in his blood. He poured another goblet of wine, draining the contents without even tasting them. Refilling the cup, he turned his back on the open door and threw himself down on a chair. The ear-shattering din outside faded in his mind to a distant drone, his eyes glazing as they fixed blankly on the glowing embers within the brazier.

Meriel glanced for the dozenth time towards the open door leading to the ante-room. The noise outside gave no sign of subsiding, except that the townspeople who had shouted out their complaints had fallen silent when they realised that several young noblemen were among the drunken revellers. Rolf had not come to her, as she had hoped he would.

Without Bella to assist her, she had struggled with the laces down her back and finally managed to wriggle out of her gown. Discarding also the silk chemise, she had wrapped a loose silk night-robe about her, tying it at her waist with a scarlet sash. There was no sound from the outer room. Unable to stand the strain of waiting for

Rolf to come to her, she moved to the door. He sat forward in the chair, one elbow resting on his knee, his chin propped on his knuckles, staring into the brazier, unaware of her presence.

'Rolf?' Her voice croaked with nervousness.

He turned towards her, a muscle throbbing along his taut jaw as his gaze roamed the length of her figure silhouetted in the doorway. As though in a daze, he explored her body with his eyes, and her cheeks stung with heat as she realised how the candlelight in the room behind her would make her flimsy robe almost transparent. She schooled herself to stay where she was, remembering Bella's advice that, to captivate a man, a woman must first tantalise and allure.

CHAPTER NINE

As MERIEL moved slowly towards Rolf, the noise outside at last ended, the knights and courtiers tiring of their sport. Breathlessly she held his heavy-lidded stare, the sudden silence falling over the chamber tangible, like a cocoon isolating them in a world of expectancy and promise. He sat motionless as she approached, and she sensed that something was terribly wrong—that he resented her coming to him thus, yet found himself caught in the same spell which was impelling her forward. Why did he make no move to take her in his arms? Her courage almost failed her, but remembering Bella's words, she knew that having caught him off guard, she must not draw back now.

His wine goblet was empty, so she picked up the flagon, and, kneeling at his feet, leant forward to fill it. His gaze slid from her eyes to the fullness of her breasts partially revealed as her robe gaped open. He swallowed hard, the hollows beneath his high cheekbones tautening as he swiftly drained the goblet, his knuckles whitening as they curled round its silver stem. When he raised his eyes to her, their topaz depths were bleak with an inner torment.

'Go to bed, Meriel,' he said tonelessly. 'You must be tired. It has been a long day.'

There was no tenderness in his voice, no soft words to soothe a slow-dawning fear. Why had he not kissed her? It was almost as though he were fighting her, and her heart thudded painfully in growing alarm. This was not how it should be on their wedding night! She had so little time left before he rode out in the morning. Her panic grew with each heartbeat.

'My lord, what is wrong?' She placed a hand on his thigh, feeling the heat of his body beneath the fine hose.

He started as violently as though she had stabbed him. Standing up, he crossed the room, turning his back to her. 'Why should anything be wrong?' he snapped. 'I have much on my mind. There are papers I must look through before I leave tomorrow.'

Her toe caught the edge of her long sash as she rose to her feet, and she gripped the side of the chair to steady herself. At a loss to understand his strange behaviour, she stared at his broad, unyielding back, pain clawing at her throat.

'But after tonight it could be months before I see you again,' she said impulsively. 'I thought...' Her voice broke as he swung round to face her, and her arms lifted in entreaty. 'This is our wedding night, my lord. Can the papers not wait?'

As she moved, the sash, which had become loosened when she stepped on it, fell to the floor and her robe parted. His eyes devoured her nakedness. Instinctively she sought to cover herself, but as she snatched the robe together, the silk slipped from her shoulders, held in place only where her hands clutched it to her breasts.

A spasm flickered across Rolf's face, and his voice was savage. 'You speak with words of such innocence—yet your every action betrays you for the whore you are!'

'That is not true!' Meriel stared at him in wide-eyed horror, shrugging her shoulders back into the robe and clasping it to her body with folded arms. 'I am a maid!'

Rolf grabbed a cloak from a peg on the wall and moved to the door, his tone scathing. 'Do not add to your dishonour by lying. God's teeth woman, you were alone with His Majesty for over an hour! How many others have there been before him?'

Her patience snapped at the injustice of his accusation. Holding the edges of the robe together, she ran to the door, throwing herself against it to prevent his leaving. Her cheeks flamed with the force of her fury.

'I do not lie...why should I? I know a man can tell whether a woman is a virgin or not.'

'And with those shrewd wits of yours, you will also know that, once the marriage is consummated, and since we are not closely related, there can be no escaping this match.' His eyes blazed. 'Whether you were a virgin, or not, before this night, would then be irrelevant in the eyes of the law. You would have what you wanted— someone to wrest your precious Wychaven from Sedbury's clutches. It was a clever attempt, my lady, but unsuccessful. I learned a long while ago that the harder a woman pleads her innocence, the greater her guilt.'

His brutal words stunned her. Gripping her shoulders, he put her aside and opened the door, his footsteps fading as he bounded down the stairs.

'Rolf!' Meriel sobbed, wrenching wide the door to go after him, but he was out of her sight. Aware of the hubbub of voices from the taproom below, she hugged her robe tighter about her and retreated into the room. In her half-naked state, she was unable to follow him and make him see reason. Closing the door, she leaned dazedly upon it. Gradually the numbness of her shock drained from her mind and she realised that she had been standing by the door for so long that her teeth were chattering with the cold. She moved woodenly to the inner chamber, her throat and breast raw and aching with the pain of his rejection.

She sank on the edge of the bed, his words whirling through her brain. He did not want her as his wife because he believed her to be a wanton? But it was something more than that which drove him to act as he had done... It had to be! She had seen for herself that he was capable of surprising gentleness and passion, and if he judged her so harshly, it was certainly not because he was a prude. What had happened to embitter him so? She wiped a hand across her cheek, surprised to find her eyes awash with tears. She should hate him for his callous condemnation, but, strangely, she did not. It was not her he was rejecting—only the type of woman he thought she was. He had proved himself too strong willed to succumb to his desire, and although on this occasion his integrity was to her disadvantage, she could not help admiring so esteemable a quality. She stood up, refusing to be defeated. It was going to be more difficult than she had imagined to convince Rolf that she was a worthy wife.

Given time, his anger at being forced into this marriage would cool, but he was on the point of leaving for France. Their differences must be resolved before then, or they could fester. First, she had to overcome his prejudices, but how? She ran her nail along her teeth, thinking hard. The best way to do that was to discover what had embittered him towards all women, but whom could she turn to for advice? Her frown cleared. Surely the best person would be the Lady Isolda?

Instantly a plan formed in her mind, and in a fever of impatience to put it into action, she hurried from the room to summon Bella. When Rolf returned, she would be gone. The moment the gates opened in the morning, she would leave the town to speak with the Lady Isolda.

Rolf pulled the hood of his cloak low over his face as he entered the street. The gesture was instinctive—he needed to be alone to still the throbbing anger gnawing him. Not that there was much danger of being recognised. The town was sleeping and the streets were deserted. His soft leather boots were silent as he strode to the city walls overlooking the river, where an alert sentry challenged him as he stepped on to the battlements. Reluctantly, he pushed back his hood. A single glance by the guard into his set features was enough for the man to lower his sword and allow him to pass.

The black rage continued to blast through him as he paced back and forth along the battlements. Finally, he paused. Gripping the crenellated wall, he stared out at the silver ribbon of river below. His anger was unreasonable, but the knowledge made it the harder to bear. When would this cursed devil stop riding him? It was not with Meriel that he was really angry, but with another, who had destroyed his illusions of chivalry and innocence.

Guilt jousted with his conscience. He had not envisaged himself married for another year at least. The suddenness of it, and the manner in which he felt it had been forced upon him, were an affront to his pride. He cursed the king beneath his breath. This was Henry's way of punishing him for his loyalty to Richard! Yet the honours Henry had bestowed upon him along with Meriel's hand were generous in the extreme. Obstinately he clung to his ideals, but in the stillness of the night, broken only by the tramping of a sentry's feet, those ideals taunted rather than sustained him.

He had not meant to treat Meriel so callously, but when she had offered herself so brazenly, he could not stop himself. It was his only defence. She was so lovely, so very tempting—she had laid bare his weakness. He closed his eyes and inhaled sharply to blot out the ache of longing. A groan wrenched his throat as his mind conjured up the seductive vision of her holding out her arms towards him, her robe tantalisingly parted to reveal the perfection of her slender body, her breasts uptilted... He opened his eyes, but her image remained, rising out of the darkness of the night to hover, ethereal and beguiling, before him. With a curse, he passed a shaking hand across his eyes and, mercifully, the vision vanished. Not so the torment that continued to thrust like a sword through his body. Against all reason—all the lessons he had learned of women's faithlessness—he wanted to believe Meriel innocent.

Hearing a door opening in the palace gatehouse which led directly on to this section of the battlements, he turned towards the sound.

'Lord Loxstead! You are the last man I expected to see this night!'

Rolf stiffened upon recognising William Marshal's voice. 'I needed to be alone!' he answered tersely.

'Then I intrude,' William said, preparing to turn back to his rooms at the top of the gatehouse.

'No, my friend.' Rolf stayed him, suddenly needing to talk to someone he could trust. Despite the difference in their ages, there had always been an affinity between them which transcended age. William was the only man Rolf had ever confided in. 'It will be dawn in another hour. I should return to the inn. Have you only just left the king?'

'Ay, His Majesty keeps the devil's own hours. He'll be in the saddle, riding hard for Dover, in another three hours.' Sir William rubbed his hip-joint. 'With every passing year I find it harder to keep pace with him. Faith, I am bone weary! Too tired even to sleep.' His austere face was lined with weariness and also concern. 'You are troubled, my friend, or you would not be here on your wedding night. How so?'

Rolf rubbed his neck, his mouth twisting with bitterness as his finger traced the line of the scar. 'You are the only one to whom I have confided the truth of how I came by this. I am driven by something I cannot explain, even to myself. It eats at me like an insidious maggot. The king has honoured me beyond my wildest dreams, yet, instead of elation, I feel...' His stare bored into his friend's, his confession dragged from him. 'I feel cheated, and that is absurd, especially since I want her—desire her—almost to the point of madness, but I cannot forgive Meriel for what she has done... for what she is!'

'You have good reason to distrust women—but sometimes things are not always as they seem. You must forget the past. Was not the Lady Meriel obeying the queen's orders by coming to Court? Would you condemn her for her loyalty?'

'No, never for that!' As Rolf studied his friend's serious face, his anger towards Meriel dwindled. The need to believe that she was incapable of falseness and infidelity intensified.

'Then reserve for Henry your anger and resentment at this rushed marriage,' William advised. 'Accept your wife for the honours she has brought you, and the obvious delights still to be discovered. Give yourself time to learn to trust her, my friend. It is the future which is important. Even I, hardened soldier that I am, can see that the Lady Meriel cares for you. There is a clearness about her eyes that speaks of an honest nature. And the way she kissed you after the ceremony!' William laughed softly. 'I could have sworn it was to prove some point to the king. You had your back to Henry, and could not have seen his eyes clouding with regret that her preference for you was so obvious.'

'Do you think it is an honour to accept Henry Plantagenet's cast-off mistress as my wife?' Rolf snarled, turning away from his friend as his anger returned.

'You underestimate your value to the king if you think Henry would use you in such a manner. He knows your prejudices too well.' William's voice sharpened with exasperation. 'The regret in Henry's eyes was for what he wanted but could not have!'

Rolf gritted his teeth against an unexpected rush of relief, the acuteness of which smote him like a stab-wound. These were the words he craved to hear, the balm his conscience needed for him to begin to trust Meriel. Could it be that she had outwitted Henry and escaped his attentions?

'I leave you to your thoughts, my friend.' William gripped his shoulder in understanding. 'But think well upon my words. You know Henry as well as I; his rewards often have a sting in their tail. We all have to bow to his wishes. Do not let your anger against him cloud your judgement of your wife. I, too, have fallen a little under your countess's spell, but I would wager my most prized destrier that if ever she should turn from you to another, it would be because you had driven her.'

Rolf watched William disappear from sight. He knew his friend spoke the truth, and his advice echoed what he had been trying to come to terms with all night. His step lightened as he hurried back to the inn. His need for Meriel had at last overpowered his plans to set her aside, and his warring feelings settled into determination. Why deny himself the pleasure of bedding Meriel? She was his wife, and while she upheld the honour of his name, he was prepared to accept her. He thrust past the sleepy-eyed landlord, who finally answered his impatient hammering at the locked door, and ignoring the man's urgent calling of his name, sped up the stairs two at a time. He could think only of the pain he had caused to Meriel and his need to comfort her—to make love to her.

Dawn was already brightening the sky as he pushed open the door to their chambers, his throat suddenly dry with the anticipation of tenderly kissing awake her sleeping figure. Shock pulled him up short at the door, the pale grey light showing him that the bed had not been slept in. A hasty survey of the room revealed no trace of Meriel's presence, and disbelief fast turned to fury at her desertion.

'Landlord!' he bellowed from the top of the stairs, after he had checked Bella's room to discover that it too was empty. 'How long ago did the countess leave the inn?'

'Not long after yourself, my lord,' the landlord answered, his eyes brightening with curiosity. 'The countess said she had received word that her mother was sick, and that you had gone to summon your men to leave at once.'

'Fetch Sergeant Kedge!' Rolf blazed, moving back into the room to take two daggers from his coffer to arm himself, anxiety for Meriel grinding through his anger. The town gate would already be open, and she could be on the highway by now. Even as close as a mile from the royal palace, bands of outlaws had attacked unwary travellers.

'My lord,' the landlord's voice sounded puzzled as he stood by the door, 'Sergeant Kedge went with the countess. I heard her telling him you expected to join them by the gate.'

Meriel fidgeted impatiently with her palfrey's reins, her escort waiting behind her muttering among themselves. Would the gate never open? At her side, looking worried and ill at ease, Bella sat hunched on her mare. Bella had accompanied her out of loyalty after a long attempt to get her to change her mind. Only by recalling Rolf's taut face and his cheekbones flagged with angry colour had she found the strength to stick by her plan. Aware of Sergeant Kedge's questioning look upon her, Meriel willed her hands to be still. She dared not betray her nervousness, lest he suspect she had tricked him. When the huge oak double gates were finally dragged open, Tom Kedge rode his horse across her path, his expression anxious.

'We must await his lordship. With only six men, it is not safe for you to ride out.'

Meriel forced a reassuring smile. 'Probably Lord Loxstead has been delayed by His Majesty. I must reach my mother without delay, but I cannot ride as hard as his lordship. He will be with us before we have travelled more than a few miles, especially since he wishes to inform the Lady Isolda of our marriage, and we are to stop at the convent. I also wish to ask her to pray for my mother's recovery.'

Sergeant Kedge compressed his mouth stubbornly, his dark brown moustache adding to the sternness of his expression. Meriel raised a condemning brow. For two hundred years her ancestors had ruled the hard and rugged coast of southern England—according to legend, there had been a fortress at Wychaven even in King Arthur's day. They had beaten off invaders and beseiging armies alike. Their blood was in her veins, and she had not come this far to be stopped now.

'His lordship mentioned nothing of this to me. The roads are dangerous and ...'

'You forget to whom you are speaking,' she interrupted, her voice ringing with the authority of those who had ruled for generations. 'I do not expect my orders to be disobeyed.'

An embarrassed flush stained the sergeant's cheeks. 'There is always danger of attack upon the roads. His lordship will flay me should any harm befall you!'

'No harm will befall us,' Meriel said confidently. 'I am no faint-heart. My mother has need of me. Every moment we delay...' Her voice broke as though with distress, and she dabbed at her eyes with the edge of her cloak. 'Lord Loxstead will not thank you, if you serve me so ill.'

'I think only of your safety, my lady,' he answered gruffly. 'Oh, by all the saints, I cannot bear to see a woman cry! Ride on, my lady.'

Meriel urged her horse forward through the crowd of beggars and pedlars entering the town. Momentarily she was separated from the men-at-arms by the press of people, and she risked a triumphant grin at Bella riding at her side.

'I pray, my lady, you will not regret this rashness,' Bella whispered worriedly. 'I still think it would be better to wait!'

'Wait for what?' Meriel answered in a clipped undertone. 'To be cast aside without a fight? When I am reunited with Rolf, either at Winchester or Wychaven, I intend to know all I can about him. For that, I must speak with the Lady Isolda.'

She fell silent as the men-at-arms rode into position around her, her heart thudding with dread lest Sergeant Kedge took it upon himself to stop her. He did not, but the grim set of his face and the anxious way he kept looking back over his shoulder showed her his unease. A pang of conscience made her regret that her recklessness would rebound upon him. Rolf would be furious at her leaving and would likely blame his sergeant for not preventing her. Not that anyone, short of physical violence, could have done that.

The day was overcast, echoing her gloomy mood, and she resisted the urge to look over her shoulder, as Sergeant Kedge constantly did. He was uneasy that his master had not yet caught them up. By Meriel's rough calculations they should have one, or perhaps two, hours' start on Rolf, and she was certain he had no intention of visiting his sister on his journey west. She prayed he would not suspect that she would visit her.

She breathed more easily as they turned on to the track leading to the convent, and, as they rounded a bend which would take them out of sight of the Winchester Road, she gave in to the impulse to glance back. Her heart jolted. Was that a blue and silver pennon she had glimpsed through the trees? Before she could be certain, her horse carried her beyond the bend and, thankfully, at that time Tom Kedge had not also looked back. But had Rolf seen them? Her spine studded with alarm. If he came upon them now, she would have failed miserably. He would never understand what had driven her to act as she did—and without the knowledge she hoped the Lady Isolda could provide, the prospect was too fearful to contemplate. Rolf would feel himself justified in putting aside a wife who had deserted him on their wedding night.

Rolf pressed his men to a faster pace, haunted by the fear that round the next bend in the track he would come upon Meriel's body, his men attacked by outlaws. He had arrived at the town gates shortly after it had opened, but an argument had broken out between two wagoners, neither giving way as the two vehicles approached the gate. Their wheels had locked, overturning the wagons and spilling their contents of cabbages and apples, so that the road had been blocked for what had seemed an eternity. His initial rage at Meriel's flight had been tempered by guilt that he could have wounded her so thoughtlessly. It was his own stupid pride that had driven him to act as he did, and now her life could be in danger!

Without pausing, he galloped past the track to the convent, giving his sister no thought, in his need to catch up with Meriel before his fears could be realised. Each mile brought with it a greater hopelessness. He looked up at the pale glow of the sun struggling to break through the layer of clouds. It was almost noon. Meriel and her escort would never have travelled so far in this time; he should have met her party several miles back. Already they had passed a dozen tracks leading off the Winchester road, and she could have taken one of them, or be hiding anywhere in this thickly wooded part of the countryside. He could search all day and still not find her, especially if she did not want to be found. He cursed her roundly. She was too quick witted for her own good. She would know his time in England was limited... His anxious thoughts broke off at the sound of a fast-approaching rider wearing Queen Eleanor's colours.

'Sir Rolf of Blackleigh?' the messenger demanded, skidding to a halt, his body swaying in the saddle from exhaustion. ''Tis good fortune I met you upon the road. The news from the queen is grave, and she bade me ride both day and night until I found you.'

'It is Rolf Blackleigh, Earl of Loxstead, now,' a soldier behind Rolf proudly informed the messenger.

Rolf gestured his men to silence and took the parchment held out to him. As he hastily scanned it, his face set into a thunderous mask. 'You have done well to reach me so quickly.' He dismissed the messenger, and smothering his anxiety for Meriel, reasoned that Tom Kedge was a good man who would guard her with his life. He turned to his men, for the urgency of the queen's summons could not be denied. There was now no time to scour the surrounding villages for word of Meriel. He, too, must ride day and night. Meriel had her duties to complete, and would return to Winchester to report to Queen Eleanor. Even she would not dare to keep Her Majesty waiting. He would leave word for her there.

*   *   *

Meriel looked pleadingly at Rolf's sister as she came to the end of her story. 'That is why, Lady Isolda, I had to ask your advice.'

'You did right to come to me.' The anchoress smiled serenely, patting Meriel's hand as they sat on the low wall between two arches of the convent cloisters. Her light gold brows drew together, her gaze sliding from Meriel's to regard the worn flagstones. 'I cannot say why Rolf so distrusts women. After our mother died, and before he went away to train for knighthood in another household, we were very close. He was the most affectionate and considerate of children. Of course the years of training are not easy, but he excelled in everything—perhaps it was his single-mindedness to be a great warrior which hardened him. I saw little of him after my marriage.' The Lady Isolda's hazel eyes flashed with a cold, hard light which momentarily disconcerted Meriel, until the older woman's voice cracked with sadness. 'It was several years later before I met Rolf again, in France. He was the adored hero of the tournaments—proud, assured, a golden knight in every respect—but he had changed.'

'The scar on his neck?' Meriel asked, striving to overcome her disappointment that the journey had been in vain. Isolda could tell her little. 'How did he come by that? Perhaps that has something to do with the change in him?'

The Lady Isolda paled, her voice strained. 'He never speaks of it. I suspect it has something to do with Rolf's cynical view of chivalry. Perhaps he fought over a faithless woman. He has, I believe, never been short of willing female companions.'

Meriel knew too well the devastating effect Rolf could have upon a woman's senses to wish to dwell upon the thoughts of his conquests. 'Then I am no nearer to discovering what drives Rolf to act as he does!'

'In that I cannot help you,' Isolda replied, her voice thoughtful. 'But...' she met Meriel's gaze, her eyes sparkling, 'I cannot believe Rolf is as cold-hearted as he

would have people think. It was difficult to draw his
inner thoughts from him, even as a boy. But I know him
better than anyone—was I not both sister and mother
to him for some years? If he really did not want to, no
power on this earth—even the threat of King Henry's
wrath—could have made him take you as his bride.'

Meriel shook her head. 'He sounded as though he
hated me.'

'Rolf is not one to waste time on words.' Isolda stood
up, moving away from Meriel so that her expression was
hidden. 'If there is a wrong to avenge—he acts!' She
turned slowly to smile at Meriel. 'For the moment, my
brother's pride is somewhat bruised, and he could be
stubborn, even as a child. But did I not say at our first
meeting how well suited you are for Rolf? Your differences must be settled before he sets sail for France, and
I shall help you all I can. I am not bound by any vows
to remain an anchoress here indefinitely. I shall come
with you to Wychaven and seek to reason with Rolf. He
will, of course, be furious that you apparently deserted
him.'

'I could not ask so great a sacrifice of you,' Meriel
began.

'It is no sacrifice.' Isolda cut across her words. 'Besides, you have also said that you fear Lord Sedbury will
cause trouble for Rolf. I am acquainted with your
kinsman—he was a friend of Sir Harold and often visited
our estates when my husband was alive. Perhaps he may
listen to the pleas of the wife of an old friend on your
behalf and that of the Lady Maude. Is it not a sister's
duty to help her brother to gain all he deserves in this
life?'

'You must care for Rolf very deeply,' Meriel said,
swallowing against a knot of emotion. She had not
expected so much from the Lady Isolda. 'You said the
very same at our first meeting.'

'Of course!' Isolda's eyes glittered with conspiracy.
'Even shut away here, the news of my brother's exploits
reached me, and I have prayed for the chance to serve

him...to help him attain life's rewards.' Her voice rose to a passionate note, then dropped as though embarrassed by her outburst. 'I was never blessed with children, and I suppose that makes me more protective towards Rolf. By helping him, I would be close to him again, as we were years ago.'

Impulsively Meriel stood up and kissed her cheek. 'I, too, wish only to make Rolf happy. It is likely that he will go first to Winchester to report to Queen Eleanor. We may catch up with him there. Will it take you long to prepare to leave?'

'My needs are simple. I shall explain everything to the prioress, and be ready to leave within the hour.'

Meriel bowed her head against the persistent drizzle that had accompanied their three-day journey. The horses' hooves slithered over the churned-up track, slowing their progress, and with each mile the air of tension hanging over her party intensified. Sergeant Kedge was tense and uneasy since learning that Meriel had tricked him, and was not at all pleased that Isolda had joined them. His curt attitude towards the anchoress puzzled Meriel. The frustrating pace of their progress, coupled with the miserable weather, echoed the bleakness of her thoughts. She had learned nothing which gave her any insight into Rolf's mind. From the villages they passed through, she had learned that he was at least one day ahead. Her heart thumped heavily. Their reunion at Winchester was likely to be bitter and stormy, and she had brought it upon herself.

They crested another hill, and the stone walls of the castle with their conical towers, and the unfinished cathedral of Winchester, lay sprawled before them. Within an hour she would have to face Rolf, and daunting though the prospect of facing his wrath was, she still longed to see him again. After spending so long in his company, the three days they had been apart since their wedding had dragged interminably. Was this bitter-sweet ache of emptiness and yearning part of loving? She had never thought it possible that she could miss anyone as much as she had missed Rolf these last days.

Bella urged her mare alongside Meriel as they rode along the single row of tall gabled timber houses towards the castle ramparts and the gatehouse. 'My lady, have you planned what you are to say to Lord Loxstead?' Her swarthy countenance was drawn with concern.

Meriel shook her head. 'There is nothing to tell him but the truth. If we had been more open with each other, many of the misunderstandings between us would never have arisen.'

'Wisely spoken,' Isolda broke in, 'but you must tread warily. I doubt Rolf will be forthcoming with any of the dark secrets that haunt his past; such is not the way of men. And you must take care not to leave yourself open and vulnerable to him. To protest your innocence and love for him overly will condemn you further in his eyes.'

Bella grimaced. 'With respect, my lady, Lord Loxstead is master of his own emotions. He will never trust you if you are less than honest with him. I was wrong to advise you to be other than yourself. Follow the instincts of your heart, they will not fail you.'

Isolda's eyes glinted haughtily. 'Meriel, my dear, I know my brother best. You really should not allow yourself to be influenced by a servant,' she dropped her voice to disapproving whisper, 'especially one who once sold herself on the streets. What would she know of decency and honour?'

'Bella did not lead that life through choice,' Meriel retorted, her impatience wearing thin. This was not the first time the anchoress had expressed a lack of sympathy and understanding towards her friend. She would have thought a holy woman would have more understanding and compassion for one less fortunate than herself, but from the first moment the two had met, a mutual dislike had sprung up between Bella and Isolda.

Isolda looked contrite. 'I had no wish to offend you. Obviously you are very attached to your servant.' She paused, and eased her weight in the saddle with a weary sigh, adding apologetically, 'It is years since I have ridden. I am tired, stiff and sore, and I fear the rigours of the journey have made me irritable. Forgive my harsh words. Of course you must confide in Rolf. Speak to him as you poured out your heart to me, and you cannot fail to rekindle all that is chivalrous in him.'

Yet, as they rode into the palace courtyard, Meriel looked about her uneasily. Some inner sense told her that Rolf was not here. Had he already set sail for France? Dear God, let it not be so!

She fretted, restlessly pacing a small ante-room as they awaited audience with the queen. The inner door was opened, and a tiring-woman ushered the Lady Isolda and Meriel into Eleanor's presence. They both sank into a reverent curtsy. Her Majesty sat straight-backed and imperious upon a carved chair, her dark brows lifting with curiosity as she looked at Isolda. 'This is an unexpected pleasure, Lady Isolda. Lord Loxstead gave no intimation that you would be accompanying his wife. It would please me to speak with you later, but first I must speak privately with the countess.'

From the corner of her eye, Meriel saw Isolda stiffen at her abrupt dismissal, the anchoress's lack of humility startling her. But Isolda's face wore smooth compliance as she rose and swept gracefully from the room.

'Well, Countess! Frankly, I am surprised that you dare show your face here.' Eleanor's voice sharpened once they were alone. 'Rolf brought me the news from King Henry's Court that I expected to hear from *your* lips. As to the rest...' her dark eyes flashed with anger, 'you show little respect or regard for the honours King Henry has showered upon you. I had not thought you the sort of woman who lets her husband of but a single night ride off unaccompanied, however arduous the journey might be.'

'Your Majesty...' Meriel flushed, 'may I know if that is what my husband told you?'

The queen eyed her impatiently. 'Rolf said nothing of the kind, but it was obvious from his manner that all

was not as it should be between you. If the marriage
does not please you, then you are a fool. What more
can you want from a husband? He is titled, young, and
too handsome for his own good! It was plain enough
from the way he watched you dance that he was far from
averse to your charms.'

'Oh, he made it quite clear that he wanted the minstrel
and dancing-girl as his mistress, Your Majesty.' Meriel
hung her head, unable to hold Eleanor's piercing stare.
'Those were not the qualities he was looking for in a
wife. At King Henry's insistence we were married with
such haste that there was no time to clear up the misunderstandings between us. And he intended to leave
immediately for France—alone.'

Eleanor frowned, her expression sceptical. 'Lord
Loxstead is adept at concealing his feelings, but it was
not my impression that he seemed eager to escape an
unwanted bride.'

Meriel stared at the queen, not daring to believe her
ears. Her heart pounded so loudly that it seemed to
drown out her nervous question. 'Your Majesty, is Rolf
still at Winchester?'

The queen regarded her carefully for several moments, then understanding softened her expression. 'You
love him, don't you? I fear, then, that this news will
come hard. Rolf left this morning for Wychaven. Apparently Sedbury, knowing that the king set sail from
Dover two days ago, ordered Wychaven to prepare for
a seige. The castle is locked against you, and Sedbury
is in residence.' As Meriel gasped, Eleanor nodded
gravely. 'Lord Loxstead has ridden out to raise an army
to recapture Wychaven. It is his wish that you remain
here until the seige is over.'

'Then it seems that once more I must disobey him,'
Meriel answered without hesitation. This was her chance
to prove her loyalty to Rolf. Her determination and confidence grew as a plan formed in her mind, and her voice
throbbed with the urgency of convincing the queen that
she must leave. 'Wychaven was built to withstand in-

vaders from the sea and the land. I know its secrets better than any one, better even than Sedbury! A siege could last for weeks, and Rolf has duties in France. There is a secret way into the castle that is not known to my kinsman, and only I can show it to Rolf. I pray the castle can be retaken without bloodshed.'

CHAPTER TEN

MERIEL STOOD gazing down at the painted wooden effigy on her father's tomb in the stone church on the headland overlooking Wychaven. She had hoped to find an answer to her prayers before meeting Rolf in the valley below, but nothing came. She reached out to touch the carved likeness of Sir Arnulf, with its long drooping moustache and coat of mail. It was so lifelike that her eyes misted with resurgent grief for the loving father she had lost. She had failed Sir Arnulf. She should have returned to Wychaven sooner. It was an insult to her father's memory that Sedbury had refused to relinquish his hold upon her inheritance. It was a deeper insult to Rolf.

Would Rolf blame her for that insult also? 'Oh, Father, what a failure I have been in every way,' she said beneath her breath, aware that the Lady Isolda was praying at the altar rail a few feet away. 'Why was I not the son you craved, instead of a weak and foolish woman?'

The effigy blurred before her eyes. She was a child again, sitting at Sir Arnulf's knee as he told her of Wychaven's past. How this church had been built on the edge of the grove of wych-elms which gave Wychaven its name. Of her ancestors who had withstood the Viking raids, and of his plans for Wychaven to thrive· and prosper. He had ruffled her dark head, declaring his pride in his daughter, but sadness had lingered in his eyes for the four tiny infant sons who had died before Meriel was born, and who were buried in the vault of this same church. Yet now the sea-green eyes of the effigy did not reproach her, and gradually a feeling of peace settled over her. She had not failed—not yet, nor did she intend to. ·

Casting a look back at the Lady Isolda, still at prayer, Meriel walked out of the church into the bright sunlight and moved across the elm-dotted graveyard to the edge of the cliff. From there, the highest point on Wychaven land, she stared along the coastline of the three rocky coves. Above the smallest inlet, dominating the rugged cliff-top, sprawled Wychaven Castle. The familiar sight brought a lump of emotion to her throat, as joy and sorrow alternately tugged at her heart. After so many years it was wonderful to set eyes upon her home, which, outwardly at least, was unchanged. Her critical eye scanned the village and countryside—all was peaceful. Too peaceful!

Uneasy, she looked back towards her waiting escort. Apart from the men, Bella sat alone on a low boulder, her shoulders hunched in dejection. Since Lord Sedbury had cast her out, the sparkle had left her. It was obvious that Bella had loved Sedbury, despite his harsh ways. His rejection, and his betrayal of Meriel, had broken her spirit. Nothing seemed to ease her pain, and Meriel could only pray that in time her heartache would heal, that she would find someone more worthy of her love. Heavy-hearted, she pushed Bella from her thoughts. She could do nothing for her now, and must concentrate all her efforts on weathering Rolf's anger and saving Wychaven.

Her own troubles pressing down upon her, Meriel tipped back her head, her veil whipping out behind her as she inhaled the tangy salt air. Shading her eyes against the bright sun, she scanned the wild coastline. The azure sky was vivid against the darkness of the rugged cliffs, and the sea was bright turquoise before it broke in waves and crashed with a roar on the treacherous black rocks. Pride filled her breast. On a summer's day like this, warm and cloudless as she always remembered it, Wychaven must rival the lost splendour of Camelot or Avalon.

Her gaze moved on to the fishing-huts on the sandy beach, and beyond to the cluster of low stone turf-roofed dwellings that made up the village. She frowned, an icy hand squeezing her heart as she realised why everything had appeared too peaceful. No smoke rose from the blacksmith's forge, and the cattle and goats were roaming the hillside unattended. The village looked deserted. What had happened to her people?

It was the same here as on the other villages they had already passed on Wychaven land. Was this Sedbury's doing, or Rolf's? Without an army, she doubted that even Rolf could have retaken Wychaven. What was he doing now? Worried, she had sent Sergeant Kedge on ahead to warn him of her arrival. Suspecting that Rolf would be angry that she had again disobeyed his orders, she hoped that by not appearing unexpectedly before him, he would have time to conquer his initial rage and be prepared to talk reasonably with her. With the bitterness of their last meeting still ringing in her ears, she clung to this faint, but sustaining, hope.

Her assessing gaze returned to Wychaven Castle, studying the turrets outlined against the vivid sky. When she narrowed her eyes to make out the colours of the standard flying from the pole over the circular keep, her worst fears were realised. Rolf had been unable to take possession of the castle. The standard displayed the scarlet and gold chevrons of the arms of Lord Sedbury. Fresh anger burned through her at the treachery of her kinsman. The Earl of Loxstead's blue banner with its silver griffin should now be flying proudly over these lands.

Over the incessant screech of seagulls and cormorants, she heard the thud of hoofbeats. Turning, her spine set more rigidly, and her body tingled with the awareness that Rolf was approaching. The moment she both longed for and dreaded had come. She pushed back the edges of her veil that had blown forward round her face, and watched Rolf's party halt by her escort.

Rolf edged his grey destrier a few paces forward, and stopped. He was dressed in chain mail, and looked magnificent in his emblazoned blue and silver surcoat, his high-domed helm topped with a plume of white ostrich-feathers fluttering in the wind. Meriel's heart quaked.

He was every inch the warlord, proud and invincible—
a stranger to her as he waited for her to approach him.
Unable to see his features through the slits of the helm,
she found it impossible to make her obeisance to him.
An unearthly silence fell over the crowd assembled on
the cliff-top. Each moment she delayed would make it
harder for her, but she could not move; it was like a
nightmare not being able to see his face and judge his
feelings.

Then the stiffness of his manner changed, and
stripping off his gauntlets, Rolf lifted the great helm from
his head and held it in the crook of his arm. It was the
only concession he was prepared to give her, for he remained seated, tall and imperious in the saddle, waiting
for her to speak. The wind lifted his mane of golden hair
away from his sun-bronzed face, clearly defining his high
cheekbones and proud aquiline nose. A rush of love and
longing crumbled her pride. He asked little enough of
her in the circumstances.

Meriel crushed her sudden impulse to run and beg his
forgiveness, and with dignified grace she walked slowly
forward. Halting several feet from his destrier's head,
she raised her eyes to meet his chilling glare. Her throat
dried with apprehension. She swallowed, her mind racing
to find the right words. So much was at stake, and an
incautious comment could dash all her hopes. Ob-
serving the way his full lips compressed at her hesitancy,
she sensed that he did not trust his temper to remain
leashed. By first leaving the king's palace, and now by
further disobeying him, she had shamed him before his
men. She must atone for that before she could expect
him to listen to reason.

Spreading her skirts wide, Meriel sank into a reverent
curtsy, heedless of the dampness of the grass beneath
her knees. She held his gaze steadily, still defiant in her
need to justify herself despite the humility of her homage.
'My lord husband,' her low voice was just loud enough
to reach his ears, 'I have come to crave your pardon for
my wilfulness, and to put an end to the misunder-

standings between us. In times of trouble my place is at your side, and never more so than when you fight for the freedom and rights of Wychaven.'

Rolf gestured to one of his men to take his helm before swinging down from the saddle, his tread measured as he closed the gap between them. Taking her hand, he raised her, his tawny eyes shadowed by his lashes as he looked down at her.

'It would seem that no sacrifice is too great if you believe it will save your precious Wychaven.' The coldness of his tone was as biting as a March wind.

'Wychaven is only part of the reason why I came.' Her voice crackled with the rawness of her pain as she continued to hold his condemning glare. 'I do not beg you to accept me as your wife, Rolf. I ask only that you listen to what I have to say. But not now—not while there is anger and bitterness in your heart against not only myself, but Sedbury, and also the king. Once you hold Wychaven in your own right—the right of conquest—we must talk.'

'A siege is no place for a woman,' he said gruffly. His brow lifted as his lion's stare seemed to probe the depths of her mind. 'It will be some days before my brother's men, whom I have called to my aid, arrive. There is no suitable accommodation for you here. Return to the safety of Winchester. We shall meet again before I leave for France.'

She thought for a moment he would say more, but the stern line returned to his lips, and the brief hope which had kindled in her breast died out, to be replaced by a growing anger at his brusque dismissal.

'I do not fear hardship or danger, my lord,' she retorted swiftly. 'If you do not send me away, I will help you to regain Wychaven.' The words tumbled out in a breathless rush. 'You will not need an army, and Wychaven can be yours this night. There is a secret way into the castle from Merlin's cave.'

'And where does this passage come out within the castle?' Interest quickened Rolf's glance and voice.

'In the heart of the keep. There is a staircase hidden within the outer wall with openings into the store-chambers at the bottom and the lord's chamber at the top.'

'Does Sedbury know of this passage?' Rolf's voice was interwoven with excitement, impatience and a note she prayed was a sign of his capitulation.

'Not even the steward knows of its existence! Only the Lady Maude and myself.' She laid her hand upon his arm, her tone impassioned, as she added, 'It is a secret entrusted only to the lords of Wychaven. You have a score of men under your command here. Wychaven has withstood past sieges with fewer than that. How many men do you believe Sedbury has?'

'It is difficult to say—the battlements are sparsely manned. I would guess no more than fifty.'

Meriel nodded, her heart thudding with building excitement. 'At night, less than a third of that number will be on duty. I shall show you the way through the cave, my lord. There is no way into the cove from the cliff—the sides are too steep—neither can we risk using a boat, which will be spotted from the battlements. We shall have to swim. And, to avoid detection from Sedbury's guards, we must go alone.'

For a long moment Rolf did not speak, his eyes speckling with topaz lights as he gazed into her face. 'I would not put you in danger, Meriel.' His voice was oddly strained. 'Tell me the way. I shall do what must be done.'

She shook her head. 'My people do not know you, my lord. They will not dare to rise against Sedbury's men unless I am there to command and reassure them.'

'Once I tell them we are married, they will fight.' Rolf remained adamant.

'Perhaps—but perhaps not, my lord. Sedbury is no fool. How do we know what lies he has told them?' Rolf frowned, his cheeks paling, knowing that she spoke the truth. 'I shall be in no danger. Whatever Sedbury's faults, he will not dare to harm me. There would be too many of my people to speak against him.' She pressed home her advantage, refusing to be deterred. 'True, it should be easy enough for you to take Sedbury a prisoner while he sleeps in my father's bed, but you do not know the layout of the castle. The gatehouse guards must be taken by surprise for us to succeed. I shall rouse the bailiff and have the portcullis raised and the drawbridge lowered for your men to enter.'

Rolf took time to digest her words, then he lifted a hand to touch her cheek. 'You have great courage, my lady Countess,' he said softly. 'It is not my wish that you should risk your life.'

'I risk it willingly. I shall not fail my people . . . or you, my lord.' Her eyes silently pleaded with him to agree, as she hurried on to outline her plan before he could order her to leave. 'Merlin's cave is in the cove beneath the battlements. As I said, the only way into the cave, without being discovered by Sedbury's guards, is to swim round this headland.' A sudden consternation creased her brow. 'I trust you can swim, my lord?'

'I can swim.' He smiled into her upturned face, and her heart quivered as she waited for him to continue. With the lines of tension eased from his face, he looked younger, less formidable and devastatingly handsome. 'It is a plan that could work, but . . .'

Her hand tightened over his arm, their bodies touching as she leaned forward in her need to convince him. Her eyes widened with entreaty. 'Do not deny me in this. We shall take Wychaven before Sedbury's men realise we are in the castle. I shall be in no danger.'

As she spoke, the muscles in his throat tensed, and his thumb moving down the line of her jaw to touch her lips, stilled her words. Hope rekindled, flaring through her. She could feel the pressure of his sword-hilt against her hip, and the heat of his thigh burned through her thin gown. Beneath her fingers, his arm stiffened—not through anger this time, she sensed, but through the effort it was costing him to withstand her plea. Then he slid one hand round her waist, and smiled. 'It shall be as you say.'

Then his head lifted and he looked past her towards the church. He stepped back, his eyes again glittering with anger. 'What is Isolda doing here?'

The tender moment between them was destroyed and Meriel drew back, once more defensive. Puzzled by the vehemence of Rolf's reaction to his sister's presence, her gaze was as forthright as his. 'I visited the Lady Isolda after I left the palace. I needed her advice.'

'Upon what?' he asked stonily.

Meriel blushed, and her gaze faltered. How could she tell him that she had gone to Isolda to learn more about him—to discover if there was any hope of winning his love?

Her arm was gripped in iron talons as he pronounced savagely, 'Isolda's place is within the convent. She will return at once. I do not want you associating with her.'

Meriel felt the colour drain from her cheeks, her blood running with ice. 'Do you think that the dancing-girl you were forced to marry might contaminate such a holy woman? She, at least, does not condemn me without a hearing.'

'That is not the reason...' Rolf began heatedly, but broke off at the sound of Isolda calling his name as she approached. He added in a harsh undertone, 'We shall discuss it later.'

'My dear brother, I am overjoyed at the news of your good fortune. An *earl*, no less, and overlord of these lands as far as the eye can see, and beyond!' Isolda dipped the barest of curtsies, taking care that her gown was not stained by the damp grass.

'A pity then, Isolda, that you have travelled so far to meet with such scant hospitality.' Meriel was startled by the coldness in her husband's tone.

'Do not concern yourself for my comfort, Rolf.' Isolda continued to smile, ignoring her brother's stiff manner. 'I have grown used to austerity in recent years. I endured this journey not only to wish you well, dear brother, but because Meriel wished it. She has been distressed that this marriage was not of your choosing.'

Meriel looked fiercely at Isolda, appalled that she should have spoken so tactlessly. It must sound to Rolf as though she were discontented with their marriage. Worse, it suggested disloyalty to him by her confiding in Isolda. Had not Isolda herself insisted on travelling with her? Her glance shifted to Rolf, and her heart plummeted. The closed look had again settled over his features, his eyes frosty. Isolda's careless words had destroyed the first threads of trust Meriel had tried so hard to establish between Rolf and herself.

'I am touched by your concern, Isolda.' The smoothness of his tone cast Meriel into deeper despair, for it proved that his anger was directed at herself, not his sister. 'I fear, however, that you have mistaken the matter. I am content enough. You will have to find quarters for yourself in the village. I appreciate that you will wish to return to the convent without delay, but unfortunately I can spare you no escort until the castle is taken.'

'I shall return to the church to pray for your success, Rolf dear,' Isolda smiled sweetly, 'but I shall not return to the convent for a week or so. You may have need of me. If you are to return to France safe in the knowledge that your lands are secure, you must first settle your differences with Lord Sedbury. As I explained to Meriel, Sedbury was a friend of Sir Harold and he often visited our home. He may listen to me.'

A pulse leapt into life beneath the puckered skin of Rolf's scarred neck, his voice low with warning. 'This is none of your concern, Isolda. I shall settle my own score with Sedbury. He has much to answer for. Your place is at the convent.' He swung round to face Meriel's escort. 'Mount up, men. We return to camp.'

Belatedly, Meriel remembered that Sergeant Kedge might also be facing Rolf's anger. A hasty scan of the men who had accompanied her husband showed her that he was not present. 'My lord, your anger against myself and my kinsman is justified.' She almost faltered at the grimness of his handsome features. 'I would speak for

Sergeant Kedge. He showed you no disloyalty by escorting me to the Lady Isolda. Indeed, he was against travelling without your orders. I worded my command in such a way that he was duty bound to obey.'

'You have a persuasive tongue, my lady,' Rolf responded. His tone remained gruff, but there was a mellowing in the tawny depths of his eyes. 'Kedge has never, in the three years I have known him, been disloyal to me, either by word or by deed. He would not speak against even you in his defence.'

'He is a good man. I would not have him punished for my foolishness, my lord.'

Rolf nodded, apparently satisfied, but still cynical. 'Foolishness!' he said in a taut undertone. 'Is that how you describe deserting your husband on our wedding night?'

Meriel's eyes flashed, but something in Rolf's expression halted her retort. Was that self-mockery in his golden eyes a fleeting shadow of remorse? Aware that Isolda could overhear their conversation, she remained silent. With the men-at-arms watching their every move, this was not the time for Rolf and herself to resolve their differences. It must be when they were alone.

As he marched away to rejoin his men, Isolda summoned an apologetic smile. 'I fear my brother's manners are better suited to a battlefield than to the company of women, but we must forgive him. He takes his obligations seriously, and being forced to lay siege to his own lands within days of acquiring them must be an enormous strain.'

Irritation stirred in Meriel, disliking Isolda's patronising tone, but she stifled it. Rolf's sister was naturally as anxious for him as she was. 'I fear you are right. We must pray that all goes well for Rolf.'

Isolda returned to the church to pray, and Meriel walked over to her mare. Seeing Bella's anxious expression, she absently smiled to reassure her, but Bella continued to frown.

'Lord Loxstead is angry that the Lady Isolda accompanies you. Why did you let her come? For all her pious words, I do not trust her.'

'My husband has such a low opinion of me that he thinks I will corrupt his holy sister. That is why he is angry.'

'Santa Maria! Corrupt that one?' Bella snorted in an unladylike fashion. 'She gives herself airs, but she is no better than...'

'Enough, Bella!' Meriel said sharply, tired of the friction between her and Isolda which had grown during their travels. She took the reins of her palfrey from the man-at-arms holding it. Once mounted, she regretted her harshness, and added more softly to her friend, 'It is clear that no love is lost between you and the Lady Isolda. But she is Rolf's sister and, as such, you will accord her the respect due to her rank.'

Bella fell silent as she, too, mounted and turned her horse towards the village. As they rode through the double row of houses, Meriel's anxious gaze sought out Rolf. He was standing in the centre of his assembled men, his hands moving firmly and decisively as he issued his orders. There was about him an air of calm confidence, but she was painfully aware of the responsibilities he now shouldered. The honours the king had heaped upon him must taste like ashes in his mouth. Not only was he burdened with a wife he did not want, but he must now risk his life to claim the lands her dowry brought him.

Her heart ached with the knowledge that she was to blame. Her wild, foolish decision to seek Isolda's advice had only made matters worse. Why was Rolf's manner towards his sister so cool? That was another problem which must be dealt with later, Meriel thought, lifting her dejected stare to the castle's impregnable walls. Tonight she would show Rolf how to breach their defences, but would she ever know the secret way to unlock the barriers guarding his heart?

*   *   *

Meriel cast a nervous glance up at the cliff-face, even though she knew Rolf had ordered his men to stay back. The night was warm, and in a cloudless sky the moonlight was dazzling, lying like a silver banner across the bay, and she still had to disrobe in Rolf's presence before swimming round the headland. Pulling off her knee-length over-gown, she hesitated, her fingers hesitating on the front lacing of her kirtle. Rolf had considerately turned his back while he sat on a boulder and wrenched off his boots.

Common sense dictated that she could not swim against the strong current in a heavy kirtle, but the silk chemise beneath would cling like a second skin to her figure once it was wet. Her skin prickled with embarrassment. She had conquered her instinctive modesty at the inn in order to try to captivate Rolf, and had earned merely his scorn. The shame of it stung her as she tried to shut her mind against the cruel memory. This was different, she reasoned. She was doing this to save Wychaven. Clinging to the thought, she freed her hair from its restraining plaits so that it fell to her thighs, then stripped off her kirtle. Quickly bundling up her clothes, she placed them in one of the two small wine-casks she had ordered to be adapted for their needs, with a crude handle fitted to the separate top. Not only would the casks keep their clothes dry as they swam, but should a guard chance to look out from the battlements, they would look like driftwood being washed on to the beach by the tide and would hide Rolf and herself swimming behind.

All at once the enormity of the task ahead hit Meriel. The danger and the consequences—too dire to contemplate, should they fail—churned within her. She swallowed, conquering her fear, but a deeper dread would not be laid to rest—the horror of failure. She shuddered. Not only Wychaven would be lost to her, but far more heart-breaking was the knowledge that if Sedbury triumphed over them, he would kill Rolf.

She bowed her head against the agony. Wychaven was not worth the sacrifice of losing Rolf. There must be some other way! She turned to speak to him, but her words checked in her throat as she saw he was looking up at Wychaven. He stood in his shirt and hose, hands resting casually on his hips. The moonlight showed the features of a man surveying his domain, and her heart swelled with understanding. There was pride in that fierce survey, and suddenly she knew that it was not enough for him to have won Wychaven as a marriage settlement. All his life he had fought for what he wanted, and now he wanted to fight for the right to be Wychaven's lord. She turned away, knowing he would listen to no words of caution. Wychaven had woven its spell about him. What would she not give for him to look at *her* one day with that same fierce pride!

Then he started to pull off his shirt. In a flurry of embarrassment to be in the sea before he could glimpse her half-dressed state, she picked up her cask and ran into the breakers. The sudden chill after the warmth of the evening air made her gasp. Regaining her breath, she jumped the last of the waves and dived into the calm water beyond, and pushing the cask ahead, struck out for the jutting rocks. A splash close by alerted her that Rolf was close behind.

His cask, with his sword wrapped in waxed cloth tied to its side, bobbed ahead of hers. Then he was swimming level with her, his hand brushing her arm as he slowed his pace. The brief touch sent a shock wave through her, and her gaze was drawn like a lodestone to his. His long dark lashes were spiked round his eyes, which were no longer hardened with anger. Their pale depths sparkled with anticipation for the conquest of winning Wychaven and, something more—a light of acceptance that sent shivers of expectancy along her spine. She suddenly lost the rhythm of her stroke and gulped a mouthful of salty water.

'Are you all right?' he asked with a throaty chuckle, as he steadied the casks that were in danger of floating away from them in the strengthening current.

Gasping, she nodded. It was not the stinging sea-water which took her breath away, but the bold intimacy of his eyes upon her. The stronger current was now running against them, and the temperature of the water dropped. They were approaching the headland and the submerged rocks, the jagged ridges of which were capable of tearing flesh to the bone. Meriel dragged her gaze from Rolf's, needing all her strength to battle against the pull of the current and stop her cask floating away. Within moments, her arms and legs ached. As they rounded the point and swam back towards the sandy cove beyond, she was disheartened to see how far away the beach looked.

Before they had covered half the distance, she began to fear she would never make it. She had never swum so close to the rocks with their swirling undercurrents, for her father had always warned her of the danger. The tide seemed to be pulling her down and she kicked out harder, biting back a cry as her thigh struck a sharp rock hidden by the sea. The salt bit into her lacerated flesh as she struggled on. They dared not risk swimming further out into calmer water, for once away from the shelter of the rocks, they would be easily seen from the battlements. Gritting her teeth, she forced her tired limbs to move. The pain of her wound was like a warning bell driving her to swim harder to escape the treacherous rocks. She would make it. She had to!

She heard Rolf mutter an oath, his voice close to her ear as he swam on strongly while with each stroke she seemed to be making no headway.

'Put one arm round my waist and hold on as best you can—and try and keep the cask ahead of us,' he ordered gruffly. He put one hand through the cord holding his sword in place on his cask, and, briefly pausing to tread water, took her hands and placed them round his waist.

The touch of his skin, and the feel of the powerful muscles along his back undulating as he effortlessly swam for the shore, sent a surge of longing through her tired body. Within moments, the current was no longer tugging at them. The water, no longer chilling but invigorating, was still warm from the heat of the sun. She did not immediately release her hold upon Rolf, stealing one more moment of the wonderful feel of his naked body in her arms.

'You should be able to see the cave from here,' she said, lifting her head to scan the shoreline. Between the main headland and another outcrop of rocks, a dark fissure was just visible in the rugged cliff. 'My lord, swim to the right of that claw-like rock. There . . .' she nodded in the appropriate direction, 'do you see a small triangle of sand? The cave opening is narrow, and barely noticeable even when approached from this angle. The overhanging cliff hides this part of the cove even from Wychaven's watchful sentries.'

Her foot struck the bottom, and as she reluctantly slid her arm from Rolf's waist, he released his hold upon the casks, which swept forward on the crest of a wave and were left high on the sand as the water retreated. She dragged herself on to her knees, but the pain in her torn thigh doubled her over and she fell back into the water. A wave crashed over her head, knocking her off balance and sending her body tumbling through the breakers.

Then Rolf's arms swung her upwards, and the solid warmth of his chest pressed against her cheek as he carried her to the shore. She could feel the powerful rhythm of his heart beneath her temple and the heady scent of his sea-washed skin filled her nostrils. Through half-closed eyes, she looked up at him. The tense set of his jaw remained stubbornly grim, but was it just a trick of the moonlight, or had the hollows of his cheeks softened and the lines about his eyes mellowed? He set her down on the sand with a reverence that brought a tight lump to her throat.

Kneeling over her, he examined her gashed thigh, his lips compressing with concern. 'Your leg should be tended. The cut is not deep, but it could become inflamed. It must be extremely painful, but you made no complaint.' He twisted round to gaze into her eyes, his voice deepening with respect. 'But you never do complain—not even when life serves you ill.'

Beneath the impact of his open stare, guilt plucked at her conscience. Now was not the time for a long confession, but she could not contain her anguish at the wrong she had done to him. 'But I do act rashly, my lord. Often foolishly, without considering the consequences. It was wrong of me to leave the palace as I did, but I swear it was not to shame you. I thought the Lady Isolda could help me to understand you better.' Her voice caught in her throat at the effort it was costing her to hold his piercing stare. 'I should have stayed, like a dutiful wife.'

She broke off, catching a bright glitter in his eyes. Was it anger or amusement? She inwardly cursed the shadows hiding his expression. 'Yes, a dutiful wife would have stayed!' He plucked a strand of seaweed from her hair. 'What manner of woman are you? Sea-witch? Siren? Mermaid?'

'I am half drowned!' she retorted, conscious of the broad expanse of his bare chest with its dusky masculine covering of hair leaning over her. A tremor passed through her body. Not of cold, for the night air was warm upon her skin, but her damp chemise, clinging to her figure, left her exposed and vulnerable to his appraising stare.

He leaned over and rolled one of the casks towards him. Punching open the lid, he drew a linen towel from within and handed it to her. From the second cask he retrieved his own towel, and after briskly drying his body, he wrapped it about his hips. Clearly his years of punishing training for knighthood and the long campaigns had toughened him against the discomfort of something as slight as the coolness of the night air. With her hair dripping icily down her back, Meriel could not suppress a shiver. Catching her movement, Rolf pulled her cloak from the cask and, carefully lifting her wet hair over its collar, placed it round her shoulders.

'Even half drowned, sweet water-sprite, you are temptingly lovely.' Rolf twirled one of her dark curls round his finger, his eyes caressing her with smouldering intensity. A wry smile tilted his mouth, then, with obvious reluctance, he drew back, his manner again that of the practical soldier. 'I shall bind your leg for you. It must be properly tended later.'

He worked quickly, ripping a strip of material from her chemise and winding it round her leg. Each time his fingers touched her bare skin, her heart capered wildly. They did not speak, but with each passing moment the air pulsated with a tangible awareness, their breathing changing, becoming weighted with the force of the physical spell evoked by the slightest touch, or the meeting of their gazes. The bandage in place, Rolf's hand lingered upon her knee, his thumb making lazy circles along the sensitive skin of her inner thigh. This was the first moment they had been alone since he had stormed out of the inn. His manner was different now, although his mood still eluded her. She only knew she had, somehow, to end the distrust and antagonism between them.

'My lord, I am shamed by the actions of my kinsman. Wychaven should have greeted its new lord with rejoicing hearts and pageantry. It is humiliating that you must enter through a secret passage to claim what is yours by right.'

'Why should Wychaven accept me so readily? Was I not fool enough to reject its brightest jewel?' To her surprise, he bent over her leg, to touch a light kiss on the skin above her wound. Her heart raced. Had she heard him aright? Was he telling her he wanted her? She had misjudged his moods too often to risk rousing that dark and frightening demon from his past by questioning him now, when his mind would be on taking Wychaven.

Already she could feel him mentally withdrawing from her as his gaze lifted to the cliff. The angular planes of his face tensed as his voice became practical. He pulled the rest of their clothes from the cask and, tossing Meriel's into her lap, he stood up, turning his back to give her privacy as he commanded, 'The castle will have settled down for the night. Dress quickly, Meriel. It is time. Show me the secret passage.'

CHAPTER ELEVEN

'TAKE THIS candle, my lord.' Having earlier taken a thick candle from the church and fastened it to her jewelled girdle, Meriel now untied it and handed it to Rolf. From a pouch hanging at her waist she drew out a tinder-box. 'At high tide the sea covers the floor of the cave, and the footing is treacherous.'

They had squeezed through the narrow fissure, no wider than the girth of a stout man, into the high-vaulted dark cave, and after the warmth of the summer's night outside, Meriel shivered in the chill dampness, drawing her cloak tighter. The air was fresh, sharpened by the tang of seaweed and wet sand, and except for the slither of moonlight through the opening, the darkness was almost complete as she worked over the tinder-box. A flint spark dropped on to the wood shavings and sheep's wool and a tiny flame flared into life, and as she shielded the precarious flame with her cupped hands, Rolf lit the candle. Holding it aloft, he frowned, seeing only a suggestion in the wavering dim light of a channelled recess no larger than a baron's hall, its greyish-green walls dappled and sparkling with a diamond-bright mineral deposit that seeped through the stone.

'Wychaven guards its secrets well, my lord!' Meriel gloated at his puzzlement. 'Is this not named Merlin's cave? A common enough name in this part of England, but all is not as it would at first appear. We must climb on to that ledge.' She pointed to what looked like a fault in the rock-face a score of feet above their heads.

Scooping up the hem of her trailing kirtle, Meriel tucked it into her girdle, and with her legs free from the cumbersome folds of her skirts, she nimbly scaled the craggy wall, her hands and feet seeking the irregular natural hand- and foot-holds. Once on the ledge, she reached down to take the candle Rolf held up to her. The light from its flame reflected the amusement in his amber eyes, and her heart leapt.

While they had been dressing, Rolf had questioned her about the castle's layout and the usual routine of the household and guards. The first was easy to answer, for every room and stone of Wychaven was ingrained in Meriel's mind. Picking up a stick, she had drawn a plan of the castle in the wet sand of the cove, explaining in detail its layout and the possible positions of the guards. But it was the latter which troubled her. It had been so long since she had been here, and Sedbury would have changed their routine. That was where the danger lay— in the uncertainty of the guards' movements.

At that point, Rolf's face set bleakly. 'It is too dangerous for you, Meriel. I must go alone.'

'Then you will fail,' she returned hotly. 'I am not afraid, and in this you need me. While you take Sedbury prisoner, someone must open the gates.' She continued to press her arguments until he reluctantly agreed. Now, as she held his golden stare, she prayed it was a sign that his doubt was melting.

'Merlin's cave is well named.' A touch of irony was back in Rolf's voice as he climbed to the ledge beside her and took the candle. 'Magical—mysterious...like its mistress.'

A blush stung her cheeks as she shook out the hitched-up folds of her skirts, her long shapely legs again demurely covered.

'Lead on!' Rolf responded more harshly than he had intended, and inwardly cursed the cynicism that had made him speak so sharply. A shadow flickered across her crystal-blue eyes, then she smiled that taunting, elusive smile and seemed to glide through the narrow opening in the wall, one hand elegantly lifting her skirt about her ankles as she picked her way over the uneven ground. Rolf followed, unable to understand her variable moods, and, for the first time in years, he wished he could truly fathom a woman's mind.

Once through the concealed entrance, he saw that the passage had been widened by the past masters of Wychaven, but every so often he had to stoop to avoid knocking his head on the low roof. Further inland the passage sloped gently upwards, and, as he followed Meriel's slender figure, his concentration began to stray from the task ahead. Each encounter with Meriel brought new surprises. Usually the unpredictability of her moods exasperated him: the complex twists of her character— at one moment worldly-wise and mysterious, the next naïvely innocent, her vulnerability hidden under proud defiance—stirred his latent chivalry. Or was it but an act? The insidious thought rose up like a many-headed demon to play upon his prejudice. A fiery passion had been there in her dancing for all to see. Was innocence but another role she played to perfection? He crushed such thoughts, not wishing to pre-judge Meriel, but his desire for her did not make him a slave to his senses. His experience of women had taught him to expect deceit, and his years spent between the warring factions of Prince Richard's and King Henry's Courts had long since made it second nature to him to be on his guard against treachery.

Rolf turned his mind to the present as they began to climb the steps carved out of the rock. They must have reached the castle keep, he reasoned, recalling each detail of the castle Meriel had described to him. During their discussion on the beach he had been struck by her fearless will, her quiet dignity in the face of adversity. They were qualities he had hoped for in a wife, yet had not expected to find. Returning anger churned through him, but now it was directed solely against the Earl of Sedbury and his seizure of Wychaven. May his soul rot in hell! Rolf seethed. Sedbury will be defeated this night!

As a younger son, without an inheritance, it seemed that all his life he had striven to prove himself, to rise above his lowly station by his wits and prowess. He had pushed himself to his limits and then beyond, gradually winning the respect of his companions until he was treated as an equal by the greatest in the land. He had carved his own destiny and now he would fight for Wychaven. The moment he had set eyes on it he had known what had driven Meriel to take her rightful place as mistress here. It was wild, rugged, the elements untamable—but it was magnificent. The villages had been prosperous in Sir Arnulf's day, and the castle... He felt a stab of pride. His experienced eye could not fault the design of its defences, or its vastness, which far exceeded his expectations. All the battle and tourney honours he had won would pale into insignificance against the triumph of having his standard flying over Wychaven. It was a prize worth fighting for, and the need to win his right to rule over it by his own prowess was a challenge he warmed to.

Meriel halted on a wide wooden platform and placed her hand on an iron lever. As the light from the candle fell across it, her stomach knotted with sudden alarm. In her father's day the mechanism had been well oiled and maintained, but now it showed signs of rust. What if it did not work?

It would work. It had to! She refused to think of failure, or to show her doubts to Rolf. Keeping her voice even, she turned to him. 'This is the way into the storerooms beneath the keep. Up another forty steps is the lever that will open a panel to the right of the lord's bed.'

Rolf laid his hand over hers on the lever, his voice taut and hoarse. 'What if the villagers are held prisoner within the store-rooms? You will be trapped behind locked doors.'

She shook her head, confident in this. 'There is another level below this one. If Sedbury is keeping the villagers prisoners, it will be in there. It is most likely, however, that he had no wish to rouse their suspicions as to the true nature of your attack. I doubt that any knowledge of our marriage has been allowed to reach them. Sedbury has probably told them that they have been summoned to the castle for their own protection against a robber-baron. The villagers are probably lodged in the hall, and to allay any suspicion, there are likely to be few guards.' Seeing the grooves of anger deepening Rolf's face, she went on quickly, 'These store-rooms are split into several chambers, and this exit leads into the smallest of them. It was deliberately kept as a room for storing empty travelling-chests and there is no lock upon the door.' She tilted her chin defiantly. 'God willing, Wychaven shall pay tribute to its true master this night, my lord.'

'And it will also honour the courage of its mistress,' Rolf said softly, taking her hand from the lever and raising it to his lips.

Her breath caught in her throat at the admiration in his tone. 'I brought these troubles upon you, my lord. If you will allow me, I would make amends in any way I can. There are many misunderstandings between us, but now is not the time to resolve them. I regret that you will begin this fight with anger and bitterness in your heart.'

'I take up this fight gladly,' he answered cautiously. 'Not just to free Wychaven, but to release people from a tyrant. I have learned enough in the past days to know that your kinsman has bled these lands dry of revenue, with little care for the welfare of the villagers. They faced near starvation last winter because of his greed.'

'You are noble and chivalrous, my lord. It makes my shame the greater.' The knowledge of the danger he faced ground through her. If anything happened to him, it would be her fault. How could she live with that guilt upon her conscience? The warmth and solidity of his hand still clasping hers gave her the courage to continue. 'I cannot deny that I went to Court to find a husband who would champion my cause against Sedbury. That is the way of the world we live in. But our marriage was not of your choosing, and I would not have you sacrifice your life for Wychaven and my pride.'

'Have you so little faith in me, my lady?' The stiffness was back in his voice, upbraiding her.

'I have every confidence, my lord.' Her voice broke. 'It is your reasons I question. I feel I have drawn you into this against your will.'

He gripped her shoulder, giving her a slight shake. 'I do this because it is my desire—and because Sedbury, and others like him, must learn that I defend what is mine.' His hand tightened as his gaze burned into her. 'I shall be proud to be lord of Wychaven. That is enough said on the matter.'

A glow of love and gratitude spread through her. She had caught the edge of excitement and anticipation in his deepening voice. But she loved him too much not to feel fear for him, her own voice catching with emotion as she answered, passionately, 'God be with you, and keep you safe, my lord.'

She lightly put a hand to his chest in entreaty, her fears for him increasing that he wore no protective chain-mail beneath his emblazoned tunic. She heard his sharp intake of breath, then his mouth was upon hers, its fierce pressure drawing an instant response from her. Beneath her hand, the steady rhythm of his heart quickened. With an abruptness that left her bereft, he tore his mouth free and stepped back.

'God keep you safe also, my lady countess,' he said gruffly, and with a grim smile added, 'Let us pray that Sedbury is in the chamber above.' Holding the candle aloft, he bounded up the remaining stairs to Sedbury's room.

The glimmer of candlelight disappeared behind a curve in the passage, and Meriel offered up a prayer for their success, and with renewed determination took hold of the lever. Firmly gripping it, she pulled it towards her. Her jagged nerves screamed, for it seemed that an age passed before, with a grinding sound, the stone slid partially open. Her breath released in a rush, Meriel squeezed through the aperture before easing it back into position.

She paused, her heart hammering in the darkness. She strained her ears for the sound of patrolling guards, but all was quiet. Her hand gripped the hilt of the dagger at her waist for reassurance. It was little protection against the thrust of a guard's sword, and she prayed that she would not have to use it. She groped her way forward, her hand brushing against the sides of stacked coffers as she moved towards the door. Once outside in the dark corridor her step quickened; she needed no light to guide her along its familiar twists and turns and up the shallow stone steps to the first floor. She paused on the top stair and flattened her body against the wall as she listened for any sounds of guards. For a long moment she heard only the sound of distant snoring within the hall, then there was a scrape of steel against stone, and a loud yawn.

'Damn Sedbury!' a tired voice complained. 'Two nights without sleep, and he says himself they'll not attack until reinforcements arrive. The villagers suspect nothing. Why can't he let us take our rest?'

'There are few enough guards on duty,' a second disgruntled voice replied. 'Someone has to keep an eye on the villagers, lest they become suspicious. Come, it's time to make our round.'

Meriel froze, dreading that the guards would come in her direction, but the sound of their tread took them away, into the hall itself. Edging forward, she was relieved to find the corridor empty. Avoiding the hall, she entered a series of small interconnected chambers where the castle officers worked, and re-emerged a short distance from the main entrance of the keep. Her heart thudding with stifling irregularity, she checked the corridor. To her relief, it was still empty, but she shivered in apprehension as she approached the great oak door. If it had been barred against attack, it would take three men to lift the heavy beam securing it. Thank God, the beam was not in place! Clearly, Sedbury was overconfident that Rolf would not attack until his numbers had swelled. That was to their advantage.

She pulled the heavy iron ring that served as a handle, a fine beading of sweat prickling her spine as the door groaned on its hinges. Opening it the merest fraction, she dared not wait to discover whether the guards had been alerted by the sound, and squeezed through the small gap, closing the door behind her. Fortune was with her; the moon was obscured by clouds and the long outer staircase was in black shadow. Lifting her skirts above her ankles, she raced down the steps, knowing that at any moment one of the guards on the battlements might swing round and see her. She was breathing heavily as she reached the solid ground of the inner bailey, her injured thigh throbbing from the strain of her pace. A hasty glance up at the battlements showed only an occasional sentry outlined against the sky. She hurried on, the urgency of her task giving her no time even to feel relief that she had not been spotted. Rolf must be in the chamber and confronting Sedbury by now. There was no time to lose. If he were not to be captured, the gates must be opened without delay.

Keeping to the shadows of the grain-store and kitchen outbuildings, Meriel edged towards the bailiff's room in the turret of the outer bailey. She knew the steward and chamberlain were Sedbury's men, but Godric the bailiff had not been replaced. His family had served as bailiffs at Wychaven for three generations—he would not fail her.

From the keep above, Rolf had drawn his short sword, bracing himself against the unexpected as he discarded the candle and pulled the lever in the secret passage. Soundlessly, the wall before him swung back. The bedchamber on to which it opened was dimly lit, and as he paused, he heard loud sobs and a woman's voice pleading. He stepped silently into the room and glimpsed the richness of red and gold wall-hangings, but his gaze centred upon the giant bed with its scarlet velvet bedhangings tightly drawn about its occupants. The woman's voice begged tearfully for mercy. Her pitiful cries kindled

Rolf's temper. Sedbury seemed to be forcing his unwanted attentions upon one of the village wenches. The
sound of a slap, followed by Sedbury's harsh command
to silence, goaded Rolf into action. Flinging back the
bed-hangings, he brought the flat of his sword down
upon Sedbury's bare heaving buttocks.

'Yield, dog!' Rolf blazed. 'The castle is mine!'

With a grunt of rage, Sedbury rolled away from the
cringing figure of a young girl who had scarcely reached
womanhood. Sedbury's eyes bulged with astonishment,
and his mouth opened. Before he could call the guards,
Rolf pressed the point of his sword against his throat.

'Silence, cur, or you die!'

Without taking his eyes from Sedbury's sweating,
angry face, Rolf grated out his orders to the girl, who
clutched the sheet to her naked body. 'Get dressed,
wench, and hold your peace.' Her eyes rounded with
relief that she had been saved from Sedbury's lust, and
his tone, softened, reassured her further. 'I am Rolf, Earl
of Loxstead, husband to your mistress the Lady Meriel
of Wychaven.'

The girl scrambled from the bed and pulled on a rough
woollen dress. Clearly she was too shaken and frightened
to be a problem to him, and his attention returned to
Sedbury.

With the sword-point still against his throat, Sedbury
eased himself up in the bed, the hatred contorting his
flushed bearded face cooling like wax until his expression
was bland. He glanced at the dark opening. 'So you and
my kinswoman must have become reconciled. Meriel's
here, isn't she? I suspected there was a secret way into
the castle, but its whereabouts eluded me. Even the
bailiff, when put to the question, could tell me nothing.'
A sneer twisted his thin lips. 'I misjudged Meriel. She
was too damned willing to swallow that cursed pride of
hers and act the role of minstrel. I hoped that pride would
be her downfall—and yours.'

'You have much to answer for, Sedbury,' Rolf retorted. He was not duped by the man's apparent dis-

simulation. Sedbury was a wily courtier, whose life was spent in intrigue and counter-intrigue. Rolf knew his kind too well and despised them for their falseness and treachery. He bit down his anger. Sedbury deserved to die, but it would not be by his hand unless he was forced to it; it was for the king to punish him. 'Get up!' he commanded tersely. 'You are my prisoner and will order your men to surrender.'

Briefly, hatred sparked again in Sedbury's eyes and was as quickly doused, his voice smooth and as slippery as a viper. 'I never argue with a man who has his blade at my throat.'

Rolf inched back, his sword still poised and ready to strike. Sedbury was too calm—too acquiescent. He was planning something! Rolf watched, alert for the first sign of danger as Sedbury shrugged his shoulders into a long fur-lined robe and belted it about his thick waist.

'This day may be yours, Loxstead,' he jeered, 'but the matter is far from ended between us. Enjoy Wychaven while you may—and the king's whore who brought it to you.'

White-hot anger stabbed through Rolf, his vows of chivalry forgotten in the fierceness of its blaze. A sharp pain jolted through his knuckles as they crashed into the man's sneering face. The force of the blow slammed Sedbury against the wall with a thud, blood trickling from his cut mouth.

'Take care how you speak of my lady countess,' Rolf warned, 'or you will answer to my sword!'

Sedbury wiped the corner of his mouth with his hand, his eyes slitting as he stared down at the blood on his fingers. Rolf leashed the rage consuming him, startled that he had lost control of his temper. Sedbury had much to answer for—not least for his treatment of Meriel and the insults he had laid upon himself. But if he were to remain true to his vows of knighthood, he could not take justice into his own hands.

'You will call off your guards, and before the assembled villagers, surrender the castle,' Rolf ordered,

his voice granite hard. With a disdainful flick of his
sword, he indicated the door for Sedbury to leave by.
As his opponent walked in front of him, Rolf pressed
the point of his sword into his back. 'One false move,
and I shall take pleasure in running you through.'

'The castle is yours, Loxstead,' Sedbury answered, a
shade too quickly for Rolf's peace of mind.

There had been no sound of disturbance from below.
How had Meriel fared? By now, he should have heard
something. The drawbridge should have been lowered
and the portcullis raised to admit his men. Without them
to support him, he could be overpowered at any moment
by Sedbury's guards, and Sedbury knew it! That was
why he was so confident. But there was no turning back
now, Rolf acknowledged grimly, showing nothing of his
apprehension as he gestured for the man to proceed.

Meriel knelt at the side of the bailiff's pallet bed, appalled at the extent of Godric's wounds. 'I cannot believe that Sedbury would do this to you! It is poor reward
for your loyalty.'

'He knows there's little love for him here, my lady. I
would not have told him the whereabouts of the secret
passage even had I known.' The gaunt face twisted into
a grimace of a smile as he drew his pain-racked body
into a sitting position. 'We knew that the troubles visited
upon us were not your fault, but there were many who
in the last months began to despair of ever being free
of his yoke. Why did you not wed before and save us,
my lady?'

'It was not possible,' Meriel said heavily, unwilling to
elaborate. 'You must rest, but I need information. Lord
Loxstead—my husband—is also within the castle, and
in grave danger from Sedbury's guards. You are too weak
to help me. Tell me whom I can trust?'

She started as the door opened and a stalwart figure
entered the room, his bushy brows drawing down as Meriel
rose to her full height, her hand ready at her dagger
should she need to defend herself against the stranger.

'This is my son, Baldwin, my lady,' Godric said proudly. 'Baldwin, 'tis the Lady Meriel come to free us. It is her husband, the Lord Loxstead, whose men are camped outside our walls, not a robber-baron seeking to plunder, as Sedbury would have us believe.'

'My lady!' Baldwin knelt at her feet. 'God bless you! But how did you get in?'

'There is no time to tell you now.' She took his hands and raised him up, her gaze travelling over his huge frame. She remembered Baldwin as a skinny lad of ten when last she had seen him. 'We must open the gates for my husband's men to enter, and quickly. How many men can you raise? We have so little time.'

'There are but two guards on duty in the gatehouse. Lord Sedbury was boasting this evening—saying that his men could take their ease, as it would be some days before their attackers would be in sufficient numbers to strike.'

'Sedbury's men must be overpowered by stealth, Baldwin,' Meriel cautioned. 'Until the drawbridge is lowered, they must suspect nothing—my husband's life may depend upon it.'

'We shall not fail you, my lady,' Baldwin passionately vowed. 'The villagers are bedded down in the hall, but Sedbury's guards watch over them. Fortunately, the castle servants have been allowed to keep their own quarters. I suppose Sedbury did not wish to arouse too much suspicion of his treachery. The grooms and stable-lads sleeping in the hay-lofts are strong men, and there are no guards posted by the stables, as far as I know. Armed with pitchforks, we can take the guards in the gatehouse.'

'God be with you then, Baldwin. Go now and rouse the grooms,' Meriel said, drawing the hood of her dark cloak over her head and moving to the door. 'I must be close to the hall. If anything goes wrong, I must be on hand to call the villagers to help Lord Loxstead, though with all my heart I pray it will not come to that. I would win Wychaven without my people shedding their blood.'

'My lady!' Godric croaked from the pallet bed. 'Sir Arnulf would have been proud of you this day!' He fell back weakly on to the straw mattress.

Profoundly touched by the sincerity of his words, Meriel crept through the shadows, her heart thudding as she approached the keep. The outer flight of stairs leading to the first floor and the hall were now bathed in moonlight, adding to the danger of discovery. But she dared not hesitate. It was a heartening sign that the alarm had not been raised, but Rolf was but one man against so many. How was he faring?

With a shudder of dread, she offered up a hasty prayer for him. Waiting until a guard on the battlements looked away from the keep, Meriel crouched low, hugging the side of the shadowed wall as she climbed the steps. With every step, she expected to hear a guard shout out a challenge. None came. Anxiously glancing towards the stables, she saw several dark figures creeping towards the gatehouse. Dear God, let them not be seen! So much depended upon their success.

She strove to master her shaky nerves as she pushed open the great oak door. Her apprehension at fever-pitch, she heard a confusion of sounds within. Holding her breath, her ears attuned to danger, she edged forward, puzzled that the guards were not in sight. Where was Rolf? Had all gone well? Was Sedbury his prisoner? The sound of footsteps from the stairs leading to the lord's chamber prickled her flesh with alarm. They grew louder; the air suddenly rent with a wild shout from Sedbury.

'Guards! Guards! To me!'

Her blood ran cold. Dear God, had Rolf walked into a trap? Although her first instinct was to rush down the corridor to peer into the hall to see what was happening, she steeled herself to remain where she was. If Rolf had been captured, she had to remain free to try to save him.

'Guards!' Sedbury thundered hoarsely. 'Lay down your arms. Lord Loxstead has taken the castle.'

Rolf had done it! Relief made Meriel's head spin as she was drawn to the hall and gazed upon the scene within. A stunned silence had fallen upon the gathering. Three bewildered-looking guards stared at their master, while the villagers were sleepily rubbing their eyes, puzzled as to what was happening. The scene was dreamlike. Lord Sedbury, with dishevelled hair and his long gown open to the waist, showed that he had been roused from his bed. Rolf stood slightly apart from him, his sword unsheathed, still wary. As the light from one of the few lighted flambeaux fell across him, his golden-haired figure dominated his surroundings. A lion among men, his voice rang out through the echoing hall for all to hear as he proclaimed, loudly, 'I take this castle in the name of Henry Plantagenet, king of England, and the Lady Meriel, Countess of Loxstead—my wife!'

Surprised mutterings broke out among the villagers, some clearly suspicious, others relieved as the import of Rolf's word sank in. A voice she recognised as that of her father's falconer exclaimed, 'The Lady Meriel, married? Why were we not told?'

Their mood changed to anger, but whether against Rolf, as a suspected impostor, or Lord Sedbury, Meriel could not tell. She opened her mouth to call out her support for Rolf, when suddenly a dark shadow appeared from an alcove behind her husband's shoulder. It was another guard, his sword raised ready to strike.

'Rolf! Behind you!' she screamed, running forward as the soldier lunged towards her husband. 'My people, for the love of God, help us!'

She saw Rolf swing round, his sword slashing his assailant across the throat, but a second soldier took his place. Then everything happened at once. Outside, the tocsin bell raised the alarm and shouts came from the courtyard.

'Dolts! Arrest the intruder!' Sedbury shrieked. 'And the woman!'

Meriel evaded the outstretched arm of one of the guards, her voice rising with fear. 'Help us! I am the Lady Meriel!' She saw Rolf dodge back from a guard's vicious sword-thrust. Placing his back against the wall, he took on the two remaining guards, his sword flashing wickedly in the torchlight. The sound of fighting in the inner bailey was louder. Thank God, Rolf's men had entered the castle, but would they be in time to save him? Throwing back her hood, her black hair cascading over her shoulders, she cried out, 'My people, Lord Loxstead's men are already in the castle. Wychaven now belongs to him. He would free you from Sedbury's tyranny!'

''Tis truly the Lady Meriel!' shouted a woman. 'Our mistress has returned to us. Help her...and our new lord.'

'He has no need of us!' The falconer's voice rang with pride as they all saw Rolf bring down the last of his attackers and in a swift lunge grab Sedbury's arm and press his sword against his throat.

'Order your guards to surrender!' Rolf snarled, as several of Sedbury's men burst into the hall from the courtyard.

Hatred contorted Sedbury's face as he spat out, 'Lay down your arms, men! The castle is yours, Loxstead.'

Sergeant Kedge and several others of Rolf's men pushed their way through Sedbury's guards, snatching their former opponents' swords from their hands, before turning to Rolf to await his command.

Only then did Rolf lower his sword from Sedbury's throat. 'Lock Sedbury in one of the towers,' he rapped out. 'And put his men in the lower level of the keep until I decide what to do with them.'

Rolf held out a hand towards Meriel, and the villagers fell back as she walked towards him. He was not even breathing heavily after the strenuous fight, but his hair was darkened with sweat at his temple, and grooves of tension still lined his mouth. As she took his hand, a light flared in his eyes, acknowledging her part in their success and, fleetingly, a deepening intensity such as she had not seen since their first meeting by the river at Eadstone. Her blood quickened with expectancy. They were triumphant. Sedbury was defeated. And that look...? Surely it must mean that Rolf truly accepted her as his wife.

There was a disturbance at the entrance of the hall. Frowning, Meriel looked to see what was happening, and saw the Lady Isolda framed in the doorway. Meriel stared, astonished. The anchoress's expression was curiously blank as she briefly met Sedbury's stare as he was being led away. At her side, she felt Rolf stiffen. What was it about his sister that antagonised him so? Meriel felt a twinge of unease. From the way Isolda had spoken, Sedbury had been her husband's friend. Naturally, in the circumstances, she would condemn Sedbury for taking up arms against her brother, but that blankness was somehow too chilling. Surely such a holy woman would show some compassion?

Rolf placed Meriel's arm on his, and the strangeness of Isolda's behaviour was forgotten as he led her to the dais to address the villagers and castle servants.

'Good people,' his voice rang out proudly, 'the tyranny of your past overlord is at an end. The time has come for Wychaven to be great again and prosper. I give you the Lady Meriel, Countess of Loxstead—mistress of Wychaven.'

A cheer rent the air, the voice of Baldwin, the bailiff's son, rising above the others. 'God save the Lady Meriel! God bless our new lord, the Earl of Loxstead!'

A tight ball of emotion rose to Meriel's throat as the tall youth bent his knee in homage and, following his lead, everyone within the hall sank in obeisance; without prompting, they swore allegiance to Rolf and herself. Deeply moved, Meriel looked up at her husband and saw his throat work convulsively, his eyes bright with the force of feelings which for once overcame him. Clearing his throat, there was the barest tremor in his rich voice as he answered.

'You have proved your loyalty to my countess this night, and you shall be rewarded. I have seen how my own demesne is well planted with wheat, while your own strips show a poor yield. Henceforth there will be no excessive work-days upon my land, and this year's harvest shall be divided among us all. Many of your houses are also showing signs of neglect. Before autumn, all shall be repaired at my expense.'

The round of cheers shook the rafters, and Meriel's heart swelled with pride at Rolf's generosity. To her, it made good sense and was a policy her father had followed. The people would love him for it, and next year the yield from Wychaven's lands would double. She scanned the room, dismayed that she could not put names to the younger faces, but the older villagers and servants, their faces a little more wrinkled, and hair greying or balding, she recalled well enough. Within a week she would know them all. Only then would she truly feel she was mistress in her father's house. Her attention was drawn to a grey-robed figure who moved with painful slowness through the crowd to the dais. When he lifted his bald head and she looked into the weather-browned, walnut crinkled face, joy warmed her.

Her hand tightened upon Rolf's arm. 'My lord, let me introduce you to Father Aethan. He has been chaplain here since my grandfather's day. He has no idea what year he was born, but he must be four-score years and more.'

As she smiled down at the aged chaplain, Meriel saw uncertainty and dread in his grey eyes. Did he fear he would be cast aside? She was about to prompt Rolf that Father Aethan drew his strength from serving the community at Wychaven, but Rolf had already begun to speak.

'Father Aethan,' he said respectfully, 'you must know Wychaven better than anyone. We must talk tomorrow, for I would value your advice upon several matters. Your duties must be many and varied; perhaps we should discuss bringing in an assistant chaplain to help with the more taxing of your duties. Now it is time to give praise for the success of this night. We shall go to the chapel, where you will take prayers.'

'It shall be my honour, my lord.' Father Aethan bowed, his step firmer as he left to prepare the chapel.

Lady Isolda came to stand at Rolf's side, smiling sweetly, her voice honeyed with warmth. 'You have won the hearts of your people with your bold promises, brother. I only pray that when you are recalled to France they will not become disillusioned or rob you blind. They rose very quickly to your help—perhaps too quickly.'

Anger stung Meriel's cheeks at Isolda's criticism of her vassals. 'The people of Wychaven are loyal to their lawful overlord. It was Sedbury who sought to steal my birthright!'

Isolda looked distraught. 'My dear sister, you take my words amiss. They were meant as a friendly word of caution.'

Rolf regarded Isolda coldly. 'Your advice, even if well intentioned, is ill timed.'

The underlying, almost warning, note of his voice puzzled Meriel. Although somewhat thoughtless in her remarks, Isolda clearly doted upon Rolf, yet his manner towards her was always so reserved. Why did he always set a ring of steel around his emotions? Would she ever break through that impenetrable barrier? Her body trembled slightly at the thought, and she was conscious of Rolf's piercing stare upon her. She pulled herself together. The dangers she had faced, and the over-whelming response of the people to Rolf and herself, had all taken their toll upon her, and her wounded leg began to ache. She was being over-fanciful. Too overcome to meet Rolf's assessing stare, she turned away with an excuse. 'Before I join you for prayer, my lord, I shall instruct the chamberwomen to prepare the rooms for what is left of the night.'

Meriel beckoned to Bella, who was standing unob-trusively at the back of the hall, but as she moved away from the dais, the Lady Isolda's voice carried to her.

'How romantic it all is—your bold capture of the castle with your lady at your side! The troubadours will add to the legend that already surrounds your name. But after such a life of adventure, will you not become bored? Still, you always have France to escape to. I doubt not the lovely Sibyl will welcome you back with loving arms.'

The low snarl of Rolf's reply did not reach Meriel. The happiness of the last half-hour drained from her as she was reminded of the reality of her situation. Forced into a marriage not of his choosing, was it not obvious that Rolf would seek solace in the arms of his French mistress, once he was recalled by Richard? Meriel gave her instructions abstractedly to the chamberwomen and to Bella. When prayers were over, she would be alone with Rolf. Her fighting spirit asserted itself. She might not have long before he was recalled to France, but she would use every moment of that precious time to break through Rolf's mistrust. Otherwise, they would inevitably drift further apart. She could not bear that, but until she learnt the dark secret which made him mistrust all women, how could she ever hope to win his love in return?

CHAPTER TWELVE

'LEAVE THE shutters open, Bella. The night is warm,' Meriel said from the doorway of the lord's bedchamber, having checked that all trace of Sedbury's presence had been removed and fresh linen sheets put on the bed. She crossed the ante-chamber to the narrow unglazed window overlooking the sea. 'You may retire, Bella. You must be exhausted after all that has happened today.'

'I will not be far if you should have need of me, my lady,' Bella answered, rather despondently.

Meriel looked worriedly at her. 'It must be difficult for you, knowing that Lord Sedbury is a prisoner here.'

'That is over,' Bella said without rancour. 'I would make a more respectable life for myself. You have given me the chance to make it possible.'

'There is always a place for you at Wychaven,' Meriel answered warmly, before Bella left her. She turned back to the window, gazing out at the towers and battlements illuminated by the moonlight. Gradually the majestic beauty of the castle and the vast expanse of sea before her soothed her nerves. After the heat of the hall and chapel, crammed with people celebrating the defeat of Sedbury and his men—now all safely locked away—the fresh breeze coming from the sea was refreshing. She ran a hand through her flowing hair. In preparation for retiring for the night, she was naked beneath the sapphire velvet robe with its loose-fitting sleeves, but, even so, the garment was too warm and she unfastened the gold cord at its high neck, easing it away to allow the cooling breeze to play over her throat.

Would Rolf come to her tonight? After the simple service of thanksgiving in the chapel, she had slipped away to make sure that those wounded in the fight had been tended to. Rolf had remained kneeling in solitary prayer by the altar, his head bent in homage, his expression rapt, as absorbed as any knight during the lonely hours of vigil. For Meriel, Rolf's piety and humility in this, his moment of triumph, had helped to ease the pain of Isolda's cruel words. But she felt no closer to penetrating the barrier that guarded her husband's emotions.

Kneeling by Rolf's side in the chapel, she had sensed his withdrawal from the closeness they had shared during their swim and the journey through the cave and secret passage. The cool control which made him invincible on the tourney field now made him an enigma she could not begin to understand. He was ruthless and implacable towards his enemies, yet every one of his soldiers would give his life for him, and tonight she had seen the ease with which his courage and generosity had won the hearts of the villagers. It was what she wanted and respected in him. Yet suddenly she was afraid, not for her people—but for herself. What if she found it impossible to break through Rolf's reserve and remained forever shut out from his love?

She started violently as a shadow loomed up on the wall beside her. Looking round, she saw Rolf bend his head to enter through the doorway, and she nervously drew the edges of her robe together at her throat. He must have come from the lord's dressing-chamber on the far side of the interconnecting rooms. Her heart leapt traitorously. He had changed into a long moss-green dressing-robe, the flatness of his stomach and his slender hips emphasised by the wide silver-work belt at his waist. As he straightened, his tall, broad-shouldered figure dwarfed the opening. One side of his handsome face was in shadow, making it impossible to judge his mood, but the candlelight falling upon his finely-etched profile set her heart catapulting with longing.

She remained by the window, desperately trying to still the frantic pounding of her heart. This time she would make no move towards him. The humiliation of his rejection on their wedding night had cut too deep. The pain was still raw, she realised, and she did not think she could bear its like again.

A muscle throbbing along Rolf's jaw added to her apprehension as he poured two goblets of wine from the silver flagon left by the chamberwomen. When he held one out to her, his eyes were shadowed by the thick crescents of his dark lashes.

'Wychaven is yours, my lady,' he stated in a quiet growl. 'You achieved what you set out to gain through our marriage.'

She gasped, shocked. 'You still believe that?'

'What else could have brought you back to me?' His stare sharpened dangerously. 'Or have you chosen to forget the speed with which you abandoned your marriage vows?'

'I have not forgotten the humiliation of our wedding night, my lord,' she returned thickly. A warning bell clanged in her mind. She must not lose her temper. He was deliberately taunting her. If they were to resolve their differences, they must talk—no matter how painful his recriminations might be to start with. Holding his gaze, she outwardly assumed a calmness she was far from feeling. Why, oh why, was she so disturbingly aware that he was likely to be as naked as herself beneath his long robe? Or, that even with anger tightening the hollows of his cheeks, he was devastatingly handsome—the vibrant power of his masculinity more threatening to her self-control than his rage? 'I was wrong to act as I did, but you are cruel to taunt me so, after...'

The formidable glint in his eyes halted her words.

'You think me cruel, do you?' His hand shot out, his fingers like silk-sheathed steel round her wrist. 'I do not like being used. Since first we met, you have unscrupulously played the tease to gain your own ends. Perhaps you think your beauty exonerates you—that I would be brought to heel by the promise of your body offered so seductively on our wedding night?'

'I never set out to trick you!' She defended in an uneven whisper. 'I was commanded first by Lord Sedbury and then by Queen Eleanor to keep my identity a secret. I did not like the dishonesty involved, but how else was I to protect my name? You should be flattered by the queen's trust in you, my lord. She knew that I would be safe as her emissary—that you would protect even a minstrel-girl from any unwanted attentions forced upon her.'

The line of Rolf's jaw set rigidly and his eyes sparked amber fire. Sensing some inner conflict battling within him, she willed her gaze to remain unflinching. She would not plead her innocence, neither would she cower from any retribution he inflicted upon her.

'Damn Eleanor—for all she is our queen!' His voice deepened savagely. 'That woman is a born intriguer.' His lips twisted cynically, then changed to a self-mocking smile as his gaze bored into her. 'But I was aware of that, and should have known all was not as it seemed.'

For a long moment tension rippled like shock-waves between them—unbearable in its vibrancy. Then, unexpectedly, she heard him drag out her name in a ragged breath. He took her chin in his hand, tilting her face upwards so that he could look down into it with a compelling hunger that pitted her soul. There was a stillness between them—the tension changing and crackling. The gap between them inexorably closed, until her whole body pulsated to the expectant thud of her heart.

'This moment, at least, was inevitable from our first meeting.' His voice held a mixture of mockery and tenderness. 'You have tempted me to the edge of damnation, but no longer...'

As his hands slid round her, she stiffened, his words of censure slashing her like winter sleet. He was prepared to accept her as his wife, but with hatred searing his heart. She turned her head aside, evading his mouth.

'Dammit, Meriel,' he rasped heatedly against her ear. 'I've waited long enough. You'll not deny me now.' His lips covered hers in a fierce, angry kiss which stopped her breath and effectively silenced her words of protest. She stiffened within his tightening embrace, her mind screaming a silent entreaty. I shall hate you if you make it happen like this!

Almost as if he read her thoughts, his mouth gentled. Now it clung sweetly, caressing her lips with slow, masterly thoroughness to destroy her defences. Whether soldier or lover, he was an expert at disarmament, and now he spared her nothing of his skill. Lingeringly, he kissed her eyelids, her cheeks, leaving a fiery trail in the wake of his lips as they travelled with sensuous slowness to the hollow of her throat. Her skin glowed with a delicious tingling warmth, robbing her of breath and setting her heart clamouring. The silky touch of his hair brushed coolly against her heated skin, the scent of him, too potently male, filling her consciousness in the most infinitely sensual way to destroy her fragile reserve. Where his mouth travelled, his hands followed, tenderly stroking her neck inside the collar of her robe and down over her bare shoulders until she relaxed. When his tongue traced the softness of her mouth, she could bear the torture of her restraint no longer, and her body ignited with the response he sought.

In boneless supplication she swayed against him, helpless as a ship on a storm-tossed sea. Her whole body quivered as though in the grip of a fever, as every nerve and sense leapt into life and she clung to him, a small moan of surrender rising in her throat.

Scooping her into his arms, he strode into the bedchamber and gently laid her on the soft feather mattress. His kiss deepened as he untied the cords fastening her robe. Sliding his fingers along her shoulders, he drew the edge of the velvet material down over her arms, his mouth teasing and tantalising as his lips moved over the rise of her naked breasts. For an instant, she involuntarily tensed. No man had touched her so intimately. Rolf's long hair was feather-soft upon her skin as he paused to look up at her, his straight brows drawing together. The topaz light in his eyes deepened.

'Meriel?' Her name was a husky rasp against her ear, his gaze scalding her as he silently questioned her innocence.

The dawning wonder in his eyes brought a strange tightness to her throat, making speech impossible. She drew her palm along the roughening texture of his jaw, every pore of her body aware of the leashed power in his iron-hard form pressed against her. Her hair spread across the pillow and was captured behind her shoulders, preventing her from lifting her head, but her arms circled his neck, drawn by a will of their own, to bind him closer. Her flesh burned where his mouth touched her, tongues of fire licking through her veins to consume her in their enfolding heat.

His lips brushed against her ear. 'Sweet water-sprite, you taste of the sea, but even that cannot wash away the delicious scent of your skin, like woodland flowers with the heady fragrance of spring. It filled the air when you danced, seeping into my bones, haunting me ever since, and driving me to the brink of madness.'

'Oh, Rolf, 'tis not madness, but...' Her words of love were lost beneath the onslaught of his lips recapturing hers, possessing, dominating, but with a finesse and controlled passion which savoured each moment, treasuring each mingling of their breaths, and drawing her into a world of sensuality she had not thought possible. As she answered him kiss for kiss, her innocence was lost for ever, his demands becoming bolder and more insistent as he expertly brought her to greater heights of pleasure. With each moment and each new intimacy shared, the fire within her gathered momentum until it raged like a furnace out of control. At last she was Rolf's—truly his wife, in body and in mind, wholly and completely.

No, not wholly—not yet! Even though he tenderly held her close, as their breathing slowed to normality, a new wound opened in her heart. How could she ever be wholly Rolf's until that dark secret which haunted him had been laid to rest? But this was a beginning, she reassured herself. She had been given an insight into the passionate man behind the hard, cynical nature he presented to the world. She lay back, relaxed and replete, her lips nestling into the curve of his throat. Feeling the indent of the scar, she kissed it. Immediately he tensed, and rolled on his side. Was the scar connected with the mystery which made him so disparaging towards women?

As though reading the question in her eyes, Rolf propped himself on an elbow, his eyes defying her to question him. She stifled her curiosity. It was too soon to probe into whatever torment ate into his soul. Instead, she touched his cheek, needing his reassurance.

'I never meant to deceive you, Rolf, about my identity. Wychaven is no mean prize. It may not be as vast or wealthy as the lands in Auvergne, but...'

'Hush, my sweet.' He stopped her words with a kiss. 'Wychaven pleases me well enough, as does its mistress. It is I who should crave your pardon for the ill I believed of you.'

Lovingly, she put a finger to his lips. 'It was my foolish pride which began it all. I should have spoken out that day by the river—but I was so ashamed that you had caught me dancing.'

'And I have travelled so far down the path to hell,' he answered heavily. 'I could not believe that a woman of such beauty could ever be untouched.'

Again she bit back the untimely curiosity raised by his enigmatic words. What had made him so cynical? Deliberately she thrust the question from her mind. Floating in a delicious languor from his lovemaking, she did not want anything to spoil this precious moment of harmony.

'I want only to be a good wife to you, my lord—and that Wychaven will one day give you the peace you seek.' She smiled at him and, emboldened by the softening glint in his eyes, rolled on her side and kissed him passionately upon his mouth.

With an amused chuckle, he imprisoned her in his arms, his voice low. 'A good wife must learn to be obedient and please her husband in every way. With you, my headstrong countess, obedience may take a little time to master, and I shall try to be patient. But...' he grinned wickedly, 'as to the art of pleasing me, the night is still young! Time enough for many lessons to be taught which will delight us both.'

Meriel stirred in the large bed and stretched sensuously with a feeling of well-being. Her body still glowed from the pleasure Rolf had given her. Gradually the early morning noises of the castle penetrated her consciousness and she reached out a hand to touch him, but her eyes shot open in disappointment. The bed was still warm from the heat of his body, but he was gone. From the lord's dressing-chamber beyond came the sound of splashing water. As she searched for her robe among the tangle of bedclothes, she heard the low urgent tones of Tom Kedge as he attended upon Rolf. There was something in that urgency that made her feel uneasy. Discovering her robe on the floor, she hastily wrapped it about her, calling out for Bella. Strangely, there was no answer to her summons, and the men's voices had also fallen silent as she moved towards her own dressing-chamber.

'Bella will not be attending you.'

Meriel spun round at the sound of Rolf's voice behind her, her welcoming smile fading as she saw the bleakness of his expression as he crossed to her side. His attire surprised her, for today was meant to be a day of feasting, yet he was dressed as though for the hunt in soft fawn leggings and nut-brown tunic and long boots.

'Is Bella ill?'

Anger brightened his eyes as he stared down at her, his voice cold. 'Bella has gone. So has Sedbury! Her guilt speaks for itself. She must have released her lover.'

'No!' Meriel refused to believe it. 'Bella would not betray us!'

'She was Sedbury's mistress, was she not?' Rolf replied scornfully, 'and most likely his spy?'

'It is true that she loved my kinsman, but she refused to spy on me. Sedbury cast her out. She would not betray me... She was my friend!'

'Little you know of a woman's faith! They have none!' he snarled.

His words blistered her. He was condemning *her* as much as Bella. Her hand shot upwards, but inches before it reached his face, the warning glitter in his eyes froze her movement. In her rage at the injustice of his words, she had almost gone too far. She lowered her hand, clenching it until her long nails dug into the flesh of her palm. Her gaze held his, matching and defying his scorn. 'Curse you, and your prejudice! Not all women are faithless. Not I! And not Bella!'

He caught her hands and jerked her towards him, his eyes blazing. 'Understandably, you are upset, but do not try my patience too far, or so forget to whom you are speaking.'

The coldness of his tone hit her like a body-blow. Last night had changed nothing. The tender lover was gone—replaced by this cold, implacable warrior. She blinked back the hot sting of tears behind her eyelids, too proud to let him see her pain. 'As you, too, forget, my lord. I am your wife—your equal in rank—but I have a voice of my own and the right to speak out in defence of my friend.' Deny it though she must, doubt seared her. Had Bella betrayed her? The dread of it cut deep. Was Rolf right? Bella did love Sedbury—so would her love lead her to betrayal? In her heart, she would not believe it.

Rolf looked down into Meriel's stricken face. He knew the pain she was feeling too well not to feel sympathy, and the last thing he had intended upon waking this morning was to quarrel with her. He had envisaged a few pleasant days in her company as they explored their lands before he must leave for France. Sedbury's escape had destroyed any chance of that.

'It is hard to accept when someone you care for breaks your trust,' he said, seeking to ease the tension between them, 'but you must accept it. Two of my men were killed without the alarm being raised. Whoever went to Sedbury's cell to release him must have been known to them. Now both Sedbury and Bella have gone. They were probably dressed as peasants, and went out with the villagers when they left the castle at dawn to return to their homes. The evidence speaks for itself.'

He felt the fight drain from her as she lowered her tear-bright azure eyes. 'If Bella is in any way implicated in Sedbury's escape, she was tricked. I will not believe she betrayed me.' The fierceness was back in her voice. 'Something could have happened to her!'

'The castle is being searched.' To his surprise, Rolf found himself moved by Meriel's stubborn loyalty to her friend. She had an uncanny knack of catching his emotions off guard. He did not want to see her hurt or to spend their last few hours together in conflict. Not liking the implications behind Sedbury's easy escape, he hid his unease and drew Meriel into his arms. 'This is supposed to be a day of feasting. Our people expect it. I leave the arrangements to you, but I must ride out after Sedbury. I shall return as soon as I can.'

Meriel looked up at him, disturbed as much by his cool practicality as by his nearness. Did nothing dent that granite exterior? 'All shall be in readiness for your return, my lord. I regret Wychaven has brought you little joy so far, only worry.'

His lips twisted sardonically. 'My displeasure is with Sedbury, not Wychaven. Would that I had more time to discover all of its delights and mysteries.' He kissed her swiftly upon the lips and left the room, calling back, 'I shall send one of the women to help you to dress.' In a moment she heard his voice in the courtyard, followed by the clatter of departing horses. An hour later, Meriel finished giving her orders for the preparation of the food and the cleaning of the hall, and looked about for a sign of Isolda.

'Has the Lady Isolda not arisen yet?' she enquired of a passing chamberwoman carrying a bundle of fresh bed-linen.

'The Lady Isolda left when Lord Loxstead rode out. He sent four men to escort her back to the convent. Did you not know, my lady?'

'I had not realised that my husband could spare men for her escort,' Meriel answered, masking her hurt that Rolf had not informed her of his sister's departure, or that Isolda had not bidden her farewell. With Rolf away, she had been looking forward to learning more from his sister about the complex man she had married. She smothered her disappointment. She had hoped this morning would see a lessening of the distrust between Rolf and herself, but obviously not! Did he still feel that his holy sister would be tainted by her company? Why else should he have sent Isolda away with such haste?

The knowledge crushed her, but the most cutting pain of all was Rolf's total disregard of her wishes upon the matter. She was half out of her mind with worry over Bella, and Rolf's hasty assumption that her maid was guilty of treachery was further proof of the low esteem in which he held women—the apparent exception being his sister, whose virtue he protected so vehemently. The magic and happiness of returning to Wychaven dimmed. Last night had held such promise, but the harsh light of day had brought with it a bitter reality.

CHAPTER THIRTEEN

MERIEL SQUARED her shoulders as a stream of village women, all dressed in their best clothes, bustled excitedly into the hall to join the castle servants in preparing it for the banquet. Smothering her own uncertainty about the future and how best to win Rolf's trust, she summoned warm smiles as she moved among them, asking after their welfare and that of their families.

To take her mind from worrying over Bella's disappearance, which, she had reluctantly to admit, implied that her friend had betrayed them and gone with Sedbury, she inspected the castle. Her anger rose as she noted the signs of neglect during Sedbury's stewardship. The limewash on its outer walls was discoloured and in many places flaking from lack of maintenance. She summoned a scribe to accompany her, and dictated to him the list of the tasks which should be tackled without delay. The thatched roofs of the outbuildings were in a deplorable condition, but worse was the sight of the almost empty store-rooms and granary. With each further sign of neglect, her temper rose. She had seen from the fields that few crops had been sown. If they were not to starve this winter, food and grain would have to be purchased to replenish the stock Sedbury had sold to fill his own coffers with gold. There was also the question of appointing new castle officers to replace Sedbury's men who had bled the lands dry. Godric the bailiff might know the whereabouts of the former steward and chamberlain; if not, others must be employed to take their places. With so little time before Rolf left for France, she would need to gather information quickly, so that they could discuss what needed to be done and how much expenditure would be necessary.

As Meriel made her way to the last of the out-buildings, the smell of roast ox already turning on its spit in the courtyard drifted to her. It was mid-afternoon, and time she changed her gown for the feast. Her worries returned, sharper now that the hour was so advanced. Rolf had not returned. Surely Sedbury and Bella could not have travelled far? Unwilling to waste time, she decided to check the last of the buildings before going to change. To her disgust, there were several large holes in the roof, and her nose wrinkled at the rank stench of rotting wood as she entered. It was the wood-store, though its contents would be little use to the estate now. The rotting logs lying on the water-covered floor were covered in grotesquely shaped fungi. She shivered in the dank air, her flesh crawling at the scampering noises in the darkest corners. The place was infested with rats!

'It will have to be cleared out—the whole store is rotten,' she dictated to the scribe. 'The roof must be repaired before it is used again.'

Seeing a rat as large as a well-fed cat sitting on top of a wood-pile, she shuddered. Then she heard what sounded like a mew of a kitten. The sound came again, and she tensed. It sounded very like a kitten, but...? The hairs at the back of her neck stirred. That was no kitten, but a human voice, weak from pain.

'Fetch a torch, lad,' she ordered. 'I want that far corner searched.'

She strained her eyes in the gloom, unable to see into the dark corner. Only the sound of scampering across the sodden floor reached her ears now. Perhaps she had been mistaken, and it had been nothing more than rats squeaking. The scribe returned, followed by Baldwin, the bailiff's son.

'My lady, you don't want to be in here,' Baldwin advised. ''Tis just a wood-store and full of rats.'

'Perhaps, but I heard something, Baldwin,' Meriel explained, unable to dispel her feeling of disquiet. In the flickering torchlight, the store looked innocent enough. 'I would feel happier if that far corner were searched— just in case I was not mistaken.'

Meriel's throat dried as the bulky young man held the torch aloft and cautiously climbed over the logs. Several slithered from beneath his feet, sending him off balance.

'Take care, Baldwin!'

He scrambled higher, held the torch above his head and peered into the corner. 'Sweet Jesu!' he gasped.

Meriel ran forward, a terrible premonition seizing her.

'My lady, stay back,' he said firmly. 'It's your maid. Better you do not see her.'

Meriel ignored his words, her knees scraping as she clambered over the logs, ignoring the dangerous way they moved under her weight. On the far side, tossed like a broken doll in the corner, was indeed Bella. Her clothes were in tatters, as though someone had tried to rip them from her. The wavering light showed her slender body covered in bites from the rats. Meriel started to roll the logs away to get to her maid, unable to drag her horrified gaze from her battered, bloody face, one side of which was distorted by a blackening lump the size of a goose-egg.

'She's still alive!' Meriel gasped. 'I heard her whimper.'

'Stand back, my lady.'

Baldwin rolled the remaining wood aside and lifted Bella from the floor. As he did so, she moaned softly. To Meriel's alarm, she saw a long wound in her maid's shoulder, clotted with blood that had dried in dark streaks down her arm and breast.

'Take her to the room next to mine,' Meriel ordered, appalled at what had happened. Who could have done it? Sedbury sprang to mind, but, somehow, despite his violent temper, she could not see him as responsible. There was almost something cowardly about Bella's injuries—especially the stab-wound. Sedbury had fought in many battles, and if he had stabbed Bella, he would have killed her. But who else could be responsible? The questions sped through her mind.

Their advance through the castle caused a stir among
the servants. Meriel dismissed everyone from Bella's
chamber, even the serving-women, saying heavily, 'If old
Sarah the wise-woman is still alive, send her to me. Other
than her, I shall tend my maid myself. And summon
Father Aethan.'

The priest arrived, his wrinkled face paling with
concern as he looked at Bella. Meriel covered her half-
naked body with a blanket, her voice strained as she addressed him. 'Everyone within the castle must be questioned, Father. In the absence of Lord Loxstead, will
you see that it is done?'

'Nothing like this has ever happened in all the years
I have served your family.' The priest shook his ancient
head sadly. 'It was not one of the villagers, I would swear
to it.'

'And I cannot believe it was any of Lord Loxstead's
men; his discipline is too strict. But all must be questioned. Someone might have seen something. Whoever
has done this must be caught and punished. Could any
of Sedbury's guards have escaped capture last night and
be in hiding? I want every room in the castle searched.'

'It shall be done, my lady. And your maid will be in
our prayers.'

Father Aethan left, and by the time old Sarah hobbled
into the room, Meriel had removed Bella's tattered
clothing and gently sponged her bruised body and face.
Throughout, she made no movement or sound, her
heartbeat so weak as to be barely discernible. Her flesh
already had the chill of death. She had lain unconscious
in a pool of rank-smelling water for hours, and it was
a miracle that she was alive at all. Meriel called for a
lighted brazier to be brought into the room, to bring
some heat back into Bella's body, and watched anxiously
as Sarah's expert fingers examined her.

'Will she live?' Meriel asked, as the old woman sat
back.

'It is in God's hands, my lady. That cut upon the head
bodes ill. Even if she lives, her mind may never be right
again.'

'Tell me what I must do, Sarah. We must save her.
Bella must not die or lose...' Her voice broke, and she
swallowed painfully. 'She will recover. She must! She is
my dearest friend.'

'She's young, and she looks strong enough.' Sarah
eyed Meriel doubtfully. 'But it is not for you to tend
her—not this night at least, my lady. Your people await
you in the hall. Tonight your place is at your lord's side.
I shall tend your maid as though she were my own
daughter.'

Meriel nodded her consent, unwilling to leave Bella,
but knowing she must. And she trusted Sarah. She smiled
gratefully at the old woman who, surprisingly, had
scarcely altered during the years Meriel had been away,
but then old Sarah had looked ancient when she had
brought Meriel into the world—or so the Lady Maude
had claimed—worn out by long hours of tending the
sick and from bearing fifteen children, a dozen of whom
she had proudly reared to reach adulthood. If anyone
could save Bella, Sarah could, Meriel thought.

It was late afternoon and time for the feasting to begin,
but where was Rolf? Had he recaptured Sedbury? Surely
her kinsman could not have got far away on foot? The
villagers had long since assembled in the castle grounds
and begun to celebrate by drinking the wine from the
vat Rolf had ordered for them. With things as they were,
Meriel felt in little mood for rejoicing as she changed
her clothes in readiness for the banquet. The laughter
from the villagers carried to her. At least they were
happy, and some good had come out of freeing
Wychaven from Sedbury's tyranny.

With an effort, she shrugged aside her dark mood.
What had happened to Bella was still a mystery, but
Sedbury must have been involved. Father Aethan's
questioning had produced nothing. No one had seen
Bella after she had supposedly retired for the night. How

could Sedbury have left her to die in the wood-store? Meriel shuddered at the memory, and prayed. Dear God, let Bella have been found in time!

Just as she was settling a jewelled girdle about her hips, she heard a trumpet-call from the gatehouse. Rolf must have returned. Her heart fluttered. She was still angry with him for sending Isolda away, and felt no triumph that he had been proved wrong over Bella's loyalty. The circumstances of that were too grim. This was far from the home-coming she had envisaged. The neglect she had witnessed at Wychaven had also taken its toll upon her. There was much to be done, and it would take a fortune to put it right, which would not be easy, for Rolf would need all the finance he could raise to build the castle, as ordered by the king, on the lands bestowed upon him.

Meriel swallowed her anger and resentment that Rolf had sent Isolda away. Her company would have eased the burdens she now had to face. With so many larger problems threatening the stability of their marriage, hurt pride could destroy its rickety foundations. She must learn patience. It could take a long time to win Rolf's trust, and deeds were more powerful than words.

Now his mood would surely be unpredictable after half a day in hunting for her kinsman. Whether he had succeeded, or failed, the matter was bound to add to the tension between them. She hurried to the hall to greet him, feeling too vulnerable to face a confrontation with Rolf in private. For the sake of their people, they must appear to be content with one another.

She entered the hall from the dais doorway at the same moment that Rolf strode into the chamber from the far end, the gathered villagers parting to let him through. To her surprise, he was accompanied by several armed knights.

As he approached the dais, her heart sank. His lips were set in a forbidding line. All the knights fell back except one, who matched Rolf's long stride, but Meriel had eyes only for the stern countenace of her husband.

'Sedbury has escaped,' he ground out. 'About a mile from here, he attacked and killed a pedlar and stole his horse. We tracked him to the coast near Weymouth, but the devil's own luck was with him. He had taken ship to France with the turn of the tide. Your maid was not with him.'

'Bella has been found,' her voice cracked with emotion, 'in the wood-store. Someone had tried to rape her... She was stabbed and beaten... left for dead...'

'Has she said who attacked her?' Rolf demanded fiercely.

Meriel shook her head. 'She's still unconscious, more dead than alive. Everyone in the castle has been questioned, but they had seen nothing. I can only think...' her voice shook, 'it must have been Sedbury.'

Rolf scowled, his eyes brittle with condemnation. 'Then she could still have helped him to escape, but refused to go with him, or else...' His expression tautened as he exchanged a troubled look with the man at his side. Meriel, following his gaze, was immediately struck by the resemblance between the two. The stranger was several years older than her husband—his hair, cropped short, was a duller blond, but the straight slash of brows were the same, and the long slender nose. A narrow dark beard emphasised the slightly heavier set of his jaw in a face that was as arresting as it was handsome. When he turned his stare upon her, she found herself facing identical golden eyes. Briefly the same pained, haunted look, which so often darkened Rolf's eyes, was also apparent, then, as his gaze took in her puzzled expression, he smiled.

'In his preoccupation, my brother seems to have forgotten his manners.' The stranger executed a formal bow. 'I am Sir Edwin. I was answering Rolf's call for arms to help him lay siege to this castle, when we met upon the road. It seems that I have arrived too late. He told me of the remarkable feat by which the two of you virtually took the castle single-handed!' Edwin's smile broadened, his more exuberant nature already apparent.

'Rolf also told me of your courage—but not that I had acquired a new sister who could rival the angels with her beauty.'

Taken aback by the extravagance of his compliment, Meriel could not help returning his smile, even if her own was strained. 'I am no angel, sir. I am too wilful and stubborn for that.'

'Rolf said you had spirit!' Edwin laughed softly, his affection for his brother obvious as he looked at him. 'I always knew he would never settle for a convent-bred mouse. Welcome to our family, my lady countess.' Before she could suspect what he was about, he had kissed her soundly on both cheeks before releasing her and slapping Rolf on the back. 'You have risen high, and it is no more than you deserve, brother.'

Aware of the curious eyes of the villagers upon them, Meriel prompted softly, 'The feast is about to begin. The people wish to pay homage to their new lord.'

'Then I must make haste and change,' Rolf replied, his voice lightening. 'What quarters are there for my brother and his knights?'

'I shall send servants to prepare rooms in the watch-tower for the knights. Sir Edwin can have those made ready in the West Tower for the Lady Isolda before her sudden departure.' She glanced accusingly at Rolf, who eyed her stonily.

'The only men I could spare to escort Isolda had to leave at first light,' he said flatly. 'She would not disturb your sleep, knowing you would understand her wish to return to the convent and her seclusion as an anchoress.'

Meriel did not trust herself to answer, her eyes alone blazing their condemnation. She knew why Rolf had sent his sister away. It was rather late in the day to consider her feelings by making excuses.

'What has our sainted sister been up to?' she heard Sir Edwin ask Rolf as they moved away.

Rolf's answer was lost to her, but her heart contracted as his brother's deep voice responded. 'Ay, in the circumstances, you had to send Isolda back to the convent.'

The rest of his words were drowned by the noise of the celebrating villagers, but they confirmed Meriel's darkest fears. Rolf still thought the worst of her and resented having her as his wife.

As she moved through the throng of people, talking by name to those she remembered and smiling at the young children introduced to her, none would know of the heartbreak tearing her apart. Rolf returned, looking magnificent in the richly gold embroidered leaf-green tunic he had worn for their wedding. Immediately he was joined by his brother, and they were surrounded by a cluster of knights, all powerfully-built men, colourful in their emblazoned tunics, but Rolf, talking animatedly to his companions, outshone them all, even his handsome, convivial brother. He laughed at something Sir Edwin said, and a faint stain of colour appeared on his cheek. Then he looked across at Meriel, and with half the distance of the hall between them, she could feel the scorch of his stare. At the same moment as he excused himself from his companions to walk towards her, a blare of trumpets sounded from the courtyard, announcing the arrival of another visitor. Rolf paused at Meriel's side, and gave her an enigmatic smile before he turned to the door. His smile faded, to be replaced by a scowl of annoyance. A travel-stained man marched into the hall and, halting before Rolf, bowed stiffly.

'Prince Richard, Duke of Aquitaine, sends his congratulations upon your marriage, Lord Loxstead.' He held out a sealed scroll. 'He awaits your reply, my lord.'

The fine lines about Rolf's eyes deepened as he broke the seal and scanned the document. When he lowered it, the scar upon his neck was livid with angry colour. 'Take some refreshment, man. I shall speak with you later.' He took Meriel's arm. 'Come, there is little time and much we must discuss. The feast must go on without us.' He led her from the hall into the privacy of the Master of the Rolls's room opposite, deserted now that the clerk was at the feast.

'I must return at once to France,' Rolf said with gruff impatience. 'Richard has taken my marriage amiss. He sees it as treachery to him.'

Meriel briefly closed her eyes against a rush of misery. Now Rolf truly had reason to resent their marriage. 'Prince Richard cannot doubt your loyalty for long?' she attempted to reassure him. 'He will realise the truth soon enough.'

'The seed of distrust has been sown, so that is why I must return at once. Like all men in royal favour, I am not without my enemies at Court. There is much I would have liked to set in order here first, but it seems it is not to be. I cannot spare a large force of men to garrison Wychaven. With Sedbury loose, he could return and attack at any time. For that reason I would know you are safe. There is a convent not far from here where...'

'You would shut me away in a convent?' Meriel burst out, her whole body shaking with outrage. 'But where better to hide an unwanted bride? You have Wychaven. You have won the people's hearts by the bold way you re-took the castle. It seems you have no need of me!'

Anger tightened Rolf's jaw. 'I am thinking of your safety.'

'That is what Sedbury said when he ordered my mother to leave Wychaven after Sir Arnulf's death. The Lady Maude believed him and became his prisoner.' Meriel rounded on Rolf, her rage her only defence against the twisting, raw ache of the futility of her love and the knowledge that he meant to send her away. 'You are no better than Sedbury! He threatened to confine both the Lady Maude and myself in a convent, should I not marry to further his own greed and ambition. Now you would be rid of me in a like manner.'

'Take care of what you accuse me, my lady!' he growled, his glittering eyes warning her of the dangerous ground she trod. 'I have not the time or the inclination to argue with you. The first duty of a wife is to obey her husband.'

'If I leave Wychaven, it will be in chains,' she flung back at him, too incensed to back down. 'Do you think I would leave my people to the mercy of Sedbury, should he return? My place is here!'

'I will not be crossed, even by you, Meriel.'

She retreated as he stepped towards her. Did he really despise her so much that her feelings counted for nothing? To her dismay, she could feel tears welling behind her eyes. She must not break down in front of him. He would scorn her weakness. She swallowed painfully, struggling to keep her voice even. 'In the eyes of the law, I have no rights. Wychaven is yours. You can shut me away and no one will question you . . . for I am your vassal as much as the lowliest serf.' Her voice croaked at the strain it was costing her to keep her self-control. 'The people of Wychaven have given us their loyalty and trust. I would rather die than desert them again. You misjudged me once, my lord—as you misjudged Bella. She needs me now. Clearly, you do not.'

She spun on her heel and fled the room, too upset to heed the muffled oath and the call of her name. Blinded by her tears, she barely avoided colliding with Sir Edwin.

Rolf was halfway to the door to call after Meriel again, when his brother blocked his passage. Reluctantly, he stepped back and absently rubbed the scar on his neck as Edwin entered the room.

'I could not help overhearing some of what passed between you,' Edwin said heavily. 'A real firebrand you have married, brother! Tempestuous—beautiful and courageous!'

Rolf eyed his brother sourly. 'Beauty is too often a shallow mask to hide a treacherous heart! There is courage, and there is wilfulness. God knows I've tried to be patient, but since the first moment we met . . .' He caught himself up, even to Edwin refusing to admit to the strange fascination Meriel had woven over him, and added wryly, 'Only a fool listens to the song of a siren. There's no reasoning with her.'

'There never is with a woman in love!' Edwin laughed softly.

Impatient with the conversation, Rolf walked out of the room. Edwin must have drunk too freely of the potent French wines. Meriel did *not* love him! She had married him, seeing him as the sword to free Wychaven, but nothing more. Had she not told him as much to his face? Unaccountably that stabbed at his pride. He halted, surprised to find himself halfway up the stairs to their room, when he had intended to go to give his orders to his officers so that all would be in readiness for them to leave with the early tide on the morrow. Heavily he retraced his steps to the hall below.

In Bella's tiny chamber, Meriel squeezed a few drops of water from a cloth over her mouth, and sat back again on the low stool with a sigh. It was not easy to put water drop by drop between Bella's lips, but old Sarah had insisted that Bella must be made to drink, or she would die. In the hour Meriel had been tending her, she had not moved.

'You should rest, my lady,' Sarah said from the pallet bed made up for her in the corner. 'There's nothing more to be done, but pray. I shall watch over her.'

Meriel stared helplessly at Bella. Her swarthy complexion was drained of all colour, and fresh blood had appeared on the clean white head bandage. She took the lifeless hand lying on the coverlet. Thank God it was warmer now, but the pulse at her wrist was alarmingly weak. 'Don't die, Bella, please don't die!' Tears coursed unashamedly down Meriel's cheeks. 'You gave me your friendship when I needed it most. This is all my fault. Saving Wychaven was my foolish dream, not yours.' Meriel hung her head, her body shaking with silent sobs, her hands tightening over Bella's as she willed her friend to regain consciousness.

'Bella is strong and young.' Meriel started as Rolf spoke from directly behind her. 'That she has survived this long is a good sign. I have seen men recover from head wounds such as hers, but it takes days rather than hours before they regain consciousness.'

Meriel looked up at him. 'She has lost so much blood from the stab-wound on her shoulder.'

Rolf bent across Meriel, easing back the coverlet to frown down at Bella's wound. He straightened, and nodded to Sarah to leave the room. Taking Meriel's arms, he drew her up from the stool. 'If I wronged Bella, I apologise, but she did visit Sedbury last night. One of the scullions saw her heading in that direction. And her body was obviously hidden in the wood-store.'

'How could Sedbury have done this to her?' Meriel choked out. 'He cared deeply for her once! But who else could have done such a thing?'

Rolf stiffened, his expression forbidding. 'Her use to Sedbury was at an end,' he answered flatly.

Meriel shivered. 'I know. But though he has many faults, I cannot believe he could have done this to her. Sarah says Bella had not been raped—it was only made to look that way, as though a guard had been responsible. Unless the man was disturbed and became frightened.'

'Until Bella recovers, we shall never know the truth.' Rolf's voice was clipped.

It struck Meriel as odd that Rolf did not defend his men. Not one of them had tried to molest either Bella or herself during their journey from Winchester, knowing that to violate a woman, even a servant, under Rolf's protection would mean certain death. So why should it happen here?

'Come, Meriel, you must take your rest. Sarah will tend Bella.'

Meriel pulled back. In her distress over Bella, she had forgotten Rolf's intention to send her away from Wychaven. 'Bella has need of me,' she said coldly.

'You can do nothing more for her, now. It is in God's hands. Wychaven needs you. If you make yourself ill, who will run the estate in my absence?'

Her eyes widened, staring at him in surprise. The warmth of his hands burned through the thin silk of her gown, his eyes golden bright as they reflected the candle-light. 'I must leave for France in a few hours. I hope to return before the end of summer, but...' He shrugged. 'The news from France is not good. Richard and Henry are no closer to a reconciliation. It looks as though Richard means to fight; in which case I may be away for months.' He wiped the tears gently from her cheeks. 'I would not have us part as enemies. You are my wife, and it is my duty to protect you. I shall not force you to it, but it is safer for you in a convent than here. Sedbury could return to England and attack while I am away. And you can oversee the estate from such a place if you have someone you can trust in charge here. Godric the bailiff knows the whereabouts of your father's steward and believes he will willingly return.'

'My place is with our people. I will not hide away while they are in danger. If Sedbury returns, he will turn his vengeance against them.'

'If you will not go,' Rolf spoke resignedly, 'I shall leave half my men with you. Whatever happens in France, I will not fight against either Richard or Henry. So you realise that I could return in disgrace—my title and estates stripped from me for refusing to fight? You could lose Wychaven after all.'

'Better that, than betray all that is honourable in you, my lord! If you do what you believe is right, disgrace will not be so hard to bear. How could you live with yourself if you betrayed your own conscience?'

Her heart somersaulted as his expression softened. 'Few women would be so understanding.' A golden fire lit the depths of his eyes as he reached out to draw her closer. 'This is our last night together. And I do have need of you.'

With a soft laugh he led her determinedly towards their bedchamber, but even in her blossoming happiness that Rolf's ardour was a sign of the rift between them healing,

Meriel could not forget her friend lying so close to death. 'But there is Bella—I should stay with her.'

'Sarah will tend Bella.'

His tone was firm, and the desire darkening his eyes sent a shiver of expectancy through her as he drew her into his arms. There was an urgency to his kisses which carried her along on a surging tide of passion. Wave after wave of sensation built to storm force until they both lay fulfilled and exhausted, locked in each other's arms, their twin heartbeats gradually slowing.

Meriel raised herself on her elbow, brushing aside the ebony curtain of her hair as she gazed at his lean muscular body bathed in the golden light of a candle. Kissing the mat of hair on his chest, she said softly, 'I wish you did not have to go away so soon. In many ways we are still strangers.'

He grinned wickedly. 'The night is still young—time enough to learn more of each other.' He rolled her on to her back and kissed her until she was breathless, but she had a suspicion he was deliberately making love to her to still her questions. Reluctantly she wrenched her mouth aside, the pain that had been nagging at her all day returning as she asked, 'Why did you send Isolda away?'

He turned from her and rested his head in the crook of his arm as he answered gruffly, 'She is an anchoress; her place is in the convent, not here.'

'Am I not fit company for her?' she could not stop herself asking.

His long lashes shielded his eyes, but his voice was suddenly cold. 'Do not compare yourself with her. You are two very different women.'

Meriel reacted as though he had slapped her. Her hands curling into talons she lashed out at him, but he caught her wrists with frustrating ease as he flipped her over on her back and straddled her. 'In God's name, woman, what's got into you?'

'You are hurting me!' She tried to twist free, but was trapped beneath the weight of his body. She could feel the hardness of his thighs pressed against her hips, her body was arched, her breasts grazing against his chest as he slackened his hold, but his grip was merciless as he imprisoned her arms over her head. 'Let me go! Even as your wife, I am not good enough to share the company of your holy sister, but that does not prevent you from bedding me like a common whore!'

'That's enough, Meriel. You know nothing about Isolda, and it is not a subject I wish to discuss.'

'Why must you treat me as though I were addle-witted?' she flared hotly. 'You will not talk, and rarely listen to anything which touches our relationship. Dear God, Rolf, there are enough misunderstandings between us ... why must you make them worse?'

'Some things are better left unspoken.' The glint in his eyes frightened her, but she steadfastly held his glare, too hurt and angry to look away.

'Then that proves how little you hold me in regard,' she said hollowly. 'I was proud to share Wychaven with you. I even believed that, given time, we could be content with one another. But you shut me out ... You would have it all—you take, but give nothing of yourself. It is as well you are returning to France—without trust, our marriage is an empty worthless shell.'

It cost her dear to acknowledge the bitterness of truth, and the fight went out of her. Still Rolf did not release her, his thighs trapping her with their iron strength. His handsome face was drawn as he stared down at her, his eyes glinting. Even now her heart clenched with the force of her love, the magnificent figure he presented making the hopelessness of it the harder to bear. She lowered her gaze and found herself looking directly at the jagged white scar on his neck, and she frowned.

His throat worked convulsively. 'It's not a pretty sight, is it?' he grated out, abruptly releasing her. 'I suppose, like all women, you are curious about how I came by it: what glorious battle-honour it marks.' The sarcasm in his voice tore at her, but she lay still, sensing that the scar was connected to the demon which gave him no peace. His lips curled back into a snarl and he rose from the bed. Pulling on his robe, he jerked the sash tight about his waist as he glared at her. 'You speak of trust as a child speaks of a dream world of shining knights—like Sir Galahad seeking the Holy Grail. A pretty tale is it not, my lady minstrel? But do not forget that Lancelot was Galahad's father, and he betrayed Arthur by loving Guinevere. Trust and fidelity are illusions—like chivalry!' He spat out scathingly. 'This scar is no honourable battle-wound.'

The bleakness in his eyes chilled Meriel as he went on with angry reluctance. 'As my wife, I suppose you deserve to know the truth, and why there is little love lost between my sister and myself—though God curse your meddling! I have Isolda to thank for this.' He jabbed a finger at his scar. 'I was seven when I caught her being tumbled in the stable by a groom—the day before she married Sir Harold. She was frightened that I would tell our father, and sprang at me with a dagger. Until then, I had idolised her—I could not believe she was a whore, or that she meant to kill me. That trust almost cost me my life. I was no match then for her strength. She was like a madwoman driven by fear, trying to kill me to stop me telling Father. Somehow I managed to twist away, and the dagger entered the side of my neck. Fortunately Edwin heard my shout and dragged her off. To avoid any scandal, Isolda was married as arranged. The groom who had succumbed to Isolda was hanged on some imaginary charge. I was too ill for some months to know much about it. When I recovered, I was old enough to leave my family home and begin training as a page. I hope your curiosity is now satisfied, my lady countess?' He wheeled about, the door slamming behind him.

'Rolf!' Meriel cried, scrambling from the bed, but as her hand rested on the latch, she checked. Rolf was driven by his demon. She would only make matters worse if she tried to talk. At least now she understood why he distrusted women. But at what cost to their marriage?

She had drawn the admission from him reluctantly. Would he forgive her for learning of his shame? Had her stubborn, foolish pride erected yet another barrier between them?

CHAPTER FOURTEEN

ROLF DISMOUNTED and absently rubbed the muzzle of his destrier as he watched the city of Le Mans burning. Already his cloak and face were speckled with soot. A year ago, when he returned to France, he would never have believed it could come to this. Three times he had acted as mediator between the two fiery Plantagenets— to no avail. Henry II and Richard were now in open warfare and, if rumour were true, Henry's health was failing fast. Rolf screwed his eyes against the sting of smoke as a party of riders appeared from the direction of the city. Recognising their leader, he drew back into the concealing foliage of the wood, disgust churning his stomach. Prince John was deserting his father, leaving him to surrender or flee from the burning city.

Wearily Rolf hauled himself into the saddle. His last look at the beseiged city showed him another party of riders in flight. King Henry was among them. No longer the proud, raging warrior who had remorselessly carved himself an empire, but an old man, slumped over the saddle, weakened by disease and betrayal. Rolf pulled his destrier round and headed for Prince Richard's lines. If it was true, and Henry was close to death, Richard must make his peace with his father. If not . . . Rolf's lips thinned in grim determination. His own first loyalty, even with Henry near to death, must be to the king.

To Rolf's dismay, he saw Richard's men already riding in pursuit of Henry's army. Digging in his heels, he urged his tired horse and men to a faster pace, but they had been in the saddle all day and Richard's army were rested and thirsting for blood. By the time he caught up with them at a bridge over the river, he thought for an awful moment that he was too late—that Henry was a prisoner.

Then, as he overtook the slowing column of Richard's knights, Rolf saw that the bridge was held by the king's men. Guarding the king's retreat was Sir William Marshal, his long shield braced against his body and his lance couched in readiness to attack. How like Sir William to stand firm against so many! Rolf acknowledged, but even his prowess could not prevent his becoming overwhelmed by the sheer press of numbers on Richard's side.

Even as Rolf slowed his own horse and watched, he was astonished to see a tall, broad-shouldered man continue forward. There was no mistaking the gigantic figure of Richard the Lionheart. At that moment, Sir William shouted out and sent his horse forward at a charge. Seeing this, the prince sawed on his powerful destrier's reins to check him, and Rolf, to his horror, realised that Richard was unarmed. His own warning shout was echoed by a hoarse cry from the prince.

'By God's legs, don't kill me! I'm unarmed!'

Rolf held his breath. A collision was inevitable. Sir William's lance was aimed directly at the prince's heart. At the last moment Marshal, with a dexterity that won Rolf's admiration, relaxed his hold upon the lance, altering its point of balance, and it struck the horse instead of Richard. The prince's horse stumbled, throwing its rider into the dust. Rolf was amazed. The Lionheart unhorsed! He never thought to witness the day.

Over the astonished gathering of knights, Marshal's angry voice rang out. 'Nay, I'll not kill you. I'll let the devil do his own dirty work!' Wheeling his horse about, the knight returned to the bridge, once again taking up his defensive stand.

No one around the prince moved as they stared at the gigantic figure still sprawled on the ground, his face puce with rage. Rolf leapt from his saddle, striding to Richard's side to help him to his feet. His hand was slapped away with a grunt of rage as the prince heaved himself up. He checked his anger at Richard's ill humour. The prince would feel humiliated at being unhorsed before his army, and with his own news, he was about to deal another blow that could well earn him the Lionheart's enmity.

'The day is yours, my liege,' he said reasonably. 'King Henry is defeated. He's ill. It would be ignoble to pursue your father further.'

'You presume to lecture me on warfare!' the prince growled, his massive chest heaving with indignation inside his steel hauberk. 'I would have what is mine by right!'

'You are England's heir—Henry will never dispute that,' Rolf said earnestly. 'John has deserted him. I saw him leave Le Mans. The knowledge will break Henry. Now is the time to make your peace.'

'God's legs!' Anger sparked in the prince's piercing blue-grey eyes, high colour mottling his cheeks beneath his cinnamon and gold beard. In the grip of rage, Richard was a terrifying sight, but Rolf had weathered these storms before, and braced himself for the tempest to break over him. 'It is for Henry to make peace—not I!'

Rolf stood his ground. 'I am your friend, my lord, but I am also Henry's vassal. With your leave, I must now take my place at my sovereign's side, or be forsworn of my vow of fealty,' Rolf answered with quiet determination. 'I have tried to serve two masters, and failed. Now it seems that there is no hope of peace between you. Therefore, while Henry lives, my first allegiance must be to him.'

'Go to Henry, you traitor!' Richard snarled, 'and when I am king, I will strip you of everything.'

Rolf held his fiery gaze. 'When you are king—that will be your privilege. I'll not break my oath of fealty, even to keep your favour.'

'Then join Henry's army, damn you, and the devil take you both!' Richard snorted, his tirade cut short by the arrival of King Philip of France, demanding to know what had happened.

Rolf withdrew with long measured strides. Dear God, he had burned his bridges now! But, in honour, he could not have acted otherwise. Stiff-backed with affronted pride, he sprang into the saddle, signalling for his men to follow him to the river.

He met Sir William's challenge coolly. 'I ride to give my support to King Henry, and, with God's mercy, to seek to find a way to end this conflict.'

'Amen to that!' Sir William answered gravely, drawing his mount aside to allow Rolf to pass.

On the far side of the river Rolf looked back, and saw Richard stalking furiously through the lines at the side of the weasel-faced French king. His hand tightened over his reins in renewed fury. Several months earlier King Philip had brought Henry and Richard face to face. For months the French king had been trying to convince Richard that Henry meant to disinherit him in favour of John. As King Philip had schemed it would be, the meeting between father and son had been stormy. Henry refused all Richard's demands to take control of Maine, Touraine and Anjou—three of the most important English possessions abroad—as he also refused Richard's request that all the English barons swear fealty to himself as heir to the throne of England, and so ensure John's exclusion from that throne. At the end of that angry meeting Richard had knelt in homage to King Philip, and, before the entire gathering, had sworn fealty to the French king. Since then, there had been open war between Richard and his father.

The conflict had gone badly for Henry. The empire he had forged was crumbling, his poor health reducing him to a pale shadow of the mighty warlord of his youth. If the war were to end, a peace treaty must be signed and the family feud forgotten. Only then would Rolf be able to return to England and Wychaven.

Dear God, when would that be? He had been away almost a year. A strange tightness filled his chest. England beckoned to him as never before. The longing to set foot on his own land once again was so strong that it left him shaken. And Meriel? Her face rose vividly before him. Was it really a year since his marriage? Strange how the thought of that marriage no longer rankled; rather, it added to his impatience to leave France and take up the new life that awaited him.

A wasted year! He rubbed a hand tiredly over his stubbled chin. He had so many plans for Wychaven and for the new castle, which, from the reports Meriel sent him, progressed well. A deeper ache pierced him. In so many ways over the last year his wife had continued to surprise him—not least by the long and detailed reports, always written in her own hand, about every aspect of the estate and its people. If he could not put faces to names, he at least knew his villagers intimately through Meriel's letters. And yet he still knew little about her herself. In that respect, her reports were impersonal. Wychaven was prospering under his wife's stewardship and her competence relieved many of his worries, but still he was unsettled. It was not just his lands that beckoned. He had not expected to miss Meriel with such a burning intensity, or find that every woman he had since met paled into insignificance by comparison. He had lost count of the nights he had woken after dreaming of Meriel dancing—almost tempting him to abandon his duty and return to England.

Sitting in the steward's room at Wychaven, Meriel dismissed the castle officers and rubbed her aching temple. The figures of their monthly reports had brought a frown to her brow. In a few weeks would be the Lammas feast. Rolf had left Wychaven before the celebrations began last year; would he return in time for this year's feast? It looked as though Wychaven's harvest would surpass anything produced for several years, but the expenditure on repairs to neglected buildings was growing by the day. And there was still the money to be found to complete the building of the new castle. The foundations had been dug and the walls to the keep and outer walls raised to twice a man's height. Upon their marriage, the king had promised to finance part of the building works, but since the war in France was now going so badly for him, no money had been sent from the royal treasury.

She stood up and strolled to the window overlooking the sea, smiling absently at her mother, who sat working on her embroidery in the light of the window. The Lady Maude's arrival two days after Rolf's departure had been a wonderful surprise, and Meriel had felt ashamed of her harsh recriminations against her husband, for the men-at-arms accompanying her mother were those who had escorted the Lady Isolda back to the convent. Although dismissing his sister, Rolf had thoughtfully planned that Meriel would have company while he was away.

Her glance fixed on the distant horizon with a pang of longing. Somewhere across that blue expanse was Rolf. His replies to her letters asking about his wishes for the estate were answered with military precision, almost to the point of terseness. There was nothing in them about himself, and only from the messengers themselves did she learn something of his life in France. It seemed that he lived much as he had before his marriage—except that now there were no tourneys at which he could win fame and glory. The battles played out in France were real, and, so far, true to his word, he had played no part in them. He was emissary between Henry and Richard—a dangerous road when dealing with two such volatile men. She heard that he was acclaimed for his diplomacy, trusted by both the king and prince. She was so proud of him, but... Her heart clenched as she wondered whether, while he moved in such exulted circles, he ever spared a thought for her?

'Lord Loxstead will return soon.' Lady Maude looked up from her embroidery. 'Why do you not go riding? You spend too long indoors worrying over the estate accounts.'

'There is so much to do. When Rolf returns...' Her voice snatched in her throat.

'He will not expect to find his wife looking pale and tired,' Lady Maude remonstrated.

'What will he expect? There are so many misunderstandings still between us. We were wed but a few days and have been apart for so long. We are strangers.'

The Lady Maude shrugged. 'As are most couples when they wed. Ahead you have all the joy of discovering each other. He is not as stern and unfeeling as you would believe, else I would not be here with you now, but shut away in a convent as Sedbury intended.'

'And I wronged him in that,' Meriel contended, regretful at the memory. 'Our parting was strained, and it was all because of my stupid curiosity. Oh, why could I not have been patient and let him tell me of himself in his own time? I ruined everything.'

'If you love him, you will put the incident behind you,' her mother gently reasoned. 'It will be a fresh beginning when your husband returns. Think only of that. I know this year cannot have been easy. That episode with Bella still remains unexplained.'

Meriel glanced across at Bella sitting quietly on a stool, her eyes large and blank as usual. 'Perhaps it is as well that Bella remembers nothing of that night. She was ill for so long...it was two months before she rose from her bed, and still she has not spoken a single word! It must have been Sedbury who attacked her. Why else should her mind have become so unhinged? She loved him.'

'The Earl of Sedbury has a terrible temper when crossed, but although it is indelicate of me to say it, he had a true fondness for Bella, or he would not have kept her with him for three years.' Lady Maude shook her head in puzzlement. 'And, for all his faults, I feel Sedbury would never attack a woman with a dagger. It is an unsettling mystery.'

Rolf stared up at Chinon Castle set high on its rock escarpment. Duty had brought him here and earned him Richard's wrath. But he held himself answerable only to God, his king and his own code of honour—and he would live and die by that code whatever the personal cost. His spirits rose as he rode through the castle gate. He had made his choice and must stand by it. The first knight he saw in the castle was his brother Edwin.

'Rolf! There was never a more welcome sight!' Edwin's grim expression lightened as he strode to Rolf's side. 'His Majesty has been asking for you. Have you come with word of a treaty? Will Richard sue for peace?'

'I come with Richard's curses on my head.' Rolf eased his aching shoulders beneath the weight of the steel hauberk as they walked into the gloom of the castle buildings. 'But I thought you had returned to England?'

'I did, and I visited Wychaven while I was there. Your land prospers. There'll be a good harvest this year. Meriel is well, and more beautiful than ever. Did you know Sedbury was back in England?' Edwin blurted on in his usual exuberant fashion without giving Rolf time to answer. 'He was high in Henry's favour before he left France, and on more than one occasion tried to make trouble for you. The king would hear none of it, thank God! At least Sedbury has made no approach to Meriel or the Lady Maude since his return. He's still smarting from the humiliation of his last tangle with you.'

'Sedbury is no fool,' Rolf said. 'I do not trust him—but since he is my kinsman by marriage, I would rather not have a running feud with him.' He turned the conversation. 'Is Lord Drogo yet in England?'

'Father returned in May. He was tired and worn out from his pilgrimage and disheartened by the rift between Henry and Richard. He is eager to meet your bride. He knew Sir Arnulf of Wychaven and speaks highly of him, but there are other matters—rather more serious—which trouble him.' Edwin paused, his expression sobering. 'It's Isolda. She left the convent, supposedly to visit the shrine of Our Lady at Walsingham, but has since disappeared. No one has heard of her for weeks. I took the liberty of warning Meriel not to receive her at Wychaven.'

Rolf paled, a sudden fear grinding through him. 'Did you warn her of the danger? I told her nothing of the incident in France.'

Edwin nodded. 'She had to know the truth.'

'How did she take it?'

'She was stunned, of course. And I think hurt that you had not told her everything. Damn it, Rolf, she deserved to know!' Edwin eyed him sternly. 'If you were not so blind, you would know that marriage to her is the best thing that could have happened to you.'

Rolf gritted his teeth. He did not need Edwin to remind him that he had misjudged Meriel, but with Richard's curses still ringing in his ears, he was in no mood to listen to any sermon. 'I do not question you upon your estranged relationship with your wife,' Rolf snapped, the defensive shield covering his emotions. 'Brother or no, you are out of line. My relationship with Meriel is my own affair. Now I must pay my respects to King Henry.'

But Edwin's words haunted Rolf throughout the following days. England seemed a far-off place and he was trapped by duty. If Henry died, and he lost everything... The thought chilled him. How would Meriel react? She would probably understand, since she counted honour above wealth and position. Just as well, since here in France the situation grew worse by the day. The king was worn out by sickness, racked by the unremitting pains of an anal ulcer that daily sapped his lifeblood and strength. Despite Richard's anger with him, Rolf had striven to negotiate an acceptable treaty between the two Plantagenets—but all possible honourable terms were dashed aside by the vengeful demands of Philip of France. In the end, it was Henry who had conceded. The man who had carved out his own destiny to become a giant among rulers had in the last year of his life been defeated by the treason of his own son. A humiliating treaty at last signed, Henry had asked for a list of those who had conspired against him.

As Rolf stood over the king's bed at Chinon, holding that same document, his throat cramped as he stared at

the first-named traitor. For the life of him, he could not
bring himself to speak.

'Read!' Henry commanded, his voice an echo of its
former self.

Rolf raised his eyes to the sunken, pallid face and
shook his head, turning aside as he handed the
parchment to a servant, who read out the first name. It
was that of Prince John!

The man got no further, his voice drowned by Henry's
tortured shriek.

'I need hear no more,' Henry murmured brokenly,
turning his face to the wall. In the next hour he lapsed
into delirium, saying over and over again, 'Shame, shame
on a vanquished king.'

Nothing Rolf or his companions said could ease his
agony of mind, and Rolf lapsed into silence, suspecting
that Henry was past hearing. Unable to ease the king's
torment, he could only wait and pray that he would rally,
but by nightfall Henry Plantagenet was dead.

In the chapel high on the mount at Wychaven, Meriel
knelt before her father's wooden image. There was still
an empty core in her heart from the loss of the bluff,
hearty parent she had loved so dearly as a child. The
woman in her missed his guidance in matters the Lady
Maude could never understand. She needed Sir Arnulf's
wisdom to see into a man's mind. Not just any man, but
that of her husband—a proud, self-assured man, un-
impressed by feminine wiles, but capable of rare moments of tenderness. Sir Arnulf had been such a man as
Rolf was.

She now knew the terrible secret that had embittered
her husband towards women. Isolda was a woman of
ungovernable passions, uncaring of anything but her own
self-gratification. Before Sir Edwin had left Wychaven
for France, he had drawn her aside, his expression grave
as he told her the truth.

'Isolda has left the convent, against Lord Drogo's
wishes. The nuns think she might have gone to France—

but I am not so sure. I must ask you not to give her admittance if she comes to Wychaven.'

'But she is Rolf's sister... How can I turn her away?' Meriel said, shocked.

'You must. Isolda is not what she seems. She hates Rolf. She will try to harm him in whatever way she can.'

Meriel cried, 'I do not understand! Isolda helped me when I needed her.'

'Because she thought Rolf resented your marriage, and that bringing you both together would ruin his plans to set you aside. She wanted to see him tied to a woman he despised. She was wrong in that. Rolf respects you, Meriel. Had you been longer together, you would have resolved your differences and found happiness. Do not be deceived by Isolda's apparent piety. She is evil. Has Rolf told you how he came by his scarred neck?'

Shocked by Edwin's revelations, Meriel nodded. How could she forget the anger her husband had shown on their last night together when she had pushed him against his will to speak of the incident?

Sir Edwin shifted uncomfortably, and lowered his gaze. 'That is not the half of it, or the worst. Isolda took many lovers during her marriage. Sir Harold's death was no accident. He was unhorsed and unarmed in a tournament mêlée. Unable to defend himself, he was struck down and killed by Isolda's then lover, Thierry d'Arbeux. To avoid scandal, Rolf challenged him to single combat on a deserted field. Isolda went to plead with him to spare her lover's life, but Rolf would not listen. At the first charge, Rolf's lance struck d'Arbeux through the heart. Isolda became hysterical, vowing vengeance upon Rolf. She meant it, and is capable of using any ploy to carry it out. Our father had decreed that her punishment, for both her infidelity and being the cause behind her husband's death, was to spend the rest of her life in a convent. She has never forgiven Rolf. If she can harm him, she will.'

Sir Edwin had made her promise that under no circumstances would Isolda be allowed to enter Wychaven.

Shaken and alarmed, she had time aplenty to think over Sir Edwin's words after he left. Was it somehow possible that Isolda had been responsible for the attack upon Bella? It was a thought too awful to contemplate—that Rolf's sister could be so heartless. Meriel sighed. While she now understood Rolf's distrust of women, she was no nearer to understanding the man himself.

Rolf rose stiffly from praying in the draughty chapel at Chinon. He was numbed by Henry's death. It seemed that once he had heard that his favourite son John had also turned against him, he had lost all will to live. Rolf's step dragged, weighted by the heaviness of England's loss. For all his quick fire and virulent temper, he had respected Henry. It was the end of an era.

An outraged shout from the direction of the king's bier led Rolf and his fellow knights to run towards it. A dead man-at-arms was sprawled outside the king's door. Stepping over the corpse, Rolf froze at the sight that greeted him, the hilt of his sword biting into his calloused palm. A wave of fury engulfed him. This was the cruellest and most ignoble desecration of all. The room had been plundered of all its finery, the king's clothes and treasure-chest robbed. Rage churned like a millrace through Rolf, almost choking him as he gazed upon Henry's corpse, stripped and left sprawled upon the flagstones.

'Guards!' Rolf bellowed. Neither he nor Sir William Marshal wasted any time in questioning the soldiers flocking to his call. Their shocked expressions as they entered the room showed clearly that they knew nothing of what had taken place. He gave his orders quickly, 'Search the castle and village. Find the carrion who did this!'

A meticulous search of the castle revealed a secret tunnel in the cellars of the keep that had been used by the thieves. A further hour of searching its length and exit produced nothing but frayed tempers. The robbers had escaped.

There was no sleep for Rolf, Edwin or Sir William
that night. The thoroughness of the thieves meant that
there were no royal trappings with which to lay Henry
out. Edwin supplied a jewelled ring for his hand, and
Rolf fashioned a makeshift sceptre, and for a crown, all
that could be found was a piece of tattered gold embroidery from a woman's gown.

'That it should come to this!' Rolf groaned as he stood
on guard at the king's bier. 'And to the greatest king of
our age.'

'Richard will be informed,' Sir William said but put
up a hand to stay Rolf as he stepped forward. 'You have
earned your place at Henry's side. I'll send another. We
both must face our new king's displeasure. Either of us
could find ourselves clapped in irons. I've come this far
with Henry and I would see him decently laid to rest.
Then Richard can do his worst.'

Rolf exchanged a knowledgeable glance with Sir
William. It was unlikely that Richard would receive with
favour the knight who had had the temerity to unhorse
him. And he could still hear Richard's angry declaration
that he would destroy him. Yet neither he nor Sir William
would apologise for doing their duty to King Henry. King
or not, Richard must accept them as they were, whatever
the cost.

A messenger was despatched to Richard to inform him
of Henry's death, but it was clear that in the July heat
Henry would have to be buried without delay. The fu-
neral procession would start for the abbey church at
Fontévrault the next morning. Throughout the day, the
knights stood in vigilance about the bier. It was almost
nightfall before Richard arrived. As Rolf and his companions stepped back to give the prince privacy, he ignored their presence.

His expression impassive, Richard knelt, and bowed
his head for barely the space of time to mutter a hasty
Paternoster. Rising, he wheeled about, fixing a cool stare
upon Rolf and Sir William. 'Both of you—attend me.'

The young king stalked from the chapel. Squaring his shoulders, Rolf kept pace with him, but for all his outward show of calm, he was chillingly aware that all he had striven for in recent years could be taken from him by a single word.

Gesturing for Sir William to remain at a distance, Richard nodded for Rolf to step closer.

'You gambled and lost,' he declared drily. 'Henry is dead.'

'And I count myself fortunate to have been at his side during his last hours,' Rolf responded coolly. 'I never made any secret to whom my first loyalty lay. You were my friend, but Henry Plantagenet was my sovereign.'

Richard rubbed his coppery beard, his grey-blue eyes steely. 'Had my father a thousand men such as you, Lord Loxstead, he would have died in glory, not defeat.'

The formality of Richard's tone boded ill, but Rolf's amber stare remained unflinching despite Richard's scowls. Standing tall and proud, he waited for the young king to pronounce judgement.

'God's legs!' Richard growled, 'You say nothing—when I could have your head.'

'If you need my head to convince you of my loyalty—take it. But it will give you empty service.'

Richard started, his scowl disappearing. 'Ay, so it would. It cannot have been an easy path you trod this past year, but you gave me no disservice. You have earned your title, Loxstead, a dozen times over. And whom but you could I trust to visit Queen Eleanor with the news of her release?'

Rolf swallowed against a knot of emotion. He sank to his knees and held out his hands in the time-honoured gesture of homage. Richard took them in his and, in a voice still gruff, Rolf uttered his oath of fealty. The massive hands raised him up and clapped him heartily upon the back.

'You were loyal to my father to the end,' Richard said warmly. 'I respect that. I have need of men who are steadfast to their sworn oaths. Leave for England at once.

Queen Eleanor must make her way to London, where I will join her shortly.'

The thought of returning to England quickened Rolf's step as he strode from Richard's presence. Passing Sir William, he shot him a reassuring look, certain that the older knight would not be penalised for having also served King Henry so loyally.

Once through the doorway, Rolf's thoughts returned to Wychaven. It was good to be returning home. *Home!* The notion was enticing after so many wandering, unsettled years. And Meriel would be there waiting for him. Another exhilarating challenge.

King Henry was dead! The news cast a sobering cloud over the celebrations Meriel was planning for Lammas. Dare she hope that Rolf would return soon? And what of his relations with Richard, the new king? Not knowing whether to be fearful or glad, she wanted everything to be in readiness for Rolf when he returned. In anticipation she had already sent to the nearest towns to hire strolling players, determined to make the Lammas feast the grandest one Wychaven had known, and it would all be in honour of its new lord.

Since early morning, when two ships had been sighted from the watchtower, her hope that they might be carrying Rolf set her heart racing, but they remained distant specks, the strong off-shore winds preventing them from reaching land. Standing on the seaward wall of the battlements, she shaded her eyes against the bright sunlight, staring at them. Her heart danced, for Rolf was on board, she was certain! A feeling deep within her sensed his presence coming nearer. The wind had changed as the sun moved to the west, and the two dark shapes were at last beginning to grow larger moment by moment. Anticipation and sudden nervousness sent a stinging heat through her body. Within the hour, God willing, her husband would be with her. Rolf would have a welcome worthy of a king. All day strolling players had been arriving at the castle, and an ox was already roasting on a spit.

Turning, she hurried back to the keep to change into her best sapphire silk gown. As Bella, clumsy since her slow recovery, fumbled with the lacings at her back, she tried to curb her impatience. She, too, seemed to have caught the excitement of the preparations for Rolf's return. In the last weeks, gradually, she had begun to speak a few words, but any mention of the attack upon her brought a blankness to her eyes and she shook her head confusedly, unable to remember what had happened. A few weeks earlier her nightmares had started, and Meriel had woken to hear her, in the truckle bed at the foot of her own, sobbing and crying out in rapid Spanish. When awakened, she could recall nothing of what she had dreamt, but her body trembled as though in the grip of a great fear. Although curious to solve the mystery, Meriel dared not risk upsetting Bella and causing a relapse by questioning her too hard. She was startled now when she spoke.

'It is good that Lord Loxstead returns.' Bella stepped back to survey Meriel with approval. Then the all-too-familiar frown darkened her brow, and she rubbed the ridge of scar at her temple as though it pained her, and her hands began to shake. 'There is danger... I must warn you!' She grimaced. 'Why can I not remember? But... danger... I know.'

'There is no danger at Wychaven, Bella,' Meriel soothed her. 'That was long ago. You will make yourself ill if you worry about the past.'

Bella shook her head in frantic denial. 'I must remember. I must!'

There was a knock on the door. At Meriel's command, a fresh-faced page entered and bowed low. 'My lady, the chamberlain bids me tell you that two ships have anchored in the bay and a long-boat has been lowered. Lord Loxstead's standard flies from it.'

Meriel's heart soared. Dismissing the page, she put a comforting hand upon Bella's shoulder. 'In time you will remember, Bella. There is no danger—not now that Lord Loxstead has returned. Come, I must greet my husband. There will be entertainments and revelry. Today is for celebration, not worry.'

The troubled look remained in Bella's dark eyes, but Meriel was too excited about Rolf's arrival to pay much attention to her melancholy mood. Her legs trembled as she hurried down the entrance steps of the keep in order to greet Rolf in the courtyard. A fanfare of trumpets sounded from the gatehouse, and cheers could be heard from the direction of the village. The long-boat had already beached, and Rolf must be walking through the village. Nervously, she clasped her hands. A year was a long time. How would he act when he saw her?

She forced herself to breathe calmly as she saw a crowd come through the gateway from the outer bailey. Her gaze was drawn immediately to Rolf, who was surrounded by cheering villagers. The tallest man by far, his bare blond head turned from side to side as he acknowledged their welcome. With the ease of a natural leader, he strode across the inner bailey, now looking straight ahead to where she waited. His skin was again bronzed from the sun, his mane of hair streaked almost white at its tips from the long hours he had spent out of doors. His step quickened as he covered the last few yards to Meriel, his golden eyes sparkling behind thick dark lashes. Her heart raced, its beat seeming to echo back from the surrounding battlements and walls as a rush of love overwhelmed her. He was more devastatingly handsome than she had remembered. Shakily, she sank into a reverent curtsy. Her hands were taken and she was raised up, his soft laugh banishing the formality of their reunion.

'God's greetings, my lord,' she said breathlessly.

His hands were warm and firm upon her own, their touch sending a delicious thrill along her arms to spread through her entire being.

He raised a dark brow sardonically. 'So formal a greeting after almost a year apart?' He drew her closer, their hands clasped tightly between their chests, his voice taunting. 'It has been a long year, Meriel. Wychaven's prosperity is obvious. You have been busy—perhaps too busy to miss an adventuring husband?'

'Oh, no, my lord, I have missed you deeply.' The brightening gleam in his eyes brought a stinging heat to her cheeks, as she realised how easily he had drawn her out. 'There will be feasting and entertainments this night in your honour.'

He brought her hand to his lips, his long lashes not quite hiding the bold way his gaze slid over her slender figure. 'After a year in war-torn France, my lovely wife, you are the only feast I need.'

Both shocked and delighted by his bluntness, her blush deepened. He linked her arm through his as they walked side by side up the steps of the keep. He paused at the top to turn back and look out across the castle, and Meriel's pulse fluttered at the evident pride in his assessing gaze.

'I can understand why you were so determined to take your rightful place here,' he said seriously. 'I have thought of it often this past year. Amid so much conflict, Wychaven beckoned as a place of peace and tranquillity. I had never thought to feel in that way of any place.' He looked down at her. 'Wychaven has a spell of its own, calling to me from afar. There was a time when I thought I would lose it all.' His voice hardened with cynicism. 'Even though Henry was dying, I could not desert him for Richard. Thank God, Richard understood and forgave me.'

'Loyalty such as you give is rare, my lord,' Meriel said warmly. 'King Richard could not afford to lose you.'

His fingers tightened possessively over hers. 'I should not be here now, but on my way to Winchester, but I could not resist Wychaven's lure.'

His voice dropped to a low pitch, setting Meriel's blood afire. It was not just of Wychaven he spoke, the desire darkening his eyes told her that. Had her wildest dream come true? Did Rolf care for her? Or was it merely

gallantry? There was a noticeable difference in him. A
lingering sadness from King Henry's death, but the
underlying tension she had always sensed in him was no
longer there. He served only King Richard now, his
loyalty no longer divided and tearing him in two.

The intimacy of the moment was broken by the restless
fidgeting of feet behind them on the keep stairs, and
with a wry grin, Rolf led her into the hall.

'Lord Loxstead!' They were halted halfway to the dais
by the shout and sound of running feet.

One of the castle guards approached. 'There is a rider
at the gate asking entrance. He said he came in peace
and would talk with you. He gave no name and is attended by a single squire, but I believe it is Lord Sedbury.'

A buzz of speculation spread through the crowd as
those nearest the messenger passed his words on to those
beyond the range of hearing.

Uneasy herself, Meriel shuddered, saying softly to
Rolf, 'What trickery is he up to now? He must know he
is not welcome here.'

'If he has come alone, he must be desperate to make
his peace,' Rolf reasoned. 'He is not popular with King
Richard and would probably have me speak for him. He
is still your kinsman, with a powerful army at his
command.'

A crowd had gathered around them, including several
of the strolling players. Rolf shot them a fierce look
which made them take several steps back. As he did so,
Meriel saw Bella acting strangely. She was weaving in
and out of the crowd, looking closely into the faces of
the strolling players as though she was searching for
someone, but her face was ashen and drawn with fear.
Meriel was about to summon her to her side when Rolf's
next softly-spoken words cast all thoughts of Bella from
her mind.

'Sedbury may make an unreliable friend, but he would
be a deadly enemy. England is far from settled. Richard
is a war-hungry king and plans a crusade into the Holy
Land. He could be away months, even years. It is an

opportunity ripe for Prince John to make mischief. At such times I would have our families united, not divided.'

His stare bored into her, its intensity compelling her to have faith in him, and she nodded her head in agreement. There was also something deeper—something he would never speak of in so public a place. But as he gazed down at her, the usual shield over his emotions was lowered. With lightening heart she knew that the glow shimmering in his golden eyes was more than desire...that the softening lines of his proud, handsome face spoke of a passion deeper than his pride in Wychaven. Fleetingly, his expression softened. Rolf did love her! It was there on his face for all to see.

But almost instantly his attention shifted from her to the stir of movement at the far end of the hall. Their year apart had given her the highest accolade she would win from Rolf, but from the renewed tautness of his face muscles, she had a suspicion that he had not yet acknowledged the full depth of his emotions. A secretive smile played over her lips as Rolf led her to the dais to await Sedbury's arrival. Their whole lifetimes were before them. She could afford to be patient and wait.

The Earl of Sedbury's stocky figure appeared in the hall entrance, and paused. Silence fell over the gathering as the villagers and servants instinctively cleared a passage for him and waited—some hostile, others, especially the strolling players, openly curious. Meriel looked anxiously round for a sign of Bella. How would her maid behave at seeing him?

Her worried glance caught a glimpse of her behind the group of players in gilded masks who were to enact a religious play at the opening of the banquet. Meriel frowned. Even for Bella, she was acting strangely. She had drawn the front of the heavy white veil, which she wore over her wimple, low over her brow and was holding a nosegay against her face—almost as though she were hiding her features as she stared at Sedbury. The depths of longing in her dark brown eyes sent a shaft of pain

through Meriel. Despite all the suffering he had caused
Bella, she still loved him.

Meriel's heart went out to her, unable to see a way to
comfort her. Her kinsman marched towards the dais,
the metallic ring of his spurs resounding through the hall.
He had swept back the hood of his cloak and a sheen
of perspiration glistened on the balding dome of his
head—the only sign that he was less than at ease. His
long gown was immaculate and heavily jewelled, the sides
of his collar-length hair oiled and set into a fashionable
under-roll. He wore his wealth and position like a badge,
but the grooves deepening the lines on his high brow
were signs of an inner worry. Uncertainty about his
future must have gnawed at him to have brought him
back to Wychaven in this manner.

'Lord Loxstead! Countess!' He bowed low. 'I come
in peace. Not only to give my blessing upon your marriage but to unite our families during the uncertainty of
a new reign.'

Meriel tensed, unable to bring herself to trust him.
Over the years Sedbury had shown no respect for Prince
Richard, openly sneering at him for a reckless war-
monger. In recent months, with the rumours of King
Henry's declining health, had come news that Sedbury
was currying favour with Prince John. If her kinsman
were seeking an alliance with Rolf, it must be to save
his own skin and estates now that his scheming had come
to naught.

'In peace, you are welcome, Lord Sedbury,' Rolf replied in reserved tones. 'A family is only as strong as
the unity of its branches. And that unity can be maintained only by like alliances.' He paused significantly,
his stare piercing as it held Sedbury's affronted glare.
Then with a tight smile, he added, more graciously. 'It
is a subject I look forward to discussing with you.'

The tension eased between the two noblemen. Obviously it would be in the best interests of their families
if an alliance could be forged, but Sedbury was as wily

as a fox. Meriel conquered her fears. She trusted Rolf. He would not be taken in by Sedbury's false promises.

The musicians began to play, and as Rolf led Sedbury to take his place at his right hand at the dais table, Meriel gestured for the masked players to begin. At that moment a high-pitched scream raised the hair at the nape of her neck. Her head shot round at the sound, to discover one of the masked players surprisingly close to her.

'Santa Maria save us!' Bella screamed. Staring wide-eyed with horror at the masked player, she lapsed into her native Spanish. *'Es el diablo!'*

Even as Bella cried out, the player leapt towards Meriel. A glint of steel flashed before her eyes. Before she could move, the cold point of a dagger was pressed against her throat and she was staring into wild glittering eyes behind the eye-slits of the mask. A devil indeed!

'Stand back!' The shout, in a chillingly familiar voice, rang above the cry of angry voices.

The blade pressed harder against Meriel's cringing flesh as Rolf swung round, his sword free of its scabbard and raised to strike.

With her free hand, Meriel's attacker dragged off her mask, and tossing it aside, suddenly revealed the pale distorted face of the lady Isolda. Bitter triumph flared in the glance she gave Rolf as she warned harshly, 'One move, Lord Loxstead, and your countess dies!'

CHAPTER FIFTEEN

'HAVE YOU lost your mind, Isolda?' Rolf exploded, his face ashen beneath his tan.

'Why do you not beg for your wife's life as I begged for my lover's?' Isolda laughed shrilly, her wild glance darting to Sedbury. 'Now is your chance, my friend. Take Rolf's sword—he is at your mercy!'

Icicles of fear stabbed at Meriel, momentarily paralysing her. Was this why Sedbury had come to Wychaven? Too late she guessed something of the truth. It must have been Isolda who freed Sedbury last year. Had she also stabbed Bella? Was this how Sedbury and Isolda meant to take their revenge upon Rolf?

Even as the horrifying thoughts formed, she was surprised to see Sedbury hold up his hands, his face stiffening with outrage as he stepped back from Rolf. 'I want none of this madness, Isolda! I came in peace.'

'Traitor!' Isolda screeched. '*We* planned this. Why do you think I helped you to escape my brother's clutches? You wanted Wychaven badly enough, then!'

'I wanted my freedom!' Sedbury snapped. 'I would have agreed to anything that night to get away. But I have not forgotten what you did to Bella!'

'Craven!' Isolda sneered. 'You never were much of a man—even as a lover. But I do not need you. I do not need anyone.'

Thinking Isolda distracted by her tirade, Meriel brought up her hands to push her captor away. The dagger-point pricked her skin, checking her struggle. Her mind raced like quicksilver. She would be mortally wounded before she could strike. Already a thin trickle of blood ran down her neck, and pain seared her throat.

Meriel swallowed against her rising terror. She must stay calm, and pray that, in her madness for revenge, Isolda would prolong Rolf's agony at his helplessness to act. Thank God Sedbury had not turned against them! All was not yet lost. Everyone within the hall was frozen with shock, the hush profound. Her only hope, Meriel knew, lay in Isolda becoming diverted. But how? Dear God, how?

'You will watch your wife die, brother,' Isolda cackled, 'as I watched my lover take your lance through his heart.' The dagger was drawn downwards to nestle beneath Meriel's breast.

'Harm my wife, and you, too, shall die, Isolda!' Rolf vowed, his eyes glinting with rage.

Isolda laughed. 'Without Thierry d'Arbeux, my life is meaningless. He was the only man I ever loved.'

Meriel felt a tremor run through Isolda's body at the force of her hatred. The woman was unpredictable and unbalanced, the more dangerous for that, her next words confirming Meriel's dread.

'I would rather be dead than spend the rest of my days in a convent, brother. But I would die knowing that you will live out your days in hell!'

As Isolda spoke, Meriel was aware that Rolf was edging closer, his movements slow and barely detectable—like a lion stalking its prey. Gradually he was closing the gap between him and his sister, but he was still too far away to disarm her. Somehow, Meriel knew she had to keep Isolda talking and distract her attention from Rolf's movements. Having waited so long for her revenge, she was the kind of woman who would milk her moment of triumph to the last drop of satisfaction. That yet might be her undoing.

Meriel struggled against the fear cramping her throat, and forced out, 'How did you get into the castle?'

'That is the best of it!' Isolda gloated. 'My idea came from you. Except, instead of playing a minstrel, I hired these strolling players and travelled with them in disguise, knowing that you would employ us when Rolf returned. It was a goodly ruse.'

'You seem to have thought of everything, Isolda!' Rolf grated out.

'Oh yes! I've waited a long time for this! Given the circumstances of your marriage, I had hoped that it would break your haughty pride, brother dear. Alas, I was wrong!'

She glared venomously at Meriel. Forcing herself to appear calm, Meriel was heartened to see Rolf edging closer. A few moments more, and he would be near enough to save her.

'I came here to see you suffer, Rolf,' Isolda went on shrilly, her eyes wild as she dragged Meriel several paces back from Rolf's advancing figure. 'But what do I find? Instead of the contempt I expected, every look, every action of yours shows that you are content with the arrangement. You, whom I thought incapable of giving your heart to any woman, are besotted with your wife.'

Isolda trembled more violently with gathering fury. The dagger pierced the material of Meriel's over-tunic and kirtle, as she laughed cruelly. 'My revenge will be the sweeter for knowing that you love Meriel! I shall take your lover from you, as you took mine!'

Rolf balanced on the balls of his feet, judging the distance between him and Isolda as he weighed the chance of saving Meriel. He was still too far away to risk a sudden attack. His blood chilled. Isolda had every intention of killing Meriel. A misjudged lunge by him now would hasten her death. Impotent rage consumed him. He was powerless to help Meriel, unless . . . A movement behind Isolda caught his attention. Hope surged through him. A flicker of his eye ordered his ally to attack.

A rush of air ruffled Meriel's veils and, without warning, Isolda was knocked sideways, Bella's high-pitched scream rending the air as she threw her arm round Isolda and spun her towards Rolf. 'You shall not kill my mistress as you tried to kill me!'

'Bella! You are alive!' Sedbury's tone showed his astonishment and relief.

Meriel absently noted it, through the hubbub of noise that had broken out in the hall, as she stumbled, knocked off balance by Bella's heroic attack. Steadying herself, she saw Rolf grab his sister, his fingers fastening over the dagger.

Screaming dementedly, Isolda wrenched her hand free. 'You'll not take me! I'll never go back to that convent!'

With the immense strength of the wildly insane, Isolda thrust herself away from Rolf, and, turning her back on him, made several downward slashing movements before he again captured her and spun her round to face them. The bloodied dagger fell to the floor, the rushes already spotted with scarlet as the blood gushed from Isolda's slit wrists.

A shocked gasp echoed round the hall, and everyone began to talk and move at once. Shakily, Meriel ran to Rolf's side as he caught Isolda, who fell forward in a faint. Meriel snatched the veil from her hair and began to rip it into strips.

'We must bind her wrists quickly,' her voice quivered, 'or she will die.'

Rolf glanced up as she held out to him a piece of ripped veil. At the look of intense emotion, faster than an arrow in flight, in his eyes, Meriel's heart rose with a resurgence of love and longing. Rolf's expression changed, once more practical as he took the material and bent over his unconscious sister. Together they bound Isolda's wrists, but even with the bandages in place, the blood already seeped through them. With a muttered oath Rolf tore a larger strip and began to tie it above Isolda's elbow, saying sharply, 'Do the same to her other arm. It is the only way to stop the bleeding.'

As they worked, Meriel was aware of the hushed whispers around them and of a soft sobbing. She glanced up and saw Bella clasped in Sedbury's arms. So, after all, her kinsman did still care for her. Some ray of hope at least had come out of these tragic events, she thought

fleetingly, her attention already returning to Isolda as
Rolf raised his sister in his arms.

The expression in his eyes was haggard, and his voice
became jagged with pain. 'This could have been you!'

Wheeling round, he marched from the hall to the
chambers above, shouting for someone to summon the
physician.

In the early hours of the following morning, Meriel rose
stiffly from the side of Isolda's bed and stood back while
Father Aethan intoned the last rites. Rolf put his hand
on her shoulder as the chaplain's voice lapsed into
silence, and they both stared down at the pale face on
the pillow.

'She would not be dead,' Meriel groaned, 'had I not
left her alone with that maid.'

Rolf squeezed her shoulder. 'You could not have
known that Isolda would trick her,' he said. 'She knew
her fate. Her days would have been spent locked away.
She was as passionate in her will to die as she had been
in life. At least, this way, she is at peace.'

Meriel looked into the shadowed face of her husband.
Despite his resigned words, his eyes were clouded with
remorse. Once he had worshipped his sister above all
women, yet, even while disillusioned, he still mourned
her death. It was a measure of his compassion.

They walked through the now sombre atmosphere of
Wychaven to their chambers in the keep. The food for
the feast had been divided up and given to the villagers,
for how could there be feasting and entertainment to
welcome Rolf home? Meriel glanced sideways at him as
they entered their bedchamber. His expression was
sombre, as it had been since Isolda had revealed herself
in the hall. He had hardly spoken on his visits to his
dying sister's bedchamber, and now seemed more withdrawn than ever. All his bold assurance had gone from
his manner as he turned to face her.

'Today has taught me much about human nature,' he
said hoarsely. 'I knew that Isolda was capable of evil,

but I underestimated her... I suppose, because she was my sister, I was convinced there must be some good in her.'

'She was all one would expect a holy woman to be when I met her at the convent.' Meriel tried to ease his pain. 'The nuns respected her. It was as though she had two sides to her nature: one capable of great good, the other... a creature driven beyond all reason by revenge.'

Rolf rubbed the scar on his neck. 'There were times when she seemed to be possessed by the devil!'

She moved to his side, placing her fingers lightly upon his chest. 'You must not let memories eat away at you.'

He took her hands in his, his golden eyes burning into her with an intensity that set her pulse racing. 'Because of her, I learnt at an early age never to trust or to confide in anyone.' His voice was low. 'Often, this last year, I regretted not telling you about Isolda. It also seems that I misjudged Bella, and my thoughtlessness there must have caused you pain.'

Meriel opened her mouth to protest, but the tautness of Rolf's expression warned her to stay silent. She sensed that apologies did not come easily to him. Her heart raced. That he felt the need to explain himself to her showed a deepening strength in their relationship. Was it true—what she had so fleetingly glimpsed at their re-union, and Isolda had cried out so wildly? In their year apart, had Rolf truly come to love her, or was it guilt that drove him to heal the breach between them? She checked her disjointed thoughts as he continued, the light in his eyes glowing with warmth and respect.

'I judged Bella only from what she appeared to be—a whore who had begun to lead you astray, if only by the provocative way she had taught you to dance. Even a whore, it seems, can show loyalty to those she loves, especially when they have placed their trust in her. She loved Sedbury, but he had cast her aside, while you had stood by her in friendship.'

Meriel nodded. They had both, together with Sedbury, listened to Bella while she recounted the details of the night she was attacked. Isolda had stabbed her. Bella had gone to Sedbury's cell, but only to take him food. She found the guards already dead, and Isolda within... From what she had seen and heard, it was obvious that Sedbury and Isolda had been lovers in the past and, from the plans they were making, they would again be in the future. Sedbury swore he had not seen Bella that night. Bella confirmed this. Apparently his back was to the door, but Isolda had seen her watching. Frightened, she had fled to raise the alarm, and Isolda, on the pretext of drugging the gatehouse guards, had left Sedbury and followed her. There was a struggle, and she was stabbed. She lost her senses, and vaguely remembered coming round, but found herself lying on the floor of a dark outbuilding. In the moonlight shining through an open door, she had seen Isolda bending over her. Then she was clubbed on the head and could remember nothing more.

It was while they were coaxing the story from Bella that Isolda had regained consciousness and sent the maid watching over her to bring her a honey posset. Once alone, Isolda had stripped off her bandages and, keeping her arms hidden under the covers, had allowed the blood to drain from her.

Remembering Bella's painfully halting speech and the way Isolda had threatened her own life, Meriel felt nothing but numbness at Isolda's death. Bowing her head, she leaned against Rolf's chest. 'Isolda is at peace, but what about poor Bella? No wonder she had blotted the horror of what happened from her mind! I knew it was more than the blow to her head that made her recovery so slow.'

'Thank God, she has recovered now,' Rolf replied, his voice softening as his arm slid round her. 'Sedbury was appalled at how she had been treated ... It seems we also misjudged him. In his own way, he still cares for her and wants her to accompany him to London and live in his house there.'

'I am glad she accepted.' Meriel smothered her sadness that she would lose the company of her friend. 'Bella has always loved Lord Sedbury. Until we were summoned by Queen Eleanor from Eadstone, and Bella's loyalty was divided, he never treated her badly. If he truly cares for her, and she chooses to find what happiness she may with him, I am happy for her. And...' she hesitated, her eyes widening with uncertainty, 'and I hope, despite her remaining Sedbury's mistress, that she will continue to be my friend—even if it will not be possible for us to meet very often.'

For a long moment Rolf was silent, and the strains of a lute from the corridor outside carried to them. 'You have a strange turn of reasoning,' he said thickly. 'And a code of loyalty that would be the envy of any knight.'

The sincerity of his tone made her breath catch in her throat, an ache of happiness welling inside her. 'That is the minstrel's soul in me refusing to be smothered, my lord,' she answered provocatively, her words prompted by a singer now accompanying the tune.

Beneath her hand still upon Rolf's chest, she felt his heartbeat quicken. Their gazes fused. After a year apart, they were as stiffly formal with each other as strangers, yet each deepening look from him set her skin a-tingle. He lifted his head to listen. He stood so still that she wondered what new disaster was about to touch them, then she heard it, too. Her eyes smiled into Rolf's, her voice breathless. 'The minstrel is singing about us!'

He grinned. 'About how a travel-weary knight was betwitched by the seductive dance of a wood-nymph who, until then, had been the prisoner of a wicked guardian.' Amusement sparkled in his eyes as he drew her closer. 'What chance had he against her wiles? Together they defied the elements and, with the ancient magic of Merlin to assist them, they recaptured her castle and lands.'

'No ordinary knight, my lord,' she taunted. 'A handsome, golden-haired warlord.'

His eyes burned into her.

'And his lady, a raven-haired siren with eyes the colour of a summer sea, who set his blood afire with her exotic dancing, her courage and beauty unmatched throughout Christendom . . . who stole her lord's heart the moment he set eyes on her.'

She touched his cheek wonderingly, her heart so full that it was difficult to speak. 'So the song says, my lord, but minstrels are day-dreamers. A ballad of star-crossed lovers is always more romantic than reality.'

Rolf's eyes darkened. 'There is much I would have changed in the last year—not least that we know so little of each other. It is time all that changed. By your faith you have shown me that it is possible to trust.' He leaned over her, his lips hovering above her mouth, their breaths intermingling with sweet anticipation. 'I must leave on the morrow for Winchester, but I shall not be parted from you again for so long. I want time to learn all there is to know about you, although, I warn you, it could take a lifetime for me to experience the wealth of happiness you could give me.'

'If I had my way, my lord, it would take until eternity.'

'Then very likely it will,' he smiled incorrigibly. 'First, though, you will come with me to accompany Queen Eleanor to London to await King Richard. There you will also meet Lord Drogo, my father. It will be a proud day for me to introduce him to so worthy a bride.' His hands tightened possessively about her, crushing her in a passionate embrace, his lips urgent and demanding upon hers. He kissed her until she was breathless, his mouth travelling to her eyes and then down to her throat, his voice throbbing with desire. 'Dear God, I thought I had lost you, my darling! That I had found love, only to have it stolen from me. The song did not lie. I loved you from the first moment I saw you . . . I was just too stubborn to admit it. I love you.'

'And I love you . . . so very, very much, my lord,' she breathed in a silken whisper, her avowal smothered by the hunger of his mouth parting her lips in a long searing kiss. She arched against him, her arms binding him

closer, every sense attuned to the mastery of his touch.
A fire blazed through her veins as his every caress be-
spoke, more potently than words, the ecstasy of loving
and being loved so completely and selflessly in return.
The exaltation wiped out the distrust and torment of the
past, the misunderstandings dissolving, as hearts, minds
and bodies joined as one, forging the pattern of their
future.

UNSTOPPABLE ROMANCE

Folly to Love
LYNN JACOBS

Take Away the Pride
EMMA RICHMOND

A Question of Trust
SHIRLEY KEMP

Designed with Love
KATHRYN ROSS

Mills & Boon are proud to present their 1989 NEW AUTHOR SELECTION

The selection features four brand new novels from some of our latest authors. Varied storylines guarantee a strong mix of love, drama and sparkling entertainment which proves that romance is unstoppable!

Price: £5.00   Published: April 1989

Mills & Boon

Available from Boots, Martins, John Menzies, W.H. Smith, Woolworths and other paperback stockists.